The Gift

a novel

Michael J. Nercessian

This is a work of fiction. All characters and events in this book are fictitious. Any resemblance to actual persons, living or dead, is coincidental.

ISBN (paperback): 979-8-9854659-4-5
ISBN (ebook): 979-8-9854659-5-2

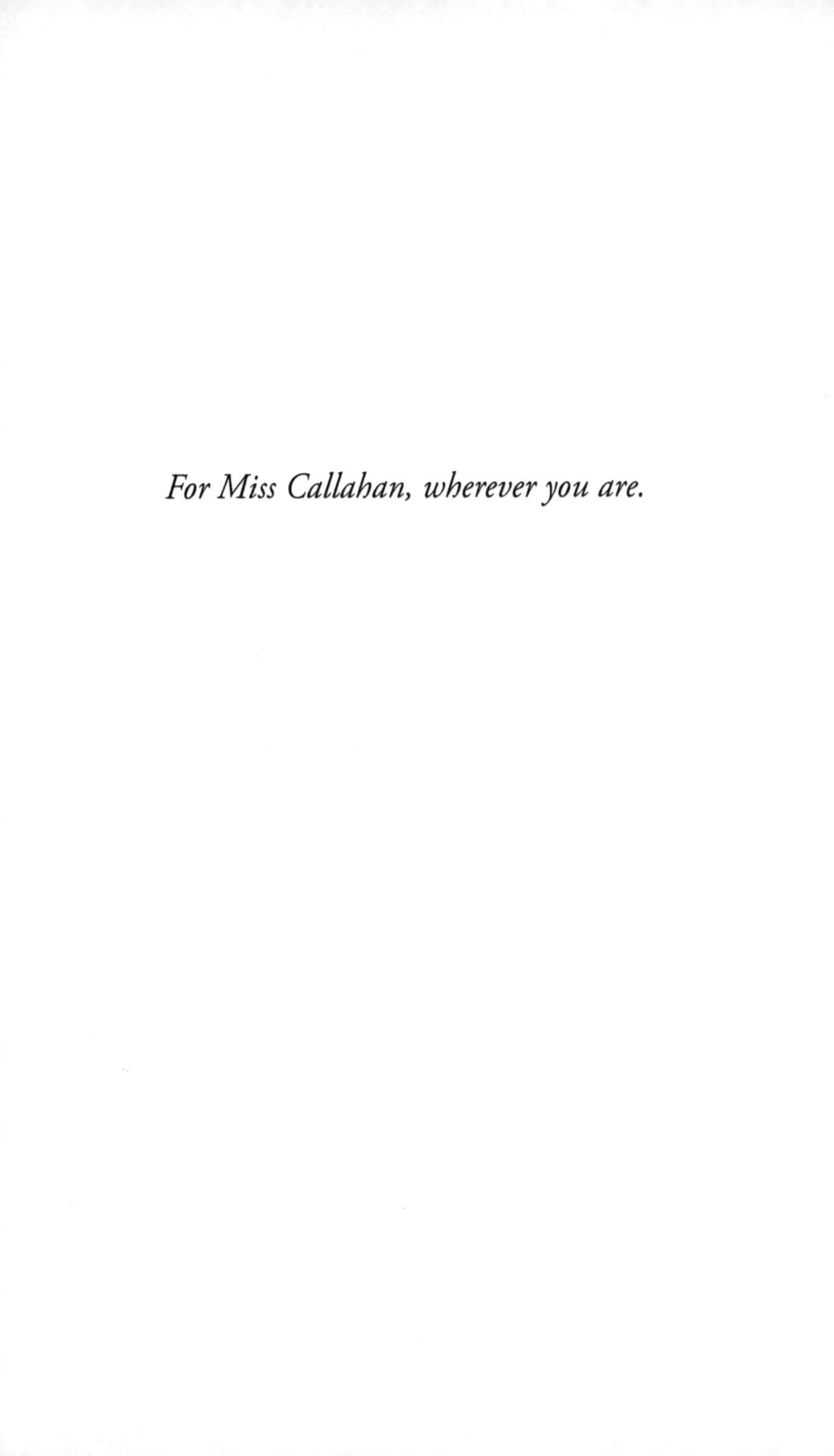

For Miss Callahan, wherever you are.

"Be careful. I am Death!"
It was Karait, the dusty brown snakeling
that lies for choice on the dusty earth;
and his bite is as dangerous as the cobra's.

—Rudyard Kipling, *The Jungle Book*

A Middle...

I'm not afraid to die; I've been dead most of my life.

"Is it AIDS? Please don't tell me I have AIDS!"

"No, we've run it twice. Both negative."

"Thank God!"

But the doctor's eyes didn't soften, his face didn't brighten. Not even a little.

"What is it then?"

He exhaled slowly through his nose and rubbed his right eye with the knuckle of his index finger.

"Something new."

The saying goes: One needs to experience lingering hardship, suffering, a tragedy, in order to evolve into an artist of some merit. Perhaps, then, it will be possible. A bright side? Undoubtedly. Things are looking up.

(Bobby)

"Ugly, yes. Though not as ugly as some."

The January that "Raindrops Keep Fallin' On My Head" hit number one on the charts an ugly child was born into the emptiness of a northern winter. On a Monday. At the witching hour.

Having set her dark-blue, disappointed eyes upon me, those ugly words, I'm told, were my mother's first in my presence. Her version of a mother gushing over her newborn. Over the years, my mother grew fond of repeating, unlike the leafless desolation of my January birth, I was "not as ugly as some." It remains mildly comforting.

When I close my eyes at day's end, I still hear her voice, clawing closer despite my extended arm, my efforts to push it away, to hold Mother at bay. And she's always with me when I awaken in the dead of night, forehead clammy with sweat, sheets soaked in tepid piss.

Before my first breath of fresh oxygen and a nurse's calloused hand smacked my damp, pink rear-end, my father had run away, escaped from my mother's clutches. Even the promise of my older sister's future was not enough to foil his scaling the wall, swimming the moat and making for the forest. Some are luckier than others. My mother and father both came from families of prolific vanishers. My ancestors were ghosts, a cold wind, gurgling water moving upstream (downstream? I still don't know the difference) – onto whatever was next. I don't know much about those ghosts, but I know what haunts me.

Let me begin.

I was born with one leg shorter than the other. Though it wasn't evident at birth, my left leg was a quarter inch off the right. My mother rolled her eyes and shook her head when, months later than expected and with considerable difficulty, I attempted to walk. For a few years, formative years, I was only comfortable walking in counterclockwise circles. I got where I wanted to go, mind you, but the route was circuitous, expectedly circular. One had to be patient.

The stunted left leg was an axis, and my world spun upon it. When you're young, you see in small circles: family, neighbors, classmates, teammates, teachers, best friends. So, to my eyes, nothing appeared out of the ordinary. There was something oddly comfortable in it – I always knew what direction I was going even when it was the wrong one.

As fate would have it, an accident that would have made things worse for most people, "cured" me.

Let me explain.

It was the year of the bi-centennial, a humid August morning in Massachusetts, a sun-filled Sunday. The trees were in full leaf and sunflowers absorbed the day's heat with straight backs and roaring lion's heads–this day of my rebirth stood in stark contrast to the day of my birth. Six-year-old me ambled the sidewalk on the odd numbered side of the street. Cares in the world? There were none. It had the makings of a perfect day. Unsurprisingly and instinctually, I pivoted counterclockwise off the curbstone and stumbled into the path of an oncoming station wagon, a white Ford with waving body fins from a bygone era. My sister, Maddy, attempted to catch me by reaching out to grab an arm or piece of my shirt, but I slipped through her fingers. There was beeping and skidding, some screaming, and the acrid smell of asphalt devouring black rubber. One doesn't forget the smell. I heard Maddy screaming, but it was tinny and far-away, like it was bellowing from a telephone receiver with a poor connection.

A family of four returning from church hadn't expected a warm body to topple in front of their Ford. They stood over me in their starched Sunday best, mouths open and scratching their heads, looking down upon the wretched creature who'd veered off the sidewalk and was now lying on the sun-warmed pavement with his good leg bent sideways at nearly ninety degrees. The youngest, a crewcut boy about my age had both hands in his dress pants pockets, a bent neck and a whistling nose that made a tweet when the air went both in and out. "Ouch" he managed between whistles. It was the only thing he said.

The impact of the Ford shattered my right leg which, when healed, had shortened almost a quarter inch! I was, of course, a quarter inch shorter than would be expected but walked normally (relatively) and none-the-wiser. My mother rolled her eyes and shook her head when I, newly released from a month in hospital, demonstrated my new, less circular gait. At least my walking was now also "not as ugly as some."

"What will I tell the other mothers?" she asked more to herself than to me.

Of course, when strangers looked at me, they still squinted their eyes tightly, trying to squeeze out the thick nose hovering above thin, pinkish lips, the fleshy, pale skin of my face, the reddish hair on my head that grew in motley coils, sideways and outward like a wide rimmed Stetson, instead of down toward my ears. To the many stares my mother would shrug and say to me, "What can you expect. They have eyes, don't they?" To her, the duckling was ugly.

My modestly improved gait didn't escape the eyes of the neighborhood children or my classmates, either. A few of them walked in wobbly circles during school recess, even though I no longer strode exclusively in that geometric shape. Sometimes I had to correct them and let them know they were pivoting on the wrong leg; I enjoyed exaggerating the steps for them. "Like this," I'd insist. The teachers and recess monitors would shoo away my demons and offer a tepid scolding, but the taunts would rise again soon after. When a few of them discovered their words and pantomime didn't hurt me nearly as much as my fist hitting their nose, things quieted down. It was easier to be brave, or foolish, when there was nothing to lose.

Maddy was destined to be an only child. She was hope: I understood this from an early age. My sister was affable and courteous, bright eyed and visually pleasing. Both of her legs were relatively equal in length. Unsurprisingly, everyone fawned over her. Blue eyes and blond pigtails carried weight. I learned there was no need to hinder her upward mobility with a younger brother who required an "And…ummmm" when being introduced. Sometimes, I wasn't introduced at all. It's strange the things you get used to; the things that become expected.

Physically, I made progress over the years, growing into the flesh of my face so it smoothed and hugged the bones, my untamable hair darkened into a reasonable brown and began to take a comb. My nose, too, became sensible and thin like everyone else's. Perhaps my nose was always this way. And I found places to hide when I needed a moment to myself. By my early twenties, I was one of you. Actually, by my early twenties, I had surpassed many and become, at worst, a warm commodity–a good catch! And a brother. And that's where I was for many years. Things had evened out.

Until that day.

Massachusetts (Bobby)

On January 4, 2010, the Centers for Disease Control and Prevention declared HIV infection was no longer of public health significance. This news was buried on page 5 of the local newspaper, beneath an ad for quality used cars.

A few days later, my sister accompanied me to an appointment. Not the first appointment, but soon after, the important one: the one where the test results were read aloud, demanding an audience. The one where everything was confirmed. It was an office visit. By that I mean it was a visit to the doctor's private office, the dark-paneled room with two fancy chairs placed across the desk from the stern bearer of bad news. It was the office used when a phone call was insufficient and considered bad taste.

"Jesus," Maddy said before the doctor finished. She looked over at me with lovely blue eyes that blinked more than necessary. I melted into the seat. I'd been trying not to listen. I was thinking of everything that didn't involve this discussion: whether I'd left the dryer running or the clothes iron on…did I lock the front door? Jesus, sometimes I forget to lock the door.

"What the hell, Bobby Shaw?" She had a bit of our mother in her and it bubbled to the surface. I tried to not make eye contact, but I felt her stare, icy and burning at the same time. Maddy knew all. Maddy the steady hand. Maddy the keeper of secrets.

Between the arm-crossed Dr. Kilkenny and Maddy's soul-crushing glare, there was no place for me to hide. The room shrank, the walls inched closer, the ceiling lowered. I smelled black rubber burning.

"In the studies I've seen, the antivirals aren't terribly effective." I liked Dr. Kilkenny, but not his voice. His voice always carried news I was reluctant to hear, like a letter from a distant relative who may or may not want to borrow money.

"Now what?" Maddy said, not to me, but to Kilkenny.

"We treat it with something new, maybe a cocktail of medicines, keep it at bay for as long as we can," he replied. He was trying on a small, half-smile, a muscle-memory, cautious-optimism reserved for these occasions. Perhaps it was a class they required in medical schools, some cross-disciplinary lecture floating between bedside-manner and marketing. I'd give him a C-minus.

Then he said something curious.

"The thing that's confusing is that it doesn't seem to want to kill you."

Kilkenny, of course, found the paradox fascinating while I almost fell off the surprisingly comfortable chair. He couldn't have missed my reaction, an amalgam of fear and hope and the sound of a toilet flushing. Despite the previous discussions, the questions, the examinations, the tests, it hadn't occurred to me that this virus might want to kill me or that it might want to take its time doing so. Or that it might not want to kill me at all.

"What I mean is, typically a virus will want to keep duplicating, that's the nature of it, keep moving forward, but this one seems content to sit and wait. It's happy to exist at its current level. Part of it is your immune system fighting back, but the other part is it doesn't seem to be in a hurry." He almost laughed to himself, but perhaps he remembered the med-school lecture and found his serious face. D-plus.

"How long?" Maddy asked while using both hands to tuck wisps of straight, blond hair behind her ears and shaking her head to dislodge any cobwebs. She was trying to be the strong and responsible one and this possible piece of good news did not change the fact I was in trouble. Unlike me, she wanted answers.

Kilkenny pursed his lips and contorted his face, perhaps thinking he was on a phone call and we couldn't see him. He was tall and lanky and never knew where to place his limbs—once he unfolded his arms it looked as though a spider or a king crab was conducting an orchestra. His wide shoulders were hunched over his too small desk like it was a prop for a middle-school play and his bald head sat heavily upon his neck, shining in the fluorescent lighting.

"I don't know," he said while running his hands over his chin, pulling on an invisible beard. "Could be years. It will depend on how he responds to different treatments and how long his levels hold. This is a fairly new disease, so we don't have the data and the treatments haven't been out there very long. It's a guess, I'm afraid. But I can say others have lived for years. My father—the original Dr. Kilkenny, he's retired now—this was his office, he's been treating the disease from the early days, so I have access to his expertise."

"You understand what you can't do," Maddy said to me as if finally understanding why I'd asked her to accompany me instead of my wife, Claire. I was beginning to regret the decision.

"To Claire?" Maddy reiterated through clenched teeth and lips stretched so thin across her face they'd lost all color.

Kilkenny crunched up his nose.

I nodded in agreement. I understood. She raised her eyebrows. I was ten-years-old again.

"I understand," I said and tucked my chin into my sternum. Her eyes didn't release me for some time. "You don't need to worry about that," I mumbled and looked up at the framed certificates and degrees that graced the office walls, celebratory magazine articles festooned with photos and toothy grins. This guy had his shit together. The place reeked of success. If he couldn't help, no one could.

When I finally gathered the courage to turn back to Maddy, she was facing Kilkenny, but looking at me out of the corner of squinted eyes like she alone understood the gravity of the situation and how we'd arrived at this moment. I was beginning to understand, too, and it hurt my stomach.

When we left the office, the clear-skied sunlight burned

my eyes. The day itself had forgotten it was a bad day, put on its best face. All was silent until we reached the parked car.

"Do you want me to drive?" Maddy asked.

"Is that where we are now?" I asked as I sat and turned the ignition. She didn't answer.

A few minutes later we were on Route 95 heading north. I thought I wanted quiet, but found myself making nervous conversation.

"What do I do now?"

"I guess forty is over-the-hill," she answered mostly to herself, her eyes glassy and red around the edges. She flipped through the report the nurse printed, making faces. "Wasting disease. Doesn't roll off the tongue as warm and fuzzy does it?"

There it was. Fate had gone one-up on me. After the score was evened when my legs were made compatible, I knew this day would come. I'd been waiting. My right leg began to ache so I rubbed it.

(Bobby)

Claire was the one that got away. Only she didn't.

I spent many evenings hunkered in the Stevens College library, especially freshman year. I needed quiet to study. I needed to study to bring the thoughts that were never completely quiet to heel. I needed to heel the thoughts to survive.

One Wednesday evening, I opened the textbook for my geography class and attempted to focus. The book was awash in colored maps and charts, photos of exotic people and places, but my mind wandered toward my feet, to the carpet, short and brownish with several round, dark stains. Then the desk, small chips in the Formica, names and their fleeting loves carved into the desktop: Millie loves Richard, Richard loves Donna, Donna loves...Back at the textbook I was reading something about a group of Aboriginal Australians who were said to have the smallest brain mass of any humans. The reason I remember this so clearly was it gave me an idea of how to respond to my mother the next time she said I was stupid: "I'm not stupid, I just have a small brain." Ha! It'd be tough to come back at that one.

It was her laugh I heard first. It wafted from the other side of a shelf of dusty library books and danced around my ears, waking them, warming them, making them wonder. It was like the first time I caught the sweet scent of fried dough at a carnival: I didn't know what it was, but I knew I had to find out. I crawled out from my study spot and stood on my side of the bookshelf leaning toward the sound, delighted, mesmerized. The laugh held me aloft for a moment, then ended as quickly as it began. I felt my ears pulling and pushing like a cat searching for a lost sound.

Thankfully, I heard it again, a laugh of child-like innocence and tears of bliss and then snorting sounds that started the joyous seizure all over again. It was the most perfect laugh I'd ever heard: polite yet uncontrolled, like someone trying to unsuccessfully hide their squeaking by burying their face into the pit of their elbow. The Stevens College library, much like the carnival, had offered something special for me to discover. Some call it love-at-first-sight. I'll acknowledge it, but with a slight modification: I didn't need to see her to know she'd make me happy.

By the time I gathered the considerable courage to walk to the end of the aisle and claim my sweet fried dough, she and her laugh had vanished again. Of course, it didn't take long to find her new location. I skulked the long rows of books, using them as cover, leaning into them to mask my pursuit, my ears scanning for waves of bliss. Using only the sense of hearing to guide me had its downside. I took a corner at too high a rate of speed and crashed into the laugher and the classmate she found so entertaining. Both of them jumped backward into the bookstacks and immediately howled in amusement! It was our own Hollywood meet-cute.

Claire had brown eyes and long, naturally straight brown hair and smelled oddly like maple syrup. Brownish freckles dotted happily below each eye, and her fair skin held a healthy hue of pink. I confess that evening in the library, I stood in front of her, unable to speak, barely able to breathe. Once her laughing seizure was complete, she said, "hi." I assume I responded in kind.

Our first "date" was to the dorm cafeteria though neither of us had pancakes or French toast or fried dough. I don't remember what we talked about. It wouldn't have mattered: I was smitten. After all, she was a mysterious and worldly junior to my parochial freshman, someone who, despite my limited conversational skills, saw the graceful swan somewhere inside the ugly duckling.

Claire was English and Scottish and New Englandish and someone in her family—a great, great, great, great somebody or other (also a fine laugher, I assume)—had arrived on the *Mayflower*, his buckled boots setting onto the sandy shore before he promptly died of dysentery. While tragic, this questionably hardy passenger remained a source of family pride for the next few hundred years.

"How did he have time to reproduce?" I asked, mistakenly believing myself a wit.

"We don't laugh at tragedy," she said. The muscles of her face went slack and the freckles on her cheek no longer appeared as happy dots. The color drained from her pinkish skin and she bit her bottom lip. I was frozen, helpless, a fool about to receive what was due for being foolish. I awaited her ancestor's buckled boot to plant itself firmly in my rear-end.

Before I could conjure a frightened, sniveling apology, she let me off the hook. "You wouldn't know that about me, though," she said before resuming a toothy smile. "Now you know."

She majored in literature and liked to read impossible verse and prose by Sylvia Plath and James Joyce. I insisted she read to me, slowly and thoughtfully, and explain the language and meanings, the between-the-lines subtleties. Some evenings, she'd read to me while we lay in bed, warm beneath a sheet and heavy down comforter, our feet rubbing together while her annoyed roommate indicated her simmering disapproval by sucking her teeth. When the weather cooperated, we'd sit on a blanket in the grassy quad of Stevens College, her reading with the warmth and passion of a true believer, while I listened behind the blind eyes of a heretic, the sun warming my skin as I awaited my long-overdue conversion. It never arrived.

After months of patient reading and listening between teacher and student, I concluded I simply wasn't smart enough to grasp either writer. This pronouncement, however honest, made her laugh, which made me happier than understanding Plath or Joyce possible could.

"An artist?" she asked when I offered to show her my drawings. "What do your parents think of that?"

"I never met my father, so he's probably fine with it," I said with a shrug of inferiority. "But my mother, she's another thing all together. She thinks artists are 'sissies.'"

"Then you'll make a fine sissy!" Claire said and laughed before placing a cold-nosed, gentle kiss on my cheek.

One day, many years later, the laughter stopped.

Over coffee one morning, she said while looking past me, "Maybe your mother was right, maybe you are a sissy."

I know she didn't mean it and she knew I wasn't. She had every right to accuse me. One day I stopped touching her. One day I stopped her from touching me. Only it wasn't what she thought it was. It wasn't why she thought it was. It wasn't because I no longer loved her. It was her laugh, or rather not hearing her laugh that morning, that hurt more than her words.

But for the fleeting years she did laugh, they were magical. I attempt to cling to those memories, that laugh, that feeling, that woman, that love. Perhaps it's enough for a lifetime. But like most selfish people, I'd hoped there'd be more and more. I always wanted more.

Claire was the only woman I ever made love to and the only woman I ever loved. Perhaps there was another. There, of course, was sex—sport and the sport of sex. But the others were nothing. Yes, fine, there were others. I couldn't help it. After all, considering where this duckling came from, when others liken you to a graceful swan, you use both hands to gather them up, all of them, then devour them. There is no other way. I always wanted more.

My mistake was simple (it's easy to see now): over time I'd placed Claire on a pedestal and, other than an occasional gentle dusting, kept her elevated high above all else. She was too valuable and lovely to be taken down and played with, too fragile to be handled often. There she sat for far too long. She was my first doll, the first statue in my mind and the inspiration for what became my life's work.

(Bobby)

There were pictures of my father left behind in his wake, memories of fleeting moments chemically sewn in the ripples of time, but not much more. I had no real memories. In these photos, his thick black mustache reflected a different era: long, dark hair scraped his shoulders, the sharp point of his paisley shirt collar barely visible underneath. He looked more folk singer than dad, more hippie than picket-fence suburbanite. Looking toward the lens as the camera worked its magic, his gaze was empty, distant and non-committal as though he were already looking toward his next adventure. His eyes, glassy and slightly sad like a doe who'd recently lost the lean year's only fawn, told me he'd already left. The pictures were old, the corners bent and chemicals breaking down, images beginning to fade. Some were black and white, snapped sometime before my ugly birth, shortly before he departed. Sometime before "Raindrops Keep Fallin' On My Head" had reached its zenith.

The pictures were unorganized, dispersed into several locations: a photo album with crushed corners, a drawer in the dining room, hither and thither. Mother never seemed particularly concerned with the photos, the memories, or their locations. One day, her mood shifted, and she began collecting pictures as she found them, condensing them into one place, one hiding place. Then, over several years, one by one, she took them out to burn in a granite mortar. She lit a match for each one and watched it for a moment as it bubbled, burned yellow and white; she stared in wonder, smiling as if she controlled the destiny of the universe. In some ways, she did. As the pictures burned, she used a pestle to work the melting acetate into a sticky, gritty powder. She leaned into it, using her right shoulder to press her weight into the mortar and her wrist and elbow to twist and grind. Her crooked smile told me she enjoyed the energy and rhythm of this small act of revenge. Perhaps the act of destroying served to create something for her, within her, filling a hole, replacing what she believed was lost. Or eliminating it. The sharp, gritty, scrape of granite against granite, pestle against mortar is imprinted in my memory like a children's television program or 70s advertising jingle.

When her rage was unfulfilled by burning effigies, her eyes would roll back into her head, her hands would begin to shake and, lastly, she'd burst into an insolent rant. "Fuck! Fuck! Fuck!" Like clockwork, she'd hurl a coffee cup or plate. The unlucky object shattered against the floor or wall with a sickening, high-pitched shriek, summoning immediately regret.

"Aunt Lucy's plate!" she'd wail like she'd hurt someone high up in her family tree more than herself or the plate.

After sweeping up the bone-white shards, she'd tearfully inspect each piece, turning it over in her increasingly bloodied hand while imagining, like much of her life, she could glue it all back together. Once she acknowledged the blood and thorns of white imbedded in her soft skin, she knew the moment was over.

As we got older, we could predict the nights when she was most likely to break something, when her rage was bubbling beneath the surface and something handed down from Aunt Lucy was in imminent danger. She'd grow quiet before dinner, almost introspective and with my father's distant gaze. Almost without looking, she'd toss our plates of food onto the table like frisbees. If you weren't expecting dinner to be pitched toward you, it would slide across the smooth surface of the table and land on your lap. We adapted, becoming lightening quick – as we learned, a plate of steaming mashed potatoes or gravy landing on your private areas was most unpleasant.

Soon after dinner, Maddy and I would evacuate to the living room or the safety of Maddy's upstairs bedroom. When we heard "Fuck! Fuck! Fuck!" and the shattering of glass, Maddy (with raised eyebrows and impeccable timing) would mouth, "Aunt Lucy's plate!" and we'd laugh until we cried. Then it was over until next time. I never knew Aunt Lucy or how close she was to my mother, but she must have bequeathed my mother an insatiable table setting for fifty.

In time, Maddy found the hiding spot for the photos: a shoebox on the top shelf of the hallway closet. Now that she could identify the shoebox, it was easier to find when the location changed (which, for unknown reasons, it often did). Maddy liberated many of the surviving pictures of my father, the ones I saw, over the course of several years by slipping them, one by one, between the pages of a well-worn copy of *Watership Down.* She was careful to take only one at a time and not become greedy. Once smuggled to safety, the photos were hidden between a loose slice of blue-whale-and-pink-dolphin wallpaper and the wall near the headboard of her bed. It was an ingenious spot; her eight-year-old self was mature beyond her years. My mother probably thought she'd burned them during one of her fits and never asked us if we'd seen any of them. Or maybe she didn't notice at all.

I imagine my father being a little afraid of mother; we all were at least a little bit. On top of the tendency to speak her mind wherever the words took her, she was prone to wild swings of mood. Learning to detect subtle hints (like before plates took flight) was an art form. Maddy was much more in tune with the atmosphere of a particular moment and on more than one occasion ushered us to safety well in front of the danger.

On one occasion, I remember Maddy whisking me to the park and swings at the end of the block in the dead of night. There, on the swings and under the combined light reflected from the moon and the soft pale of streetlamps, we played and bided our time. When I asked Maddy why we came to the park so late at night, she said "mother was having one of her moments," and it was best for us to be scarce. The calm of the night, the quiet, save the song of crickets, was soothing.

I do remember some of her rant that night, her voice rising toward someone, something unseen:

"You ruined my body and now you're leaving?"

The sound of a frying pan crashing into the sink.

"Go! I'll make sure you never see your children again!"

A water glass shattering on a wall.

"Fuck, fuck, fuck!"

Something passed down from Aunt Lucy meeting its end.

This display of ungainly rage was always followed by a particular, perhaps even peculiar sound. Often two particular and peculiar sounds. The first was the unmistakable sound of a vacuum seal being broken on a jar of pickles. The second, a clink of the pickle jar, just a little lighter in weight, being placed on a wire refrigerator shelf.

Wash, rinse, repeat. If nothing else, my mother was predictable and Maddy was a student of the game.

Her
(Bobby)

The first (and only other) time I fell in love I was ten years old. My first instinct was not to use the word "love." Writing it felt odd, misshapen, too weighty a word for youthful exuberance–what did I know at the age of ten? But, having had time to reflect upon all these years since, after everything, I believe it's the right word, an appropriate usage. What I do know for sure is once I saw her, I couldn't look away. She wouldn't let me. She called to me, a siren's song, demanding to be looked upon, studied, admired and, above all, loved. She needed to be loved as much as I did. To this day, I see her in my dreams, her confidence pulling me forward, the firm, guiding hand of a deity. Such was her immediate and lasting power and my desire to follow her wherever I would be led.

Where does one find such love?

We were on a Saturday trip to the Museum of Fine Arts in Boston, an afternoon my sister earned for us through a combination of good grades, good behavior and the requisite amount of begging. After navigating through Boston traffic, swearing at other drivers with a truck driver's aplomb, my mother herded us up the stairs and through the heavy doors of the museum, paid the admission, placed fresh currency in Maddy's hand (for lunch), and handed us sketch pads and charcoal. Hands on her hips, she lectured us on the meeting time and place, before invoking her well-oiled family trait and vanishing.

"Four o'clock," Mother said, wagging her index finger like a schoolmarm before pointing toward a single black tile on the tile floor in front of the ticket counter. "Be right here at four o'clock."

"What time?" she asked rhetorically, her eyes narrowed to slits and lips pursed, head turned slightly to benefit her ears, arms crossed tightly on her chest.

"Four o'clock," we repeated in dull, mocking unison.

Her brow lifted high onto her forehead as she considered our response before her face and eyes softened, "Have fun," she said, then poof! she was gone.

Maddy pinched her nose with her thumb and index finger and asked in a high-pitched, funny voice, a slightly elongated, "What time?"

"Five o'clock?" I asked.

"Five it is…" Maddy nodded while giving her silver Timex a tepid, thespian's glance. Sometimes, at mother's expense, a little game emerged, a way of wrestling some control over our existence.

"Miss Anthrope can wait 'til five o'clock," Maddy said with a flip of her hair. "The sign says the museum is open until five."

That was Maddy's nickname for mother: "Miss Anthrope."

"Miss Anthrope is looking a little haggard today."

"Miss Anthrope is in rare form, watch yourself."

"Miss Anthrope has locked herself in her room again."

I didn't recognize the cleverness of my sister's words, the small act of rebellion, until many years later. Despite Maddy's physical advantages, her sharp mind, there were times when she, too, was ground down with mortar and pestle. Mother didn't take drink—she was perpetually sober—so her anger, her harangued persona, was organic and long lasting, and no one escaped the net it cast, at least not for long. Not even Maddy.

That morning, in a great square hall well lit, I stumbled across the bronze cast of *Little Fourteen-Year-Old Dancer* by Edgar Degas. It was spot-lit with the care of a jeweler showing off his prized diamond and given ample real estate in the white hall, room to breathe, to dance. I fell in an immediate love, deep and unconditional. I'd never seen anything so beautiful, so confident, so perfect. She held me in her charms, unable to move for fear the moment would end. She danced for me though she never moved, she was smiling at me, though she never smiled.

Maddy witnessed the moment the dancer caught my eye, heard my sneakers skid to a halt, echo, on the tile, watched the bend in my neck as I studied her, rising on tip-toes to gain a higher angle, a better view. If there was a perfect vantage point, a golden view, I would find it. I would attempt it all that day.

Years later, Maddy laughed as she described the moment

I saw her, the moment her light filled me. "It was like she grabbed you and pulled you in for a hug."

"She did," I admitted.

Although I was unaware at the time, the dancer too, at least in sculpture form, had been considered ugly in her day, an assault on the senses, a duckling in a world that demanded the grace and beauty of swans. It was a match of destiny. I walked no further.

Perhaps the dancer *was* ugly, like me, but she was not ugly *to* me. Is that the personification of love? There was something I could only assume was beauty, for I did not immediately recognize it. After all, what did I know about beauty? Yet, there it was, something at least that made me warm and damp with tears I hid from Maddy. So, it did exist. She was a duckling who, given time, would evolve into a swan.

Despite her initial hesitation, I sent Maddy away to explore the rest of the museum. I was a fastidious child who chewed his fingernails to the quick with utmost concentration, often until the skin was swollen and bleeding. In other words, she knew If I told her I was staying put, there was little doubt I'd stay put. She would find me precisely where she left me, floating, oddly smug.

I spent the day admiring Degas' creation, studying her, attempting (unsuccessfully) to sketch her graceful lines in charcoal. A hundred different angles were explored, pivoting on my left leg (just like old times) to garner a different view, sitting on the floor or a bench, resting on my knees until both legs ached. At one point, at least until museum security put an end to it, I'd sprawled myself into a position normally reserved for sleeping. In the end, and not unexpectedly, I couldn't capture or replicate Degas' magic. To this day, no one has. That's how you know the magic is pure.

Could it be the dreamy dancer was simply an infatuation with, at the time, a poised and determined, older woman? I considered it (since I would repeat it with Claire), but the sculpture has remained a part of me. It wasn't fleeting. And I became determined not to simply attempt to replicate the "magic," the emotion of another's work, but to light my own way, to machete my own path through the jungle. Someday, would my creations summon in others the raw, beautiful emotion Degas conjured in me? Although I would never tell them, while my friends spent their nights dreaming of pitching for the Red Sox at Fenway, this is what I dreamed. I was, and remain, an odd duck.

The hours of the day passed in an instant. I stood in front of her, wide-eyed, until 4:58pm when Maddy fetched me and announced in her pinched-nose funny voice, "It's 5 o'clock and Miss Anthrope expects us at 5 o'clock." By 4:58pm, I knew what I would become or at least what I would strive to become. She became my reason, Degas my light, my must, and my camouflage from the world. She was why I persevered. If not for her, there would be no me. At night, my mind still takes me back to that day, the day my innocence was lost because I discovered beauty. It did exist! I'd now seen it. There was no turning back.

Mother met us on that one black tile in front of the ticket window. She was attempting to remain calm, arms crossed, the tap of her toe echoing into the empty foyer. Maddy had won and Mother knew she couldn't wrestle back the hour lost. What would be the point; the hour was gone, evaporated. Poof! She didn't speak to us all the way home, and we didn't attempt to speak to her. Her form of road rage picked up where it left off. And, if I'm not mistaken, she learned some new words while we were in the museum, words that made the other drivers blush. Even if, between gestures to her fellow drivers, she'd lectured us on the value and virtues of respecting time, it wouldn't have made a difference to me. I was happy. It was my time.

(Bobby)

Mother liked to hunt mice, which is to say she trapped them, which is to also say our house, partly due to years of neglect, had a mouse problem. They were gray and brown field mice, quick and healthy, and their reproductive verve put the local rabbits on notice. They'd crawl and dig and chew their way into the cellar, a rodent-friendly wonderland of soiled antique furniture and water-stained cardboard boxes that no one remembered storing, the contents, whether junk or treasure or both, long forgotten.

Once everyone had gone to bed and the house settled into quiet, the mice made their way upstairs via a labyrinth of hollowed walls, flattened insulation and aging electrical wires. They followed their noses to a bounty of unwashed spoons and plates in the kitchen sink and poorly washed spoons and butter knives in the utensil drawer, both promising a tidbit of leftover dinner or the tasty, fossilized residue of peanut butter. The trash can, if unemptied, offered another treat.

There was a fraternal bond between the mice and me, a

kinship of sorts where both of us balanced the danger and safety of the house on Bradley Street. The traps were set for both of us, though the mechanical, spring-set ones awaiting them were more lethal. Or at least lethal more quickly. I wonder why mice would want to come in to that particular house on Bradley, why they would enter the very place I myself was so keen to escape. Regrettably, they snuck in, made themselves at home, and none of us, including Maddy, ever really left. Perhaps the mice were simply seeking a finality, a relatively painless end, one that escapes me still. It's easier to see now, of course, it's always is easier at the close.

At the top of the cellar stairs, near the door to the main floor, Mother kept a chalkboard ledger of kills for the year, scratching one short line for each of the dead and a diagonal slash over the lines when she had four dead plus one. It was a handsome, framed chalkboard, black slate with a red painted trim, better suited to a grocery list than a death count. At the top of the board were two words, lowercase, written in heavy white chalk by a steady hand: "little fuckers." I imagined one day I would be a slash upon her board, the ticking off of a dead man well short of his prime, felled, if not by his mother's hand, then by her design. Naturally, Maddy would escape, over the wall, across the moat, into the forest. I would make sure of it. She was hope, and someone needed to survive to tell the story. Someone needs to be the keeper of secrets.

In the cellar, mechanical traps were placed in between the cardboard boxes and in the spidery undersides of old couches, near the small rectangular windows which teased in sunlight. The minefield of traps wasn't mapped and the lighting was woefully insufficient. If you drew the short straw and were sent on an errand to the cellar to retrieve Christmas decorations or the like, you counted your toes, pulled on your sturdiest shoes—the ones with the hardest leather toe—and hoped for the best.

The wire guillotines were baited with dollops of peanut butter spooned directly from the jar. The metal spoon scraped and scratched against the trap's small metal platform: the trigger, shaped, expectedly, like a two-dimensional slice of cheese. Mother used her hitchhiker-strengthened thumb to push the springy wire down and set the wire arm. The arm trembled against the upward push of the spring, awaiting the slightest touch, the most insignificant reason to unfurl its fury. Her face brightened each time a trap was set; each time the wire quivered in anticipation.

Mother became so adept at setting the mechanism, so nimble of finger that she was able to accomplish the task with one hand, sometimes without looking. Maddy and I both awaited the day her fingers would fail; a butter-greased digit would miss the mark and she would fall victim to her own machinations and the miniature guillotine. But it didn't happen, at least not yet and not due to this particular guillotine.

Be careful. I am death.

Mother also spoke to the dead. When she found a corpse, corpulent and slightly warm, its black eyes bulging out from the skull like antennae or intestines shot out of its anus like a shoed-foot had stomped on a full tube of toothpaste, she'd give them a little lecture.

"Tell your friends," she'd say with a snarled upper lip and pointed index finger, bending at the waist with her head down. "Tell them if they don't want to make my board, they should stay outside. You tell them I mean it. I don't crawl into their homes, no I don't!"

There were times I worried her warnings were really meant for my ears, or Maddy's. It was difficult to know where the fury would be unleashed next. After the speech, she'd march the cooling body outside, the thin wooden base of the trap pinched between her thumb and index finger, and pull up the springy wire. The body, now unencumbered by its wire assassin, fell free and landed on the ground with a soft "thud," released back into nature. Then she'd lean back on her hips and with a deep, guttural hack, pull phlegm upward and swish it around her mouth before thrusting forward and letting fly a thick ball of spit. It was a "good riddance." Over the years, the neighborhood kids treated our yard with a cautious forbearance, like ours was Bradley Street's haunted house and mother the phantom lurking in the shadows.

Despite being high season for vermin, each New Year's Day she washed the chalkboard with soap and water, using a thin, worn rag to wipe it clean of the previous year's ticks and slashes. She left the two lowercase words that inspired the board untouched along with a number written in the upper right-hand corner that represented the prior year's total. I'm not sure of her record catch, but I do remember the number "55" scratched proudly in white chalk high in the corner. It may have been easier to get a cat—maybe two cats considering the volume of visitors.

People remember the holiday season in different ways: trimming the Christmas tree each year or baking cookies with their grandmother—perhaps the scent of hardwood burning in a fireplace. My memory is the chalkboard and the marks of the dead. Maddy puts a positive spin on her chalkboard memory. Instead of ticks and slashes, she has a chalkboard that's hung on the wall the day after Thanksgiving; each day she updates the number below the words "Days 'til Christmas" written in her looping, optimistic script.

And how do I remember the holiday season? How do I remember using spoons and spoonsful of peanut butter so vividly? Some things you can't forget. Some things stay with you—biding their time, waiting to become your demise. Probably more than once, I reached for a spoon from the drawer in the kitchen and, without much thought, spooned out a mouthful of peanut butter. And, to my horror, I'd feel the hardened residue of mouse droppings fused to the bottom of the spoon, scrapping across my tongue, dragged across my dried lips.

Was it possible I ingested a rodent virus on one of these occasions? Swallowed the very poison that plagues me now? Is it possible it remained dormant for thirty years only to fulfill its destiny as wasting disease? I can't help but believe its possible. Perhaps the mice have had their revenge at last.

Be careful. I am death.

I sometimes paint mother as a (mostly) harmless court jester, someone to take lightly and smirk and smile and pity: Miss Anthrope. But she was not such. This fabrication, this persona, was all for Maddy and me to hide behind, a magician's cape to wield and, with a flick of the wrist, *abracadabra!* make things disappear.

The metamorphosis into this comical figure was primarily to dull our pain. It was easier to see her as a bit of a joke, as someone to almost feel sorry for, than for what she really was. It was easier to laugh than to loathe or fear. Although we wouldn't recognize it for many years, it became its own form of therapy.

But mother was consistent. And she was persistent. There was always another insult, another emasculation waiting to reveal itself, to be pulled from a black hat standing on its bottom. One evening during semester break, before I was meeting Claire for a date, Mother informed me that I "smelled." More precisely, I smelled like "ass," and Claire was sure to be offended.

"What do you mean I smell?"

"You stink. Something foul."

I couldn't figure it out. I'd showered with a normal and expected soap, washed my hair with the available shampoo, dried thoroughly and dressed in (presumedly) fresh clothes. I double, triple, quadruple checked my deodorant.

"I don't know what it is, but you bathed in something pungent, rolled in something like a stray dog," she continued. "I'm surprised this girl likes you as it is, she may not soon enough."

Then, with her usual aplomb: "No girl is going to like you with that leg and that nose, anyway."

As it turns out, I'd found an old cologne bottle that had once belonged to my father and sprayed a bit on my neck, trying it on for size. Having so many years to ferment was perhaps not best for such things, though I didn't recall the scent being unpleasant. As a matter of fact, I thought it both mature and appropriate, a manly, musky fragrance. The cologne did not go over well with mother.

I scrubbed my neck with a washcloth until it was red and painful, the skin rubbed raw from the friction. A trace of the offending scent remained, but I'd diluted it as much as possible. The bloodied cloth could remove no more, the remainder pulled into my blood and spread throughout my body. Claire either didn't notice or was too fine a person to mention it.

As for mother, would it not have been easier, less painful to let me be? Or to explain what offending scent had singed her nose and why it remained offensive? Could she have chastised my decision to take the green flask from the bottom drawer and dare to spray it on skin of my neck? Instead, it was necessary for her to question my fitness in Claire's eyes and make me wonder if I would find myself satisfactory in anyone's eyes. And for that, and a thousand stings of the wasp, I die a little each day.

The Calloways (Bobby)

Unsurprisingly, Claire's homelife was different than my own. Perhaps that was part of the allure, my habit of reaching out to grab something valuable when it was in reach. She grew up playing polo (at least her family did) and riding horses and reading books. Her family had a gray-shingled vacation house nestled in Nantucket Town.

Over the summer, I was invited to spend a week at the Nantucket house. When Claire extended the invitation, I embarrassedly explained that I didn't have money for such a trip. I was yet to find a summer job and a week's vacation was out of reach and out of the question.

"You don't need money," she said and laughed to indicate just how silly I could be.

"I don't?"

"Of course not. You're my family's guest."

"What about a sleeping bag and pillows?"

Another laugh. "Just bring clothes and a toothbrush."

"Do I need a bike?"

"Clothes and a toothbrush," she said slowly and a bit louder, forming the letters with exaggerated movements of her lips.

Mr. Calloway, Judge Calloway, was a judge or a barrister or an attorney—he was someone with a mysterious "Esq" hanging off the end of his name. As far as I know, he was the first "Esq" I'd ever met. Did that mean he'd inherited a title from some dusty European kingdom: like the Duke of Tuscany or the Prince of East-Southern Wales or the Esq. of Bavaria?

The first time I met him—and Claire's mother—was at a dinner at their house on a Sunday near the end of my second semester at Stevens College. Claire drove us from campus, over to Route 1A and down into Ipswich. It was a beautiful drive filled with saltmarshes and fields and other natural wonders. I wore an argyle sweater, blue with red, my only reasonable piece of clothing but the day turned out to be unseasonably warm. Under the sweater I had a stained button down that couldn't be shown the light of day. My nervousness, the sweater, and the heat of the day made me even more uncomfortable, damp, swampy.

"Art?" Esq asked over dinner. It sounded more like he was double-checking if my name was Arthur than inquiring about my future profession.

"Yes," I said and sank into the chair. "Probably sculpture," I managed to squeeze out before my throat closed from panic.

He thought for a moment.

"So, I assume there's a trust fund for your day-to-day?"

"Oh, yes! Big trust fund!" I said and laughed.

I'd thought he was making a joke, but he wasn't smiling.

"No, Dad, there's not a fund set aside." It was Claire to the rescue.

I wasn't sure where to look or who to look at.

Her father nodded his head and took another bite of his dinner, giving him time to think and me enough time to locate the exits.

"Are you planning to teach?"

"No, sir," I said. "I hadn't considered it."

"You'll need a way to pay back any student loans."

"Thankfully, I don't have any loans. My father…" I hesitated. "It's just my mother and my sister. The financial aid office was very kind."

"He's done well for himself," Claire explained.

Her father nodded and raised his glass of wine in my direction in congratulations.

"The world needs art and, therefore it needs artists. I sincerely wish you well," he said as he raised the glass.

There was a glass of red wine in front of me and I lifted it.

He continued. "I support any endeavor as long as your heart's in it and you keep at it." Then he laughed. "Of course, a trust fund would've helped."

I nodded in agreement.

The Calloways lived on several acres of wildflowers and stone walls, a watercolorist's dream of May yellows and greens and blues. The house was large, but modest, a New England colonial, five windows across the second floor and painted a deep, antique red. It looked like it hadn't changed in two hundred years. It probably hadn't. The sturdy furniture, too, matched an age long past, with its dark wood; yet it remained both useful and dignified. It held an elegant, museum quality but was warm and inviting, much like the Calloways themselves.

Claire instructed me to bring my sketches to that first dinner.

"My mother will want to see your work," she explained.

"I'm not sure I want to do that," I answered.

"Don't worry," she said. "My mother's probably the most positive person you'll ever meet."

And Claire was right.

"Teaching is an honorable profession," Mrs. Calloway explained. "Perhaps the most honorable."

Claire was smiling along as her mother spoke from a flowered couch across from us.

"If you ever decide to teach art, to go down that path, don't consider it a failure or a reflection on your talent. Think of it as the opportunity to share your passion with the next generation. A utilization of your talent—certainly not a waste."

"Are you a teacher?" I asked.

"Almost thirty years," she admitted with a laugh. "What gave it away?"

"Boundless optimism."

"You need it!" she said before slapping her knees with the palms of both hands. "Did you bring any of your work?"

"I told you she'd ask," Claire said as she elbowed my ribs.

I reluctantly handed over one of my sketchbooks I'd placed in a backpack. It contained my safest, most mundane work—it was selected, on my part, with duly, conservative care.

Mrs. Calloway flipped through it with aloof indifference, one leg crossed on the other, delicately bouncing. Her eyes scanned each page twice before she flipped to the next. About halfway through, she stopped flipping pages and looked up at me.

"Bowls of fruit? Flags? Shelves of books?"

"Class work," I explained.

"No, no, no," she said and shook her head. "Where's your real work? Where's the soul of your work? Where's Bobby? I want Bobby. Show me."

Claire lifted her eyebrows and smiled.

I extended my hand to retrieve the sketchbook and opened it to a blank page. I found a piece of charcoal in one of the pockets of my backpack.

"May I?" I asked Mrs. Calloway.

"Of course!"

I began to draw Mrs. Calloway, her brown hair that settled on her shoulders, brown eyes that drew me in—a long, stately nose over pink, narrow lips. A long, angular neck. It was effortless, flowing from my hand with an ease I'd never experienced. Claire watched over my shoulder, smiling, looking down at the paper and then back to her mother. She could have predicted the entire affair.

When I'd finished, I handed the sketchbook back to Mrs. Calloway.

She stared at the page for several moments then smiled. "Ah, there's Bobby," she exhaled in relief. "There's the talent. Can I keep this so I have something when you're famous?"

"Please," I said and gestured my hand toward her to indicate it was for her.

"By the way, this is how I get all of my art for free," she said and giggled.

My mother's reaction to Claire, or the news that there was a Claire, was slightly different than that of Claire's family to my existence.

"Mom, I met a girl."

"A girl?"

"Yes."

"Does she like you?"

"I think so."

"Are you sure?"

"No, but I think so. I'm pretty sure."

"You might want to make sure," she scoffed. "A girl has never liked you before. I don't want you to be disappointed."

Then she said:

"Do you remember what happened last time you were disappointed?"

"No."

"Elementary school?"

"No."

"Mrs. Wilson's class?"

"That was a long time ago."

"It was, yes. But you do remember?"

"I remember you having a conversation with her."

How could I forget the conversation they had during a parent-teacher conference while I sat meekly at my school desk, trying to hide under it, playing with a pencil to keep my mind busy and trying to evaporate into the atmosphere. That school year, I was having trouble seeing the blackboard, and despite my protest, my desk was moved toward the front of the classroom. While it resolved the issue of being able to see the letters, numbers, and facts and figures that were written in chalk, it took me away from my social group—my friends with good eyesight. It was a difficult transition, but one which was slowly working its own way through.

My mother, ever the concerned parent and always feeling the compulsion to humiliate me, told Mrs. Wilson that she would watch for signs of stress at home as I had a tendency to wet the bed during times of stress.

How dare you! I thought to myself. But the words could not squeeze between my clenched teeth. They were fighting to escape, my tongue circling my mouth ready to spew forth my true feelings or at least my true feelings of the moment. Yet I held back; I did not make things worse.

Was I growing up? Was I learning the rumored self-control of the mature self? Was I realizing she was damaged, and

I couldn't allow myself to submit to her demons?

It was none of it. But I kept silent anyway and walked away. Like I always did.

"We're opening the Nantucket house on Memorial Day, did Claire extend an invitation?"

"She did, yes."

"I hope you'll join us."

"Thank you, Mr. Calloway. That's very kind."

"Is this *girl* offering you sex?"

"What?"

"You heard me."

"We're just hanging out, Ma."

"That sounds like sex to me."

"Is that really any of your business?"

"Everything is my business. Maybe she'll try and get pregnant to trap you. Then you'll have no choice but to marry her."

"What? Why would you say that?"

"Because that's what some girls do."

"She's not *that* type of girl."

"Yeah, well, you don't know that."

"If this is what you want to do for the rest of your life, you need to not only work hard, but find something that makes you unique. You'll need to stand out from the crowd."

"Yes, sir," I nodded.

"This is not a traditional career like finance or engineering, the expectations and the opportunities are somewhat limited, but they exist if you look hard enough. Your goal will need to be 'I'm going to change the world!'"

"Yes, sir."

"My wife has a good eye and she likes what she sees."

"Thank you."

"You'll have to give it everything you have. Are you ready to do that?"

"Yes, sir. I believe I am."

"Then," he said with a smile. "I admire you. Never give up and never let anyone tell you that you can't do it."

His stare morphed into something more, a connection, a direct portal into my mind. I could hear him even though he wasn't speaking.

"Are you sure?" he said without moving his lips.

"I'm sure," my mind answered back.

His smile remained and I dared to smile back even though I was afraid it would dampen the moment.

"It's known that all artists must suffer for their art. They have to go through something traumatic in order to find their path."

"I have heard that," I said.

"Are you prepared for it?"

"I believe I've suffered some."

"But have you suffered enough?"

"How will I know?"

"You'll know. It will be impossible to not know."

Quickly, his smile turned over into a frown and his eyebrows floated high on his forehead. He took in a deep breath through the nose and said, "And don't hurt my daughter. She's a trusting soul, like her mother."

Then: "Did Claire tell you my brother-in-law, her uncle, was an artist."

"Oh?"

"Yes," he said as his frown continued. "He killed himself after working on a single painting for three years, a bowl of fruit. He was driven mad by it, the shapes and colors, shadows and light, by his own pursuit of perfection."

My eyes widened and my mouth hung open.

"I'm just kidding!" he said and laughed. "He's a pediatrician."

The Story of The Claw (Bobby)

I'm told there are two sounds so grotesquely terrifying and unique they can neither be mistaken for other sounds nor ever forgotten. The first is the greasy thud of a human body striking a sidewalk after a freefall from a particularly high place. The second is the sound I heard on a snowy afternoon in February.

The light of morning unveiled a classic Nor'easter, a blizzard, gray, blinding and stubborn, a time to hunker down in front of the warmth of a wood stove and enjoy the day off from school. But the snow was piling up, two feet of it by midday, and almost five feet of windblown white leaned heavily against the garage door, threatening to collapse it inward. The wind-driven snow *tap-tapped* against the picture window sounding more like small grains of sand than white flakes. With each gust of wind, the cold penetrated the small spaces where the window met the frame, driving frigid winter into the room. The oil burner in the cellar coughed and wheezed, desperately trying to keep the house at temperature. I couldn't get warm.

Mother sat at the kitchen table with a hot cup of tea, staring at nothing in particular. She was worried about the electricity being knocked off, especially once the early winter sunset pulled us back into darkness and the temperature dropped. The electrical grid had proven unreliable in past winters, failing during lesser storms, failing when you could least afford it to fail. Mother readied the wood stove, arranged the wood inside and sent me to fetch a half dozen extra logs from the garage. Safety matches were ready to be lit in a pinch. In the past, the wood stove had proven a reliable ally.

"Grab the shovels," she said as much out loud into the room as to Maddy and me. It was time.

We'd already assembled our heavy socks and boots, thermal underwear, hats, scarves and gloves, our quilted winter coats. All these garments were gathered in the hours before the storm hit, pulled from drawers and closets, dug from the dusty underneath of beds, from bins in the attic, all in anticipation. In order to fuel the task ahead, I woofed down a bologna sandwich with yellow mustard and washed it down with chocolate milk.

There were four aluminum-bladed snow shovels in the garage, two fully broken and two partially broken. I fumbled through the shovels and found the least broken of the lot for myself before handing Maddy a partially disfigured one. She rolled her eyes and sighed at the sight of her flaccid shovel. "Thanks," she offered though both of us knew she didn't mean it. There was a snowblower, an old cantankerous model that shook and belched blue smoke and may have come with the house. That was mother's weapon, not to be touched by untrained hands.

We had maybe an hour of daylight before the dark stole what little warmth the February sun provided. Thankfully, the wind calmed a bit as we began to free the garage door from the weight of the snow. It was what I'd call a medium weight snow—neither fluffy, light and back saving, nor slushy and back breaking. It was slightly wet, perfect for snowballs and Maddy and I spent as much time sneak attacking one another as we did the task at hand. The distraction did not go unnoticed by our mother, though she didn't make a comment or attempt to refocus us.

It wasn't a small driveway, though it wasn't large either. There was enough space for four cars and since our car was parked safely in the garage, the entirety of the driveway needed to be cleared. Mother fired up the snowblower and cut a small path out the side door of the garage. The blades ate large chunks of snow and a stream of digested white flew out of the top of the machine. But the problem was the snow itself. If you were looking to have a snowball fight or build an off-kilter snowman, it was ideal. However, if you were running a snowblower, it was just gluey enough to clog the chute, just sticky enough to prevent meaningful progress. Mother's body language indicated her frustration was building. Her body was angular, ridged, unhappy. Yet she continued forward, pushing and pushing, straining behind the weight. She leaned into it, pushing, attempting to will it forward, but the machine bogged down.

The snowblower struggled, strained, whirred, as equally angry as my mother appeared. Streams of gobbled snow no longer spewed from the chute on top. It was now barely a trickle despite the abundant snow directly in its path. Mother began to push and prod the machine with a gloved hand, clearing the chute and restoring a healthy arc of blown snow. This was repeated several times over the course of clearing the driveway. Progress slowed to a crawl.

This is what I heard next:

A bump.

A bang.

A clank.

A thud.

A crunch.

A wet tree branch being cut.

A wet tree branch being severed.

A wet tree branch being maimed.

A wet tree branch being fed into a wood chipper.

A scream.

This is what I saw:

A gloved hand pulled downward.

A gloved hand released upward.

A torn glove.

A ripped glove.

An incomplete glove.

A body shaking.

Red.

This is what I smelled:

Gasoline.

Exhaust fumes.

A civet scent of sweat.

A sweet, metallic scent of blood.

A scent of raw lamb.

Mother stumbled away from the machine, her executioner, in wobbly, plodding steps, taking great gasps of air like a goldfish raised from its bowl, using her left hand to hold the right by the wrist. She inspected her hand, eyes searching for what was no longer there, one glove finger missing, one empty glove finger still attached, dangling by a thread.

"Fuck, fuck, fuck!"

The snow beneath her looked like a cherry snow cone.

"Find the fingers!" she bellowed, half command, half call of desperation.

"How many?" Maddy asked instinctually.

"Find them! Two fingers! I don't know!"

Maddy, ghost white, ran in circles, stumbling over her shovel before falling to her knees, crying, patting the snow with her hands in helpless search.

I stood motionless, unable to comprehend the scene before me, as useless as the severed digits themselves.

"Bobby!"

I looked toward the direction of the sound, but I couldn't be sure of the source. All the day dissembled and darkness began to envelope the outer rims of my sight, closing in as I was about to lose consciousness. I was brought back by the scream of specific instructions.

"Bobby! Find the fingers!"

Two pale yellow eyes of a city plow truck illuminated our block, scraping the pavement with a growl as it pushed along a curling wave of filthy snow. Mother bounded through the snow we'd yet to clear, down the driveway toward the eyes, waving two hands and eight fingers above her head. The plow came to a whistling, sliding stop. She yelled something to the driver, at the driver. A man leaped from the truck and pulled my mother up into the cab.

"Go into the house you two! Go get warm." he yelled. "I'll look for the fingers and get her to the hospital."

Maddy and I stood still, silently staring into the now increasing wind and snow and cold.

"Go! Now!" he commanded, his silhouette against the yellow lights of the plow truck breaking our trance.

We watched from the window as he turned off the snowblower and walked in unbalanced, shrinking circles. A minute later the truck pulled into our driveway to reverse direction, easily traversing the pavement despite the still accumulating snow, the red taillights disappeared into the evening. The plow driver never found the fingers or if he did, they were too damaged to reattach.

The house was warmer than I expected. Maddy made us pancakes for dinner, mixing batter with a wire whisk before pouring it onto a giant pan to form frisbee-sized cakes. We drenched them in an inch of both corn and maple syrup, watched it creep over the sides, causing the plates to stick to the table. We didn't speak. We didn't say what we were thinking. It didn't need to be said. Before bed, I didn't brush my teeth.

While Mother was at the hospital, drenched in her own Hell, I never felt more at peace.

A neighbor brought her home late that evening, dumped her on our doorstep, absorbed our gratitude while refusing our invitation to come in for tea or coffee. The snow was still falling, the neighbor explained, and she needed to get back to shoveling before "everything froze solid."

"Nothing freezes in Hell," Maddy said under her breath.

The hand was set in a plaster cast so I wasn't able to see the full extent of the damage. The white cast, square and dense, made it look like she was wielding Thor's hammer on the end of her arm. Her face was gaunt, older and there were deep, purple crescents under each eye. She was groggy from painkillers and possibly blood loss and stumbled through the house like a drunk on a bender. Maddy brought her to bed and gave her a glass of water and covered her with blankets. We set the bottle of painkillers on her nightstand next to the water and Maddy wrote down the approximate times she was supposed to take another dose.

Lying in my bed that night, I didn't dream of playing for the Red Sox, or of sinking the winning basket beneath the rafters of Boston Garden. I didn't dream at all. Instead, I thought, *We are the two children, the digits. We are the fingers, they are us, severed at the base, marred, useless.* We were lucky the electricity hadn't failed and the house remained reasonably comfortable. At some point during the night, someone plowed the driveway clean down to the pavement, so clean, in fact, it looked like someone had swept it with a broom. When I sensed the driveway was clear and the fingers were gone, I slept soundly. I never heard a thing.

She took a week off from work and swallowed pain pills like they were breath mints. A few days later, the plow driver stopped by to check in on her. The driver was a short man with small black boots, thick around the waist and a heavy, dark beard that pulled his face downward. She hugged him until his eyes grew wide and his mouth hung open like he was attempting to catch an elusive breath. Once free of the hug, he shuffled, red faced, back to his city truck and never returned. Perhaps under the fog of pain medication she'd whispered something into his ear, an offer to square the favor one way or another and, like my father, he'd made a break for it.

For the rest of her days Mother stared in wonder at the space where the index and middle fingers of her right hand, her dominant hand, were missing, ground down to useless, pulpy stumps, pink and red and calloused. Now she possessed a claw from those funhouse games, the ones that ate your quarters and failed to grab the elusive toy from atop the corpulent pile of fuzzy, elusive toys. From that day forward, my mother, too, had her own brand of funny walk.

Some years ago, Mother took a correspondence course on how to draw. She found an advertisement in one of her glossies and wrote a letter (and, I assume, cut a check) to sign up. The advertisement had her draw a duck named Teddy or Lucky or something or other, with his large baker-inspired hat and wide, buckled belt. Once completed, she sent her version of Teddy or Lucky in for a professional evaluation. Yes, she too had talent, so she reminded me. But the realities of a clawed right hand put an end to that dream. If only she'd used her left hand to reach into the mouth of the monster during that February blizzard, she could have joined a long line of sissies.

It wasn't drawing she missed most, however. She was a great consumer of pickles (and sometimes pickle juice): sweet, sour, bread and butter, dill, kosher—she loved them all. But now that her right hand was damaged, nearly useless, she could no longer grip the jar and cover at the same time. There wasn't enough strength to twist. By default, I became the designated opener of the pickle jars, the extra hand, the saving grace. I believe she missed being able to open the jars more than the digits themselves.

Bobby's Mother (Claire)

I wasn't looking forward to meeting Bobby's mother. I'd heard stories—odd, heartbreaking stories—and none of them gave me a warm, fuzzy feeling. During the drive, I picked at my cuticles until my index finger was bleeding and I was afraid I might get blood on my white sweater. It was, until then, my lucky sweater. I didn't want blood on my lucky white sweater and I didn't want to explain why there was blood on it. Bobby didn't attempt to comfort me, to tell me it was all in my head and there was nothing to worry about. He didn't suggest thinking happy thoughts, of wandering far away in a dream, or even breathing deeply. I considered barricading myself in the car when we pulled up to the house, but I knew the opportunity for protest was days in the past. I took a deep breath and licked the blood off my finger one last time.

Instead of comfort, Bobby warned me this first meeting might be a little unusual, a bit awkward; his mother might say something strange or ask questions that one wouldn't expect to be asked when meeting someone for the first time. It wasn't his best sales pitch, but he'd already met my parents, and fair is fair. Needless to say, I was nervous.

The house itself was stout and low to the ground, bungalow style, brown with brown shutters and a heavy front door painted Satanic red. There were two small windows built into the pitch of the roof, bedrooms, I assumed, and likely hot as hell during the summer. In a past life, the house was likely a vacation home for Boston eccentrics, a trimmed-down escape out to the woods (which were long gone), away from the hustle and bustle. Whatever his reason, Bobby insisted on knocking on Satan's door and waiting for his mother to answer rather than simply opening it and walking inside. Perhaps he wanted her to see for herself that he'd actually brought home a girl, just like he said he would.

"This is Claire," Bobby said when our eyes, his mother's and mine, met. She had Bobby's eyes, dark blue, like an uncrossable ocean. She must have had her hair done recently, as she kept touching it admiringly, making sure to show it still had the requisite bounce and not a hint of gray.

"Pleased to meet you," I said in my best voice, my formal voice used for church and dinner with my father's colleagues. I extended my hand, but she didn't seem to notice it.

"Nice to meet you, Claire," she said and offered a lukewarm smile indicating she didn't really mean it. "Welcome, welcome. Can I get you something to drink?"

A few minutes later she delivered a cup of tea, tepid, but not unreasonably, served in a fragile cup, generations old, with a small chip on the rim.

She smelled vaguely of pickle juice or vinegar, old attic wood, and a scarcity that was foreign to me. Bobby had mentioned the accident and her hand so I did my best to not look at it even though I was curious. I'd met Maddy, a lithe, attractive young woman and I expected the same of the mother. But she was short and slightly round and skulked around like she spent the better part of her day waiting for three billy goats to cross a bridge.

We, his mother and I, took seats on two separate couches. The couches themselves were separated by a rectangular coffee table and faced each other in the small living room perhaps set up to encourage debates or card games, possibly arm wrestling. It was late afternoon, but heavy drapes blocked most of the natural light and the lightbulbs of two small lamps were barely adequate. The room reminded me of a day darkened by thickening storm clouds and trepidation. I awaited my opportunity to attempt a bridge crossing.

Everything she said, each question she asked was accompanied by a smile, slightly crooked and insincere, but a smile nonetheless. I imagine she'd honed this habit as a way of pivoting toward a joke should she be called out for insubordination or accused of ulterior motives. It was unsettling, and she was very good at it.

Bobby went into the kitchen and banged things together like he was cooking a meal for twenty. This clanging about provided just enough cover for her smile to set its sights on uncovering *my* ulterior motives.

"I hear your father's a judge," she began.

"He is, yes."

"That must come in handy."

"Handy for what?" I asked.

Her face grew stern, the thick skin of her cheeks hidden behind the many shadows of the room, behind the safety of the red door. She looked me up and down like we were on opposite sides of the butcher counter. However, she caught herself and resumed the smile before speaking. She pounced.

"Are you pregnant?"

"What? No!"

"Are you having sex with my son?"

"I…I…ummmmm."

"You don't need to answer that. I already know."

Smiling.

"I can tell," she said with a curled upper lip and a dismissive wave of her good hand, the left one. "I can always tell by the way a girl sits."

I placed my hands on my knees and pulled them in closer together while looking around the room, an infant searching for help. If there was a couch blanket, I would have crawled beneath it.

She took a sip of tea, picking up the delicate cup with the motley remains of her right hand. "You can always tell," she said under her breath.

She stared at me for a few moments, almost through me, like she was thinking of something far away or long ago or perhaps whether she wanted the butcher to trim off more fat.

"That one, he's like his father," she continued and shook her head. "Not to be trusted."

"In what way?" I squeaked after swallowing the bile built up in my throat.

"He'll be the master of disappearing. A ghost. A breeze that will rustle the leaves of the trees before it blows off to somewhere else. Somewhere new." She spoke like she'd rehearsed this speech a hundred times, learned it cold should this occasion ever arise. I heard her breath, pushing and pulling through her nose.

Somewhere in the darkened, stormy, living room, a bolt of courage struck me; the words took charge before I could hold them back. I pounced.

"Perhaps I'm the one who can't be trusted."

Her crooked smile morphed into a giant grin and she began to laugh, a gorgeous, toothy, belly laugh.

"Bobby!" she shouted over her shoulder, over the clammer of pots and pans, toward the kitchen. "Bobby! I like this one!"

Maddy's Story (Bobby)

Maddy was many things including the keeper of secrets.

Maddy was the girl everyone wanted their son to date and court and marry, one of the good kids that had her shit together and smiled a great deal, even when everyone else had given up. But there was only one Maddy and her heart belonged to David and David's heart to her. It was quite lovely, really.

They met in the fourth grade, Mrs. Callahan's class, and through the awkward growth spurts and braced teeth, the sting and fury of puberty and adolescence, they remained inseparable. Their teachers found it cute and called them the "class couple."

By freshman year of high school, Maddy had blossomed into a young woman and it didn't go unnoticed. The popular boys began to follow her down the hallways on her way to class and wait by her locker in the hopes she'd provide some attention or reveal her phone number. Sometimes they'd show up at our house after school or on Saturday afternoon under the guise of asking a question about a class project or appearing in desperate need of tutoring. She'd smile and touch their arm and politely inform them her heart belonged to David. Her offer to "be friends" left them mostly unsatisfied, but her sincerity usually put an end to any and all questions.

My friend, Jack, (and likely David's friends, too) would say, "David won the lottery!"

Or, "David's just a schmo who got lucky."

And, "What does she see in him?"

David's teeth were tinged with a thin layer of green pond scum and he had rouge brown whiskers, his only whiskers, growing from odd places and straight out from his face like a feral cat. His ears were crusted with belly-button fuzz and brownish, aged wax. And he spoke in a whining, high-pitched drawl which made him difficult to listen to and the origin of his paint-peeling accent impossible to gauge.

Actually, none of that was true.

But even if it were true, none of it mattered. It didn't matter what she saw in him or what people believe she saw in him, because it was clear she saw something and the subject wasn't open to debate.

In truth, David was perfectly acceptable. He was polite and smart, clean and well dressed— things that mothers, even our mother, loved. And he came from a good family.

He was always nice to me—his girlfriend's little brother—and there really wasn't anything bad I could say about him. He wasn't unattractive, and he didn't drench himself in cheap cologne or use scented shampoo or otherwise make himself difficult to be around. He was smart enough. He was fine. Just fine. It's just that he was kind of a weenie, a yawn; and girls like Maddy don't get their hearts broken by weenies. And in the end, I hated his fucking guts.

The trouble began when Maddy was in her early teens. I overheard my mother say to someone on the other end of the green plastic telephone, Maddy's monthly visits by "Aunt Rosie" were becoming more and more problematic. There were trips to this doctor then that doctor, then a specialist in Boston who had a fancy office and a dozen nurses who spoke softly and smiled a lot and called everyone "Honey": as in "Don't worry, Honey, it's very common" or "Honey, the doctor wants to put you on the pill."

Over time, they forgot I was listening, which enabled me to become more in tune with the vernacular. They gave Maddy "the pill" for this common malady in order to better control visits from "Aunt Rosie."

My mother begrudgingly gave in. It was for the best. Or so she convinced herself. But it took some time. "They'll think she's a hussy," she barked into the green plastic telephone.

In the end, despite the appointments, the treatments, the pills and scans, "Honey," a surgery, Maddy's system with her tubes and wires, was unsuitable, unfriendly, unwilling, effectively barren.

This family secret, for the most part, was kept secret. Despite the phone line buzzing and Maddy crying and me spying, it remained quietly in the background through Maddy's school years and her college years. When there came a time to discuss a future, it finally crawled out from its dark hiding place out into the light. For when David was ready to make her his wife, she was compelled to tell him that she was unable to conceive. With this news David became glum and unsettled, less clean and, if it was possible, more boring.

"What will I tell my mother?" he asked. "She'll be crushed."

"I know the feeling," Maddy responded.

"How long have you known?"

"Ten years, more than ten," she replied with a shrug that said it was none of his business.

"Why didn't you mention it?" he asked.

"Because it was none of your fucking business," she answered quickly. Then, softer, "Now, it's your business."

"I asked you if you wanted kids, and you always said 'yes.'"

"I do want kids, that hasn't changed."

"Everything's changed," he said, his voice trailing off into the distance. He turned away from her, twisting his body toward the far corner of the room. She touched his arm.

He was sitting on our living room couch, sunk into that flower-print abomination from another era. His hands were together as if in prayer, but with his thumbs placed over his nose forming a dorsal fin. His head was leaning down and his elbows dug into his thighs. She was pacing from one end of the room to the other. The room was so small and warm, it was impossible to escape the claustrophobia.

I was spying from the hallway, listening, peeking, biding time, perhaps. What was I going to do? Was I going to leap into action, cape fluttering in the wind behind me, to protect my sister? I have no idea.

After a few moments, David began to fidget, unsure where to look. His hands, released from the dorsal fin, flailed about into the air in front of him. "I need to think about this," he said. "About everything. It's all changed."

Maddy stopped pacing and stood a few feet from him, hands firmly on her hips. She matched his fidgets with stoicism, her voice pure and unshaken. "I understand," she said. "Take all the time you need."

When the front door banged shut, I watched through a window as he ambled down the walkway, hands deep in the front pockets of his jeans. Maddy called to me.

"You can come out now, Bobby."

The next day, via the green plastic telephone, the weenie told her he'd had time to think and it was over. All of it. It couldn't go on. That was it. He loved her, but…

She listened to the voice; the curlicue cord of the phone stretched from the kitchen into the living room as she prowled the same four corners, snarling at the empty couch, his indentation in the cushion still warm. She hung up the phone having only uttered the word "hello" then listening silently for a minute, maybe two, maybe more. Her gentleness in hanging up the receiver belied her devastation.

I'd been spying again and, as usual, Maddy was aware of my presence. "You can come out now, Bobby," she said again.

I slinked into the open. "What are you going to do now?" I asked.

"I don't know."

For the first time I can remember, I gave my sister a hug. And she hugged me back.

The house was quiet that night, lighter, no voices barked into a phone. No droning television or hissing and beating vinyl records. No horns from passing fire engines or screeching police cars coming for other people's problems. Shackles were released, and a weight was lifted. The world had rolled down from Maddy's sturdy back and onto the living room floor. There it came to rest and sat, raw, for all to see.

Though she was free of her secret, she never truly trusted a man again.

Maddy, at least, had her reasons, and I would forgive her those. If anyone had reason to be bitter and frightful and full of bile, she did. Yet, she didn't and she doesn't.

Around the time David faltered, Maddy discovered a hobby, something that helped keep her thin fingers and brilliant, wandering mind at bay. She checked out books on origami at the Free Library (which she never returned) and began to fold and fold and fold and fold. In short order, she evolved into a talented, creative artist of the paper-fold. Soon, small winged cranes and butterflies spilled from the shelves of her bedroom. Soon after, she became something akin to a crazy cat lady. I called her the Insane Witch of Origami but never to her face. It's likely this small skill, this small miracle, saved her life many times over.

Jack, Tammy and Annette (Bobby)

What makes us hateful and resentful? What plunges us into misery? I've spent more time than I care to admit considering, pondering my friend's life. His unfair life.

Jack was my best friend. Unsurprisingly, my mother saw something in him she didn't like. Of course, she didn't like anyone, not really. Of Jack, she said in her patented matter-of-fact tone, "the world needs ditch diggers." And once, "And those freckles! Whoa!" Jack was doomed from the start, but my mother was the least of his worries.

Jack lived on the next street over with his mom and sister and sometimes his dad. I didn't know his dad, but Jack's mom both scared me and intrigued me at the same time. She was forbidden and seemingly available and curiously toxic: the apple you shouldn't bite into. She offered cookies and such and somehow always had a few slices of cake in the refrigerator.

"There's cake in the fridge," she'd say. "Chocolate. Help yourself."

Sugary drinks were her specialty. Hawaiian Punch and Kool-Aid were served at room temperature: the deep red kind that stained fabric and linoleum and turned your tongue and spit so ruby red you thought you might be bleeding from the inside. There was so much to like about Annette—that's what Jack called her even though she was his mom.

"You can call me Annette," she told me. I felt uncomfortable calling her Annette in her presence so I didn't call her anything.

"How's your mom?" she'd ask even though I knew she didn't know my mom.

"Good."

"And your sister, Melonie?"

"Maddy."

"Oh, Maddy!"

"She's good."

Then she'd smile at me and cross her arms while leaning her rear-end against the edge of the kitchen counter. Annette was tall and lean, like Jack was going to be, and had so many freckles it was difficult to know if she had white skin and brownish freckles or brownish skin and white freckles. She had thin, almost translucent lips and green eyes with long, clear eyelashes. Her wavy hair flowed halfway down her back, fiery like her temper. She carried the scent of stale cigarettes when she breathed, the blue smoke lucky enough to fill her lungs if only for a moment. Her husband hadn't been around in a long while.

Jack's sister, Tammy, was a smaller, less angry, clone of

Annette. She was two years older and a head taller than me with the same fiery hair and deep green eyes as her mother, but no trace of a temper. Tammy wanted to be a doctor and one day while hopped up on Hawaiian Punch whispered with hot breath that she wanted to practice on me and, if I wanted, I could practice on her.

Jack was one of the taller kinds in our class and was hounded by the basketball coach/physical education teacher every week before the season. Eventually, Jack agreed, if only to keep the coach quiet. Every Tuesday and Thursday, Jack had basketball practice until four o'clock and Annette worked a part-time job at the grocery store for extra money. By the time Jack had walked the two miles home and, assuming he didn't stop at the convenience store for penny-candy and birch beer, it was four-thirty, sometimes five.

Although we took buses from different schools, I was home around two-thirty and Tammy around the same time. To my own delight, when I closed my eyes, I imagined she was Annette. I can't be sure, but I think Tammy knew.

Their house was a modest ranch, white with black shutters and a garage and was shaded by two maple trees, one on either side of the walkway. Tammy's bedroom was at the front of the house and overlooked the street; despite the overgrown shrubs, we typically could see Jack on the sidewalk before he passed beneath the maples. Jack had a tendency to misplace his keys and, once he found them, fumble and scratch around the keyhole for several seconds. This provided just enough time to act like I was simply waiting for him to come home from basketball practice so we could hang out.

Each Tuesday and Thursday for the better part of a year Tammy practiced on me and I practiced on her. She told me the best way to take my temperature was to put my thing in her mouth and each Tuesday and Thursday afternoon she told me I was a perfect 98.6 degrees. I took her temperature, too. The mechanics were quite different, but she was a good teacher, thorough, and I assumed, based on her expertise and enthusiasm, she would make a very good doctor.

"I wish I could fix your legs," Tammy said softly one afternoon while my head was on her lap. She swept my hair back from my forehead and looked at me like I was a child, her child. "Get rid of all the scars, make the pain go away." Perhaps my legs made her uncomfortable, or maybe she wanted to save me. As it turned out, I wasn't the one who needed saving.

In the summer it was a little more difficult to find time alone at her house—we had to dodge Jack and, since her mother was a teacher's aide, Annette was home more during the summer months. Tammy told me Annette had made a comment that lately I was paying more attention to her than to Jack—after all, I was Jack's friend. Perhaps she was on to us. It was becoming increasingly difficult to steal moments away from everyone, but we managed. Sometimes, after sundown, we'd meet in Annette's garage and trade lustful surgeries and treatments and listen to each other's heartbeat afterward—all in the name of medicine. We had to be quiet, exceptionally quiet, keep the giggling to a minimum. Practice made perfect. We tucked a blue beanbag chair into a corner and made the best of things.

That September things changed. Our meetings became more infrequent—every other week, sometimes only once a month. Finally, we had to address it.

I told her I liked when she took my temperature and she said she liked taking my temperature, but her new boyfriend didn't like the way we looked at each other and was growing suspicious. He was a mop-haired senior who wore black t-shirts emblazoned with the names of Swedish heavy metal bands. He also had a car and gave her a ride to school in the morning, and so she didn't want to screw it up. It became clear to me she was now taking his temperature more often than mine. I needed to find a new doctor.

I thought maybe Annette—her fiery hair and lean body stuffed into tight jeans, her ass leaning against the counter while asking me if I want cake, her on-again, off-again husband and the way she looked at me while twisting the phone cord around her finger as she gossiped to her friends—would be interested in taking on new patients. A fantasy to be sure, though at the time, it seemed attainable, possible, even imminent. And I wasn't the only one who noticed.

"You can't fuck my mom," Tammy said casually while simultaneously reading my mind and taking my temperature. It was a bonus appointment, a cancellation courtesy of a fight with mop-head. Bonus appointments were becoming more frequent of late. *That schmuck.* And could Tammy have known I was fantasizing that she was Annette at that very moment?

"Who, Annette?"

"Yeah, Annette!"

"I can't?" I asked.

"No, you can't."

"Do you mean I shouldn't or I can't? Those things are different."

"I mean you can't and you shouldn't."

"I have to say I'm a little disappointed."

"I'm sure you are. I see the way she looks at you and puts on that red lipstick and the way you leer at her and that's just not going to happen."

I hadn't noticed the red lipstick or rather hadn't noticed it having any hidden meaning. But what happened next made me realize that Tammy was right. It wasn't possible.

And Jack (Bobby)

Where was Jack while I was sullying his sister and dreaming about sullying his mother? The thing was, more often than not, Jack was there, sometimes in the next room. He knew I was spending time with Tammy but was apparently having trouble remembering it. He'd changed over the course of the last school year, become more apathetic and sedentary, even lazy. He wasn't overly interested in basketball anymore and his grades were slipping to the point where he might need summer school or even to repeat a year. Along the way we'd slowly grown apart.

As for me, my drawing skills were progressing rapidly, and I always had a sketch pad with me. Sometimes I would show Tammy things I'd drawn, dragons and warriors and the like, boy stuff, and she'd feign interest and sit near me with her hand on my thigh and nod along. Sometimes she'd say "Oh, I like that one!" even though I knew she didn't really care one way or another.

One Tuesday afternoon she said, "I think it's time you draw me."

"Now?"

"Of course, now."

"Jack will be home in like twenty minutes."

"So?"

"So?"

She stripped off her clothes then lay on the bed, her hands tucked under her cheek, her nude body stretched to its full length while yellow light streamed through the bedroom window. Her hair burned bright against her ivory skin, and I began to see her not as Tammy, but as something to be discovered and captured with charcoal, something to immortalize. There's a level of trust that's necessary for any model to allow themselves to be discovered by an artist. Something happened that day. For me, everything changed. Yes, I'm sure I'm romanticizing the moment, making more of it than there actually was. But this was the moment—my first moment as an artist. It was magnificent.

I traced the outline of her body in one continuous line, her head, shoulders, torso, curve of her hip, thigh, calf, feet. The air in the room became fresher, drier, cooler. I sketched her face. I'd never noticed her nose, sharp and elegant, and her lips—thin, translucent, ever inviting, much like Annette's. Her hair flowed down the side of her face, draped along her neck before covering her shoulder. I was mesmerized.

I'd barely grown comfortable with my subject when the door burst open and a seething Jack filled the doorway. He was breathing heavily like he'd seen a ghost (or had just run all the way home after seeing a ghost). He must have heard us talking.

"What the fuck are you doing?" He screamed and raised his arms in the air like a referee signaling a touchdown. I was petrified.

"Jack, get the fuck out!" Tammy returned forcefully.

And something strange happened. He did get out.

That's something you don't forget: your sister's white skin with her brownish-red nipples and each breast that fit perfectly in one hand and her belly-button, deep and mysterious and a puff of flame-red between her legs. No, that's something you wouldn't forget. But that's exactly what happened. There was no telling Annette that her daughter was sprawled out nude and his best friend was leering, sketching her, and if she allowed him to sketch her nude, who knew what else she was allowing him to do to her?

"Believe me, I'm not complaining that we didn't get in trouble and certainly not complaining about not having to face my mother, but I am confused. Why didn't he tell Annette?"

"He forgot."

"How could you forget seeing your sister naked while your best friend is standing over her?"

"Annette has a temper. She hits him in the head a lot."

I don't know if Tammy became a doctor or if Jack's

memory improved or if Annette and her husband got back together in a meaningful way.

The last time I saw Jack he was wearing a bandage over one of his eyes, a kind of flesh-colored patch that looked like he'd fallen asleep at the breakfast table and a pancake had stuck to his face.

"What happened to you?" I asked.

"Ah, nothin'," he said and turned his face so the damaged eye was hidden.

"That doesn't look like nothing," I said and gestured toward my own eye.

"Oh, that?" he said. "Fell off my bike."

He was so sure of himself.

"Did it hurt?"

"Nah."

A few days later, Tammy told me Annette had lost her mind when she found out Jack had stolen her cigarettes then caught him smoking in the garage. She'd smacked him around with a leather belt. Only she was holding the wrong end and the belt buckle split open his eye. "A complete shitshow," Tammy explained. She wasn't sure if he'd be able to see out of it.

Afterward, there were police and social workers, a crushing writeup on page three of the local paper and threats that Annette should lose her job. A shitshow.

A few weeks later the house was for sale and they were gone. In the middle of the night, they disappeared, moved on to somewhere else, someplace new, likely a place where no one would know what happened. The three of them had vanished: Jack with his one good eye and Annette with her mean streak and tight jeans and Tammy with the wonderful way she checked to see if I was running a fever.

"They were white trash anyway," my mother scoffed when I told her they'd moved. "I never liked that woman, always looking for attention from other people's husbands."

Like you have a husband for her to chase, I thought to myself.

"I liked Tammy," Maddy offered then winked at me. "And she sure liked Bobby!"

That was the last time I ever saw them. Or heard from them. Or heard about them. There were no letters from Tammy with ruby lipstick prints and hand-drawn hearts pledging her love. No late-night phone calls from Jack asking for money. No dropping by ten years on in a rattling car with a little one in diapers just to say "hi" and let me know they came out on the other side.

Is That How You See Me? (Bobby)

Flirting, unsurprisingly, is not a skill I developed quickly or fully understood. Or fully understand, now. You can chalk up such ignorance to the secrets and mysteries of life, but it was more than that—it was a myopia, a blind spot. Even on the rare occasions I was aware, I was either too clumsy to maneuver or too distracted to notice another's maneuverings. I was learning, but slowly.

"If you come to my studio, I'll sketch you," I offered.

"That's awfully forward of you," Claire grinned.

"It's my best line, my only line, really."

She considered my predicament, hands on her hips and nose toward the sky.

"Then I have no choice," she said with a jovial air of superiority. "I will allow you to sketch me."

I nodded. "You've made a good decision."

"And where is this studio?"

"Fulton Hall, basement."

"Do they place their finest artists in the basement?"

"That's where they put the freshman."

"Wait! You're only a freshman?"

My body began to heat and my clothes felt tight, suffocating. One eye began to twitch. I'd blown it.

Claire noticed my discomfort. She tried to ease my suffering by saying something smart, quoting someone else who was also smart. I had no idea what any of it meant. "A joke," she said and released a laugh. Her laugh. Her wonderful laugh.

I exhaled.

"You have to use small words with me," I said. "I'm only a freshman."

"Sorry," she laughed again.

"And speak slowly."

The college called it a studio, but really it was a corner of a basement room shared with ten other freshman and sophomores of varying talent, levels of hygiene and musical tastes.

"Smells like a locker room," Claire said and crinkled her nose the way I like. "Actually, like the basement of a locker room. After a chemical spill."

The once gray cement floors were covered in drips, drops and splashes of every color paint imaginable. Reds, yellows, greens, blues—the floor reminded me of Annette and her freckled, (though less colorful) skin. The walls were in a perpetual battle to remain white and once a month we were required to whitewash them as part of our semester grade. Lightbulbs of every wattage hung hither and tither, creating an uneven wash of dull, yellowish-white and shadow.

In several areas, black lights illuminated a student's latest florescent creation. In one corner was a trash barrel filled to overflow with crumpled papers, discarded paint brushes and greasy food wrappers.

"Smells better than old books and dead poets," I said. She stuck out her tongue in response.

"Overflowing trash really brings the room together," she noted as her eyes scanned one end to the other. "I would never have thought it would, but it really does.

I didn't have a place for her to pose, so I borrowed a filthy looking stool with a black top and metal legs from the cubby next to mine. She looked down at it with an understandable measure of suspicion, like a feline presented with a new, unfamiliar flavor of kibble at her morning feed. I dusted off the top of the seat with my shirt sleeve and patted it with my hand.

The rest of the session remains vague and dreamy, like I was more a witness than a participant, morbidly watching my demise from the neighboring cubby. I was happy, of course, I must have been. Here in my makeshift studio was the girl with the magical laugh, a girl, a young woman, of fine New England stock, handsome and learned. And I had her full attention.

The finished sketch itself, too, is vague, as is its creation. It's said magicians and the very pious can place themselves into a trance-like state, allow their consciousness to transcend both the physical self and the moment in which they exist in order to become the part of the moment itself. It's possible that I, too, had entered that realm. That's not to say

I'm particularly magical or pious, but rather at that moment in time I'd become more than I was capable of being.

Others would disagree.

"Is that how you see me? I look like an old woman!"

I panicked and borrowed from Picasso: "It's how you *will* look."

"Why would I want to look old? What have you done to me?" She turned the paper this way and that, perhaps hoping a new angle would improve the image it contained. She put one hand on her face to make sure her skin was still smooth and tight.

"An old book is one of your favorite things," I said. "Warmth. Character. Wisdom."

She stared at me, mouth hung open and eyes wide, like the village idiot had just revealed himself.

"Are you a complete idiot?"

"I just might be, yes"

"And who raised you?"

"All of this would probably make sense if you met my mother."

For several days this budding romance balanced on the edge of a razor. And I had doubts I could resuscitate it. There was a degree of groveling, apologies met with tepid indifference. One of her friends did me a favor by presenting my sketch as being the amateurish work of someone who "just might not be a very good artist." It felt like a moment from my childhood.

As it turned out, Claire was the forgiving type. Or perhaps she wanted to save me. Years later Claire admitted that

I was right, after meeting my mother everything began to make sense.

At the time, I didn't know what came over me: Why would I sketch her as I believe she would be? How would I know what she was to become? There was no simple explanation, and it remains hidden to this day. Was I simply destined to screw up my relationship with Claire?

But it gave me an idea and something deep in my memory led me back to Boston, back to Degas and the statue of *The Fourteen-Year-Old-Dancer.* What would the dancer be like at thirty years old? What would she be like at fifty? All of this would be part of her story, her existence, her experience, her life. This was the next moment, the one after I sketched Tammy, the beginning of my life's work.

Claire had an old boyfriend at Stevens College who I thought was a prick. I didn't know him, but he seemed like a prick, and she said he was a prick—so I didn't need any more evidence. He wore corduroys and wool sweaters and knew which side of the plate the fork and spoon were supposed to be set. I imagined in the summer he wore a striped shirt and funny hat and captained a yacht out of Nantucket that took Boston Brahmins and New York financiers out on the ocean for gin martinis and shortbread biscuits. His name was Warren.

Claire told me he called me "hop-along" so I punched him in the nose at a fraternity party on a Saturday night, right in front of his friends. As I was being roughly handled by two or three brawny fraternity brothers and shown the door, I heard my mother's voice saying "What can you expect? They have eyes, don't they?" I was too angry to be upset. Old habits are hard to break.

I wondered if Claire wanted me to punch him in the nose and that's why she told me what he said. Maybe she wanted to see if I would do it. Maybe she wanted to see if she could channel my rage into something useful to her. Maybe he didn't say it all.

But what was clear was I was attempting to find a flaw in Claire. I wanted to find a flaw, a scab I could pick at with a dirty, serrated fingernail; a weak bruise; a weak point in the fence. I'd found ways to be disappointed in the past, manufactured disappointments or otherwise. The problem was, I could find no flaws in her and I searched desperately. Yes, I was blind, I'm sure of it, but it was better to be blind in love than to scorn it out of fear of disappointment.

That Monday morning, I found an official Stevens College letter in my mailbox, one hand placed, without a postage stamp—I'd earned a meeting with my advisor. The meeting was in one of the buildings meant for alumni and donors, not students: stately, high ceilings and dark wood panel walls and a magnificent staircase that wound up toward somewhere I'd never see. Atoning for your sins, at least in a secular sense, requires being seated in a waiting area while contemplating the moments to come: What was your fate? What did the future hold? What would your statue look like? Would I recognize this future?

The receptionist greeting me warmly and offered me water or coffee. I accepted neither. Behind her shoulder length gray hair were bright brown eyes staring through gold-rimmed glasses. She gazed at me and carried a perpetual smile as if the entirety of the student body were her children and she was happy I'd come to visit. I'd dressed in my good clothes, a white button-down shirt and blue tie, dress pants and black wing-tips. The receptionist seemed very proud of me.

The waiting area carried the unspoken weight of those who came before me: those who'd been judged and dismissed, those splayed upon the alter stone with pleas of forgiveness and hopes of redemption. There was an odor of a hundred years and old money and books Claire would like. Sunlight fought its way through heavy drapes and leaded windows forming an elongated rectangle of light on the red woolen rug. I sat in a stiff, antique chair that hurt my back. I began to fidget with my tie and check the buttons on my shirt. I studied the bluish veins and white skin of one hand, then the other. My fingernails needed a trim. Which side of the alter would I fall upon?

"Don't worry, dear," the receptionist said warmly. I expected her to continue with, "It will all be over in a minute," but she didn't. I was also hoping she had cookies, but she didn't. While awaiting my comeuppance, I heard my mother's voice in my head: *You're not private college material. You'll screw this up eventually.*

A few minutes later the receptionist said, "He's ready for you now." When I looked up, he stood silently, filling the entirety of the doorframe, casting a burly shadow across the waiting area that merged with the sun-filled rectangle on the rug.

My advisor, Professor Adler, was a giant man. He was six and half feet tall and six and half feet wide with black eyes. He had a shiny shaved head that he probably took to the local bowling alley to have professionally polished. It's possible the college found his desk at a big-and-tall professor furniture supply because it was somehow to scale when he sat behind it. The leather-trimmed, wood chair, however, creaked and complained beneath him each time he shifted his weight. If you closed your eyes when he spoke, you'd think the whole of the room itself was speaking to you. If he wasn't a professor, I thought in the moment, he'd probably be a professional wrestler nicknamed "The Professor."

Professor Adler pointed to another backbreaking antique chair, this one across from his desk and I took a seat. There was no small talk.

"What's this mishigas from the weekend?" he began. He checked his watch and looked up at the ceiling. It was clear he had better things to do than deal with me.

"Just boys being boys," I answered with unearned confidence.

"Hmmmm…My understanding is you hauled off and popped another student at a party. As you might imagine, that's frowned upon at the college." He flashed a fake smile while his chair groaned.

"Yes, sir."

"Care to explain yourself?" His eyes were wide and his eyebrows sat high on his wrinkled forehead.

And I did. As far as I knew, he'd earned a punch in the nose. The room took notes on a yellow legal pad with an elegant gold pen I'd never be able to afford. It looked like a yellow toothpick in his great paw.

"Do me a favor," the room said after a few moments of silent writing. "Stay away from fraternity parties for the rest of the semester."

"Yes, sir."

"Off the record, it sounds like he needed a kick in the ass."

"I know how to quiet a bully," I said.

"I'm sure you do."

But it wasn't true. I could still hear my mother's voice.

Dolls (Bobby)

"Mrs. Richards," I began. "Welcome."

"Lydia," she said as she crossed the door threshold with a windy grace. "Call me Lydia."

"Of course, Lydia," I said and bowed my head to indicate I understood.

Lydia she stood very straight and purposeful, like she expected to be noticed. Her hair was light gray, almost white, and cut short and purposeful. After a few steps she spun herself around like she was the first to arrive to the ballroom of a Newport mansion and expected the camera to capture her entrance. "Remarkable! I LOVE this studio!"

"Thank you," I said. "It's comfortable."

"It feels like a museum," she smiled. "But a museum where you can take your shoes off and run around in stocking feet."

In one corner of the studio was an antique gold Victorian sofa with red velvet fabric. The sofa always caught their eye and, over time, became a popular posing spot. It was elegant, though not necessarily comfortable. Lydia couldn't take her eyes off it.

"Lydia," I began again. "We'll meet three times, three sessions, including today. You'll wear the same outfit you have on… it looks wonderful, by the way."

"Thank you." She said and dipped in a respectful curtsey.

"There's a dressing room, through that door over there," I said and pointed. "You don't have to wear the gown here, you can just get changed, change your shoes, fix your hair… make-up if you like. Completely up to you—whatever makes you comfortable."

"There's a little kitchen area with bottled water if you're thirsty. Sometimes there's snacks. When I remember I stock snacks, but I don't always remember."

"You'll pose on the sofa," I said.

"Oh, I do like that sofa," she offered with a laugh.

"You'll also pose standing," I continued. "Standing is more taxing, but I want to see your body, I want to follow the curves—"

"Curves?" She said and raised her eyebrows.

"Curves are beautiful! The human body has curves, and we're going to celebrate them."

She wore a purple satin trumpet gown, sleeveless with a draped back. The V of the neck came together into a flower made from the same gown fabric. Timeless, graceful, and, I assumed, well beyond my income level. I had yet to tell her the gown would be sacrificed for the cause.

"Each time we meet, I'll make a sketch and once I have the three sketches, ideally, I'll be ready to immortalize your beauty in bronze. You'll live forever."

"Do you really think I have beauty?"

"I do. Your face, your neck, everything about you is timeless."

"I'm an old woman."

"Nonsense. Get rid of any mirror that has the audacity to make you feel old. Throw it out, throw all of them in a river or the ocean. They're cursed. I see beauty and I think you'll agree, I'm the expert."

She blushed and looked down at her feet. "You're a smooth talker, Mr. Bobby."

Around her neck was, I assumed, an antique necklace, the metal darkened over time, ornate with fine, interconnected strands like a spider's web. It rested low on her collarbones.

"Tell me about the necklace," I said.

"Oh this?" she said like she'd forgotten her purposeful wearing of the family heirloom. "My great-grandfather had it made for my great-grandmother's birthday." She laughed a bit to herself. "That seems like a long time ago, doesn't it?"

"She had a thing with spiders, the complexity of the webs, the genius behind them. I'm told she'd watch them work for hours when she was a child, weaving their trap and waiting for it to snare them dinner. She was a bit of an amateur zoologist, I guess. I'm sure she sketched them—right up your alley."

I nodded in agreement.

"This fascination must have continued into her adulthood and caught my great-grandfather's attention."

"Keep the necklace on," I suggested. "It works."

"Now," I continued. "We may need to meet more than three times; it depends on if I've managed to capture your essence. That's the most important thing and it doesn't always happen quickly."

"Not to worry, Mr. Bobby, I'll sit for you as many times as you like."

"Perfect."

The gears were turning in her mind and she puckered her lips.

"Do I pose nude?"

"Would you prefer to pose nude?"

"Will it be warm in here?"

"As warm as you like. Either way, the statue will be nude and dressed in your gown. Sometimes I call it a doll, but really it's a statue."

"And how will you create a nude statue if I'm wearing clothes?"

"I have a good imagination," I said and winked.

She blushed, then laughed. "Well, I have been dieting for this. Maybe. I'll let you know."

She adjusted her gown and said, "I bought this gown on vacation, Monaco, how will you duplicate it?"

"I meant to speak to you about that," I said and laughed. "I'm going to cut the statue's gown from the gown you're wearing."

"You're going to ruin my gown!"

I reached out and touched her shoulder, gently rubbing the fabric between my thumb and index finger. "I'm going to make your gown immortal. There are always sacrifices."

"What about the necklace?"

"Not to worry," I laughed again. "That I'll duplicate."

"Tell me, why are there three sketches?"

"That's an excellent question! The first sketch captures the present, who you are today, the curves of your body," I winked. "Your hair, your bone structure, all of you. The second is you as you were in the past and the third is who you'll become. The second and third, of course, are based on what I see in your past and future. I'll merge the sketches to create a statue of Lydia, your essence, who you really are."

I had her attention.

"If we simply wanted to capture you as you are today, we could save a lot of time and expense, snap a photo and find a nice frame or even capture you in oil paint and hang you on the wall. I'm not sure what fun that would be, but we could do it."

"If we want to capture your essence, your soul, if we want to immortalize Lydia, we need to capture who you are, who you were and who you'll become. You're all of these things at once and that's much more complicated, but it can be more beautiful than a photograph."

"Can you do that?" she asked.

"It's my life's work. Let me show you something. No one else has seen this—other than my sister."

I immediately felt a pang of regret, but perhaps it was time.

There was an antique wardrobe, dark and beautiful, placed against the furthest wall from the door. It looked like, as Lydia pointed out, a museum piece in a French palace, ornate and unapproachable, a work of art meant to house works of art. There I stored the three wooden pedestals holding the statues of my own life. I took them out and placed them on the large square wooden table that owned the middle of the studio.

The statues were still in wax form, nude and unpleasant, the way my mother saw me. The first wore an unflattering square of black fabric cut from a bedding sheet. The legs were severed, crushed, broken, like the spirit of the boy, twisted like the anguish in the boy's face as he screamed, his heart existing outside of his chest. As strange as it sounds, It was still difficult for me to look at it.

Lydia placed a warm hand on my shoulder.

Her eyes focused on the second, the one I wanted her to see. I hoped she hadn't taken more than a cursory glance at the first, my past. After all, the second stood tall, confident, muscular and lean, one hand shading his eyes from the sun as he rose toward the sky, leaping on one strong leg. His fabric was silk, skillfully draped as a toga.

The third was a scorched lump of wax, featureless, ambiguous, unable or unwilling to take recognizable form.

"When the third is finished, perhaps it is finished," I considered. "At some point, I'll combine the three into one."

"These are your versions of the sketches."

"Yes, exactly."

"And the third? It looks like you've been avoiding it."

I couldn't look at her. "I'm afraid of the future."

"Of aging?"

"Maybe of not aging. Not having enough time."

I'd started and stopped my future statue several times over the course of a few years, but I was never able to reconcile it, never able to form it into something tangible. Like many of us, I found it easier to see others than to see myself. The mirror of my mind was unjust. I was making others immortal while I withered. Not physically, not yet, but soon enough.

Before she could ask more questions, I clapped my hands together and said, "Let's get started, I'm looking forward to discovering Lydia. Today is about Lydia!"

When I helped her on with her coat it rubbed against my cheek, mink and soft as the morning sun. She said to me, "You have quite the reputation."

"Oh?"

"Yes. They say you have a gift."

"They're very kind," I said and took a moment to reflect. "If I do have a gift…it's something I want to share with you."

"I'd like that," she said. "How did you find your talent—when you were young?"

"I was an ugly child," I said.

"I find that hard to believe! Though by the looks of the first statue you must believe it."

"It's true," I admitted. "And when you're an ugly child you see the world differently than most. You learn to appreciate the beautiful things that appear to be out of reach. You learn to reach out and grab them when you can because they may not linger for very long."

Lydia sized me up for a moment before she turned toward the door. "I left you a check," she said over her shoulder, her purposeful, confident walk on full display. "This," she said while twirling a finger above her head. "Is a birthday present from my husband."

II
The Ghost
(Maddy)

Hospitals make me anxious. I suppose most people, at least the ones that don't work in hospitals, are anxious to be in one. There's a sense of dread each time I enter the building, like this is the last time I'll see someone, a sort of "beginning of the end" premonition. Each time I see Bobby, three days of stubble on a sinking face, pallid skin against white sheets, I wonder how much time he, we, have left. You don't think in terms of time—how much time—until time is running short, like counting the hours, the minutes, the seconds until a favorite lover must rise from your warm bed to catch a train—a train that will whisk them away, perhaps home, their home—likely never to return.

The hallways of hospitals, too, they have an effect on me. The stark walls remind me of a college dorm: cleaner, but without the hope of tomorrow, without the payoff awaiting the hard work. There's machines, lifesaving, life-monitoring, and life-extending, tubes and wires and beeping sounds meaning either someone's blood pressure has critically dropped or their popcorn is ready. Either way, they're popped.

Dr. Kilkenny is in the lobby coffee shop loading up on caffeine for his rounds or perhaps the drive home. I see his gangly arms waving about as he orders, pointing to something, then something else. While his arms flail about, his red tie remains perfectly straight.

I attempt to avoid him. I act as if I don't see him even though he's stepped directly in my path to the elevator. Don't get me wrong, I like Dr. Kilkenny, he's a fine man and a fine doctor, but sometimes you don't want to talk about what you're about to see. And sometimes you don't want to see what you're about to talk about.

"We're keeping him comfortable," he says without me asking. He gives his patented shake of the head and looks through me like he's already moved on to somewhere else, another point in time, perhaps. His head is always in the clouds. I smile politely.

If I were his wife and his mind wandered off like that all day long, I'd have to kill him in his sleep, I think to myself and laugh. Yes, smother him with a pillow or strangle him with that impenitent, perfectly straight tie.

"The real worry, at least for the moment, is pneumonia," he says and takes a small sip from the paper cup. The liquid is too hot and he pulls his lips back and squints his eyes.

"Do you see any signs of it?" I ask.

"No, no," he clarifies. "It's just that his body is weak and, if he were to contract it, he'd have trouble fighting it off."

"Is it ok for me to see him?"

"Oh, yes. He has an oxygen mask," he explains. "Even better than you wearing a mask."

"And, Maddy," he says as I turned to walk to the elevator. "You've done all the right things."

I nod a thank you.

"Sometimes, there's just nothing else that can be done."

He doesn't respond, just closes his eyes tighter when I speak.

"Bobby, It's me. It's Maddy." I take his hand. It's cold. Not too cold, but cooler than I expect.

His normally bright skin is damp and dulled to a cloud gray as if he's just been pulled aboard in the net of a North Atlantic trawler. His brown hair, starting to fleck with gray, is greased flat against his head and peaked on top like a haggard dorsal fin. He weighs maybe 110 pounds. Less than last time, which was less than the time before.

Things have progressed quickly. After several years of reasonable health, he's fallen off a cliff. At Christmas, he polished off a bottle of Chianti and held court telling stories about the time he sketched Claire in his college art studio. "She didn't talk to me for a week!" he laughed. Claire laughed, too. It was good to see them getting on. Bobby's final train is running on schedule and Claire doesn't want him to catch it.

By Easter, his body had deteriorated to the point he needed hospitalization. His weight and energy plummeted. His hands shook and eyes grew glassy, hollow. At times, he couldn't control his bowels. I never thought it would catch up to him, this menace. He was too slippery, too smart, too determined. And he didn't appear to be done with the world.

"Claire?" he asks though it's muffled by the mask and the hiss of oxygen. Black crescents bore deep under each eye, growing darker and deeper by the hour, like they might collapse and swallow his eyes into nothingness.

"It's Maddy," I answer. "I sent Claire home."

"Does she hate me?" he asks. His voice is echoey and lost, like he's asking the question from the bottom of a well.

"Who? Does who hate you?"

"Claire. Does she hate me?"

"No, Bobby," I answer. "Of course not. Claire loves you. She's always loved you."

"That's good," he says with a rattling laugh that sounds like a vacuum sucking up fifty cents worth of pennies. "That's good."

After a few moments, he opens his eyes, dark blue like the deep ocean. They haven't suffered the same fishy plague as his skin—they're still clear, alive. They're not done. They haven't given up, at least not yet. But, gone are the days of his confident tone and wandering eye. Those were finally drowned in the swirling glasses of Christmas Chianti.

There's a book on the dinner cart, a heavy glossy of art—

Bobby's art. It's called *The Gift–The Art of Bobby Shaw*, photos of his work, and Bobby at work, with commentary by some innocuous museum type who's pictured on the back cover wearing a plaid wool blazer and weighty handlebar mustache. I remember the interviews and the paperwork, the contracts and, of course, the disappointing royalties. I can barely lift the book off the cart. His life's work weighs more than his life.

"What's this paperweight doing here?" I ask before the book drops back down on the cart with a thud.

"One of the nurses brought it in. Wants me to sign it for her daughter. Or her mother. Sign it for someone."

"You have fans everywhere," I add.

"Evidently."

I've gotten used to the sound of his voice through the oxygen mask, like a heavy accent, given time, becoming more natural to the ear.

"I guess you should sign it or she might not take the best care of you," I offer as a joke and place my hands on my hips like I'm his wife. Or his mother.

"Yeah, but if I sign it, then she'll lose the motivation to keep me alive."

I nod in agreement. "Can't win."

"I need you to do something for me," he says, then pauses to breath in deeply through his nose.

"I'm listening," I say.

"At the studio, in the wardrobe on the far wall, you know the wardrobe. Inside there's two pedestals, there's three, but you only need to bring two…"

(Bobby)

The envelope was big, and the bigger the envelope, I'd been told, the better. Bad news typically arrives in small envelopes, single-page letters were succinct and to the point, so as not to rub it in. The mailman knew I'd been stalking him, watching for his arrival through the small, curved window to the right of the red door. I'd attempted to remain unseen, stealthly, cool and apathetic to the arrival of mail. He was likely used to high schoolers awaiting their college decisions this time of year, which would explain his understanding smile each time I peeked through the opaque curtains to watch him climb the front stairs.

He seemed a generally happy person with round, reddish cheeks and a pleasant nose that refused to take up too much of his face. Each step he took was as much a bounce as a step and he placed each handful of mail into the mailbox like he was delivering hope, not bills or circulars from the local grocer. Somedays, I imagine, he was delivering hope.

The envelope from Stevens College was large, exceptionally large, and weighed like it cost an unnecessarily large sum of money for postage. He didn't place it in the mailbox, instead he waited for me to come out to the porch and collect it.

"Feels like good news," he said as he lifted the envelope in his hand to gauge the weight. His smile told me he loved his job on days like this, delivering good news like a proud parent or a military general presenting weekend leave to battle-worn troops.

"I hope so," I said and nodded a thank you. My hand was shaking as I took the envelope from his hand.

"Was this the one you were waiting for?" he asked.

"Yeah," I said, a little embarrassed.

He started to turn away, then said, "It's okay to be proud of your accomplishments. You should be."

I wondered, briefly, if his smile—ear to ear, toothy, from the heart—was to be the largest smile I'd see that day.

I didn't open the letter right away. I placed it on the kitchen table and returned to my room, to a sketch I'd been working on for the past few days. What was my intent? Why would I leave it on the kitchen table? I wanted my mother to see it: the grand envelope addressed to her son, the future artist. It was certainly a risk, as I couldn't know what was inside or what the news was from the ivory tower until I read the contents. Until someone read the contents. I'd pulled in a deep breath, fluffed my feathers, and puffed out my chest.

During my portfolio review at Stevens, the man in the gray wool suit, the man from the admissions office, had given me reason to have confidence. He sat across the conference table, reviewing each drawing in my portfolio, breathing through his nose, turning each page slowly, his brow moving slowly up and down as he made mental notes. About halfway through the portfolio, he looked up at me, or at least toward me, as if trying to place this potential student in a class, envisioning him in the studio, boiling cauldron and waving wand, working his magic. When he realized he'd been deep in thought and looking toward me, he smiled and then returned to the drawings, his lips moving like he was reading the words in a book out loud to himself. Someone believed in me. That was all I needed. It was all I wanted. Stevens College was the place for me.

When Maddy received her acceptance letters, my mother was giggly, all smiles. She was the star, the light, after all. And Maddy deserved to the be the star. She'd done everything right. And I was happy for her, too. She would fit in anywhere, flourish anywhere, succeed anywhere. That was her superpower.

Now it was my turn. At dinner time, the table was clear of everything except the grand envelope of Stevens College. It sat in the center of the table awaiting its moment, a time to shine. I sat down across from Maddy and attempted to ignore the envelope.

"Aren't you going to open it?" Mother asked.

"Oh, I didn't know I had mail," I said.

"Uh-huh," she replied.

I reached to the center of the table, took the envelope and placed it on the floor next to me, standing it on edge, leaning against the leg of my chair. "I'll open it later."

"We're a public college family," she began.

"I know," I said. "The numbers don't add up."

"And Maddy turned out fine."

"Yes."

"Private colleges are expensive."

"I've heard that from the accounting department."

"I don't think you should get your hopes up," she continued. "And art, that just won't give you the skills to pay back any loans you might need to take out. Or support a family. Even buy a house."

"Ok."

Having survived the speech, what did I have to lose by opening the envelope, the grand, heavy envelope sent to me from Stevens College? Private, expensive, ostentatious, Stevens College. It was a college for others: bluebloods, rich folk, non-sissies who could afford to major in philosophy or anthropology—whatever their heart desired—before joining the family business as vice presidents.

"You know what, I will open it now."

"Go ahead," she said with a dismissive wave of her hand. "Why not?"

The contents slid out of the envelope and were heavy in my hands and on my mind. There was a cover letter with the thick green logo of Stevens College at the top; the paper, almost tan in color, had a presence, a heft, the finest I'd ever held. It was from the man who'd reviewed my portfolio several months ago: he turned out to be the director of admissions.

"Read it out loud," Maddy urged. Her legs were crossed under the table, and I could feel the vibrations as her foot bounced on her knee.

I took a deep breath.

"Dear Mr. Shaw," the letter began. "It's our great pleasure to offer you a place in the Art Department, Stevens College Class of 1992."

My voice began to crack.

"It is with even greater pleasure that we award you the President's Scholarship, our highest honor, a scholarship which includes full tuition for four years. I congratulate you."

"Oh my God!" Maddy cried.

Mother was silent. News of a full scholarship folded her lips, released the scowl she desperately attempted to hide. She had no retort. She'd missed out on her dream, and her only son (no, not her only son, I know that now) was going to live his, an irony I was not keen to bring up at the moment despite it twitching on my lips, the curl in my fisted fingers.

"Not bad for a sissy," I said as my eyes filled with tears. I stood up and dismissed myself before anyone saw me crying, leaving the letter face up on the table.

As I stormed off, I thought I noticed a twinkle of light in mother's eyes, a softening. She'd been bested and perhaps now would show a little pride in her son, as much as she would allow. But, as I walked toward my bedroom, I heard my mother say to Maddy, in a tone I'm unwilling to describe, "probably because of the legs."

The Funeral (Bobby)

Mother died during the emptiness of a northern January. The brown grass, despite being frozen into crusty waves, refused to take a fresh dusting of snow. The house, once thoroughly airless, exhaled a humid breath, blew thick, dusty drapes away from the leaded windows. For the first time in many years it allowed the fickle sunlight of winter to warm its rooms. At noon, the long silent wall clock in the formal living room mustered a newfound strength and began to chime. Perhaps it chimed each day or even each hour, but for the better part of my life, I hadn't been listening.

Oddly, surprisingly, she died peacefully in her sleep. Her arms were folded neatly across her chest and her legs were straight out. I'd expected her to fight Death, to wrestle and tumble, roll onto the floor, a finger poke to Death's eye or a knee to his groin. She'd had so many things to say, so many opinions about so many things, so much anger, it was expected to be a prolonged battle, peaks and valleys, close calls and bitter setbacks. Peaceful was out of character.

A few weeks prior, she'd invited Maddy and I over for coffee to make a comment she'd made many times in the past, a wasp sting: "So, no grandkids, huh?" We'd been stung on so many occasions, our pierced skin had grown calloused and thick, our blood mostly immune to the poison.

Out of the corner of my eye Maddy frowned, so I took this one. "No, I guess not," I smiled.

Mother exhaled in dramatic, shoulder drooping fashion, her mouth sagged as her eyes bounced between us. "The end of the family line."

Maddy chewed her lower lip.

"Afraid, so," I said. "But, hey, we'll go out with a bang!"

She wasn't one for gatherings, and most of her contemporaries had either died themselves, had been interned in homes for the aged or moved away. Some of them did all three. When her breathing became hoarse and unsettled and we assumed the end was near, we asked if she had any final wishes. Her answer wasn't unexpected.

"What would be the point? I'll already be dead."

The living room furniture was removed and stored in the bedrooms, the vents in each corner dusted and her lacquered black casket placed against one wall of the now barren room. The elegant casket shone under the lamplight like the polished handles of the daggers she threw about in life without haste or regret. Despite the polish and the clean corners, the fuss and the occupied casket, the room remained lonely.

The funeral director, a tight-assed penguin, stomped

around the tiny room. The heels of his shoes struck the oak floor, echoing off the paneled walls. He shook his head and looked at his watch, mumbled something snarky about a "house call" and charging us 15 percent extra. With a pithy exhale, he unfolded two plastic chairs and placed them in the center of the room, buttoned his black jacket, straightened the chairs and insisted, mostly to himself, the casket be closed. He looked a little like he was late for his own mother's funeral.

I'd not told anyone about Mother's passing, and Maddy didn't tell anyone. No one, save Claire, showed up. What is a "celebration of life?" Yes, we could have gathered neighbors and friends, new and old, and shared stories, anecdotes, memories fair and not-so-fair. Instead, we chose an insular gathering, a reflection of her meager existence. After all, there was a danger our father, if he still walked the earth, might show himself. Mother didn't want a spectacle or want him looking for money.

What would be the point? She was already dead.

We played around with the idea my father, our father, might show up to say farewell. It was another opportunity to lighten the mood, to avoid the fact there might be some pain in the moment.

"I think he'd look like an aging rocker, long, greasy hair, mostly gray, held in a loose ponytail, uncooperative strands poking out here and there," Maddy said. "Skin aged from hard living and persistent worry he'd become irrelevant."

"Or a mad scientist," I offered, "dress lab coat with black handkerchief stuffed into the chest pocket, balding on top, but those same uncooperative strands of gray sticking straight out from his ears. He'd use thick-gloved hands to try and pat down his hair before he entered the room, but the gray would refuse, returning to shape with a cartoonish spring. Boing!"

"When he sees us, he says a familiar 'hey,' and gives us a nod like we saw him only last week," Maddy offers.

"Struts in like a hero."

"Pinches the rim of his fedora between his thumb and index finger."

"Acts like she was the best thing he ever knew."

Then we laughed.

At some point in the evening, Maddy used the sleeve of her dress to erase the chalk marks of this year's mouse kill. She replaced the ticks and slashes with a large number "1" before opening the cellar door and yelling "all clear," to the mice hiding below. I couldn't help laughing again and was a little disappointed I hadn't thought of it.

Claire paid her respects, tapping on the casket with an open palm, leaving a damp, ghostly print of her hand that faded slowly on the shiny black surface. Her cheeks were slightly reddened, but her eyes were dry, and so we sent her off—there was little need to ruin her entire day. She said she didn't want to go, didn't want to leave us, but I insisted. When she said her goodbye to Maddy, she didn't know whether to cry or hide or stare blankly or look happy. Claire kept looking back at the casket like it wasn't the end, and mother might leap out and ask us why we had the heat set so high. Claire wanted to be ready for it. We were all a little prepared for it, sneaking bite-sized looks at the casket, eyes wide, ears pointed: like nervous Chihuahuas on the Fourth of July at dusk. Even in death, Mother had a way.

She never knew what to make of my mother and my mother of her. Claire, by all measures, was destined to marry a doctor or lawyer, a professional with an expense account, heavy oak desk and liquidity. Her parachute failed to open, and she couldn't have crash-landed more off the mark. After all, no parent has ever said to their child they should settle down with a "nice, stable" artist. In Mother's eyes, Claire was too nice to be caught up with me, running with the wrong crowd and running fast. Claire was more like Maddy: bright, put together, sensible, in demand. My mother was right, of course. More than she could know. I told Claire not to attend the funeral. She began to argue and then thought the better of it.

After Claire went home, Maddy and I sat in the two plastic folding chairs staring at the fancy, polished casket. It stood stark against the modest, brown-paneled wall behind it. On the wall above the casket, more than slightly off-center, was a framed 8x10 of young Maddy and me decked out in our Sunday best, grinning widely, gap-toothed and ill-styled hair. In the photo, Maddy was in a floral dress, her hair pulled tightly behind her head. I was in a brown polyester suit, shirt collar much too large, wild hair recently wrangled with spit and a black plastic comb. The colors of the photo hadn't aged well, giving the scene a light amber patina, like the camera had captured us fifty years earlier.

"Maybe we should have taken that down," I said while gesturing toward the picture with a heavy hand. Maddy smiled, blinked and nodded in agreement. I took her hand, and she leaned over and placed her head on my shoulder. Her breathing slowed, more and more, until I was unsure if she'd also left me, my only sister. We stayed seated in front of our mother as the January light faded and the cold winter night scratched at the undraped windows and knocked against the doors and a chill filled the room. Maddy may have fallen asleep.

That evening, I opened Mother's last pickle jar, kosher dill. It was in one of the kitchen cabinets, behind several cans of chicken noodle soup, lonely and no longer with purpose. The jar gave a satisfying *pop* when I turned the cover to the left. I placed a wicker pot holder on top of the casket and gently rested the pickle jar on it in case she needed a snack during the night. I'm not sure if the mice got in it, though I'm sure there was a celebration.

Early the next morning, several strong penguin men arrived to pry the casket from the living room and carry Mother to a hearse waiting in the driveway. I wondered what they thought of the open pickle jar—no one mentioned it. One of them tightened the lid and moved the jar to the kitchen table. There it rested, lonely again. I imagine they've seen stranger things in their profession. Or maybe they just thought I'd needed a snack and wasn't one to clean up after myself.

The director from the previous night, fresh off a 15 percent commission bump, instructed us to follow the hearse in our own vehicle. A small, purple funeral flag flew from a tiny mast attached to the hood of my car, flitting in the wind as I drove, signifying we'd lost someone and that we were allowed to ignore the rules of the road. To an onlooker, the truncated procession of two cars with emergency flashers on the road to her resting place must have been a sad sight, an end to memories few would remember.

The cold stung my earlobes and tip of my nose as we walked to the plot where, once the ground thawed, my mother, or at least her body, would spend eternity. The strong men had dispersed and the three of us, Maddy, Mr. Commission and myself gathered around a few square yards of innocuous frozen earth. The ground was bare and the brownish-green blades of frozen and gnarled grass crunched under each step. The was no sneaking up on the burial plot.

Mr. Commission stood at the top of the triangle the three of us formed, straight back and stiff neck. The morning air reddened his pointed nose and he wiped whatever was leaking from it onto a bleached white handkerchief he repeatedly pulled from and stuffed back into the coat pocket of his dark wool trench coat. I imagined the skin of his face cracking if he dared smiled at a happy occasion.

The three of us looked at each other, each set of eyes bouncing among the two others. No one spoke. My feet were cold in the thin leather of my black shoes and the tips of my gloveless fingers were numb and mildly blue in color. I imagined my teeth freezing solid and snapping off near the gums, dropping one by one onto the stiff grass like white cubes of chewing gum.

"Would either of you like to say anything?" Mr. Commission asked looking first at Maddy and then at me. "Or would you prefer I said something?"

"Goodbye, Miss Anthrope," Maddy said as much to herself as out loud.

"Goodbye, Claw." I added.

We hadn't used those nicknames in quite some time. Sometimes when you punch something sad in the face, it can make you happy. At least temporarily, and Maddy and I smiled at each other.

Mr. C. gave us a thin lipped, up-and-down look, sizing us up for judgement; then, for a fleeting moment, his face drained of color, and his eyes widened like he was a little sad for us. A forced smile festered below the reddened nose, though the skin didn't immediately crack.

"If you need anything, please call me," he said. He gave our hands a cold, fishy shake, one hand shaking and the other covering the backs of our hands, and then he was off. But before he made his leave, he said one last thing to us—something that was, I assume, meant to provide comfort.

I watched as the hearse, black as night, made its escape along a road lined with leafless trees, steam from the muffler trailing close behind but never catching up.

Likely defying the demand of Hades, a cold wind swept

in from the north and broke over us like a frigid Atlantic wave. I placed my arm around her waist as we stood side-by-side in silence. Another minute passed before Maddy asked, "We done here?"

"We are," I nodded.

That was it. Our mother was gone. I was hungry.

I could count the shed tears on one gaunt hand.

On the drive home, as I attempted to shift my attentions elsewhere, memories of my mother wrestled their way into my head like barbarians storming the front gate. A conversation returned to me—I must have thought about death when I was a boy. Why? I can't be sure. But I had barely begun my life, yet I was asking how it ended, what might be in store for me, presumably so I could prepare. I was panicked. "You're a strange little boy," my mother answered. "A strange, odd little boy."

There was more: memories of itching and redness, skin bumpy and sore from scratching, my body curled into the fetal position in the corner of my room, except for my left leg which didn't quite bend like the other. My pants were wet with urine–I could smell it. A lonely child, yes, with crushing weight placed upon himself and lacking a faucet to turn to the right and squeeze off the running thoughts.

The drive from the cemetery was lonely and even though Maddy was sitting next to me and Claire was waiting at home, I was lonely.

Upon my mother's passing, one would assume a great weight had been lifted, that this event was a cathartic end and, ideally, a new beginning. But things would only get worse. Now I knew how life ended. Dr. Kilkenny knew how it ended, and Maddy knew how it ended, too.

And, as I learned the day of the funeral as I stood in the dry winter air, there was another one of us, a boy of July born in a sea of red, cold and slippery as a seal. A prince, Marcus, never to breathe on his own or see the light of day with brightened eyes. "Now she'll be with Marcus," was the last thing the funeral director had said as we stood in our frigid triangle. "Together again, now and forever. Per her request, his name will be etched upon the stone with hers."

I caught Maddy's shiver, a slight tremble only, a twitch of a finger, nothing more, before the words rolled down her dark wool coat and were swept away by the January wind. She didn't make eye contact, though I glared in her direction. She knew, she always knew. The keeper of secrets. Now, I knew. This Marcus, wedged between Maddy and I and buried somewhere in cold dirt beneath frozen grass: I was his disappointing replacement.

Maybe our father was a bad person who vanished, abandoned his family, left his wife and hid his grief.

Or maybe he was just a person.

(Maddy)

While Claire's ancestors sailed into history on the *Mayflower*, I imagine mine, at least on my mother's side, were strolling the decks of the *Lusitania*. There were warning signs during their passage, rough seas, U-boats, an atmosphere of fear and danger, but all were ignored and, as history teaches, many were lost. Some are still lost.

My mother's family was angry, very angry, which made my mother angry, too. It was their way, a family trait like a cowlick or freckled cheeks or a gap in their front teeth. Every perceived slight became a burgeoning feud, every side-eyed look opened a rift too wide to dare cross. The branch of the family with the most deep-rooted public anger was the winner and attempting to dethrone them became a sport. Healing, when a rare something was able to pass, was to take place in private, alone, without the prying eyes of those who might hold it against you in the future. "Take yourself" was the term used to banish those who shone too brightly in public.

There's a patter to the angry, a pace and rhythm that,

to the trained ear, can be deciphered. No, not deciphered, predicted. And if you can predict things that are harmful—tornadoes, hurricanes, blizzards, fits of violence—you can sometimes minimize the damage. At least you can try.

My mother was born in April 1945, a month before Germany surrendered, several months before Japan. It was a time of hope—a great collective exhale. It was also a time when girls weren't supposed to be good at math. Except my mother. She shined when it wasn't in vogue to shine, when it wasn't expected for girls to excel in math. I heard the story from my mother many times.

"Arithmetic?" my grandmother asked. "Why would a girl be interested in something like that?"

"Because I like it."

"Liking it is not a good reason. You have to be practical. There's plenty of work with the telephone company or at the bakery for someone willing to do it."

"But I have a gift, my teacher said so," my mother countered.

"Gifts don't pay the grocery bill, do they?"

"No."

She wasn't really looking for an answer.

"Right, they don't" my grandmother said almost before my mother answered. "Now change out of your school clothes so you can help with dinner. And they can use some help at the bakery tonight, so if you have any 'arithmetic' homework, better to get it done beforehand."

A few days later, during the overnight shift, my grandmother slipped while atop a small ladder and caught her foot in an industrial bread mixer. She'd been dusting the top of the whirring machine and reached for that final square inch of dusty metal, stretched to her length, she overextended her weight. The ladder tumbled in one direction, my grandmother the other. The leg was nearly severed just above the ankle as the mixer came to a grinding halt. Within the hour, the surgeons amputated the mangled mess just below the knee.

Lying in bed, she looked half a person even though only a tenth of her was physically missing. The other four-tenths, the missing four-tenths was due to her spunk being gone, taken, her personality, however dour, was left twisted in the reddish pulp of the mixer. Soon after, my grandfather vanished along with the neighbor's mousy wife and what little was held in a Christmas club account. My grandmother was left with a small disability pension and a lingering anger. The bakery was prepared to claim bankruptcy if sued for anything more.

"It's not the mixer's fault I'm a klutz."

Her bed rest gave her time to think, perhaps for the first time in her life. "Maybe," my grandmother said softly, "you'd be better with the arithmetic than working in a time-bomb like the bakery. There are more missing body parts on the night shift then at a veteran's parade." She almost laughed at the thought.

"If you want to follow your dream, go ahead, follow it," she said. "I won't get in the way."

Two operations and six months later, my grandmother died of an infection in her leg. The hospital insisted the infection hadn't started on their watch, implying she hadn't taken care of the wound when she was at home. By the time my mother noticed the skin around the wound had turned purple, almost black, it was too late. My mother insisted my grandmother died because she felt useless and that her leg was waiting for her somewhere beyond.

"Don't cry for me when I'm gone," my grandmother said as she faded. "What would be the point? I'll already be dead."

News of my grandmother's passing shook my grandfather from his hiding place, an uninsulated, waterless shack on Plum Island. The rattling Chevy he used to commute to Lowell each day once again shook the neighborhood, its unmistakable zest and billowing tailpipe smoke a familiar, almost welcome, sight. He deposited the neighbor's wife back with the neighbor and moved back into his old bedroom, all in one afternoon. There was a new respect between them, my mother and her father: he would allow her to study math and she wouldn't make mention of his treachery. The neighbor too—a tall, thin man with a sparse, unremarkable moustache and forgiving nature—had somehow developed a respect toward my father, tipping his cap like he was grateful my father had noticed the poster nailed to the telephone pole and brought home the man's lost dog. My mother was twelve.

On her eighteenth birthday, my mother got the ol' heave-ho. "Get out." His time as a family man had come to an end. Her father, my grandfather, said he was moving to Maine, way up, near the border with Canada, and he was taking the neighbor's wife with him. He wanted to live off the land, off the grid, to disappear from society, to vanish. He was good at it, at least until he grew bored of the other man's wife. By late that afternoon, there was a FOR SALE sign hammered into the front lawn.

The few belongings he had to his name were stuffed into unmatched suitcases and packed into the trunk of the Chevy or tied to the roof with fraying rope he'd kept in the basement should this same opportunity arise. He tossed anything belonging to the neighbor's wife into the cavernous backseat: black fabric duffle bags, flat bottomed, brown paper bags reused from a visit to the grocery store, one of her husband's old green army sacks that she was sure he wouldn't miss. She was barely in the passenger seat when the engine rattled and roared as the car exited the neighborhood. He didn't wave goodbye.

The neighbor's husband stood on his front porch, hands on his hips, staring them down and shaking his head in disappointment as if to say "not this again." He looked over at my mother, her hands likely on her hips and without saying a word told her, "She'll be back." He sat on his porch every day after work and on the weekends, all day when he retired from his job as a leather cutter at a local belt factory. But she didn't come back and neither did my grandfather.

The neighbor died of heart failure on a Sunday in October, still waiting for his wife to return to him. No one had seen him on the porch for more than a week before someone called the police to say they were concerned for his well-being. The police knocked and knocked, then cupped their eyes with their hands as they attempted to look into the house through the glare of the windows. Eventually, they knocked down the door with a sort of battering ram that echoed through the neighborhood after each attempt, before it finally gave way with a woody snap. An ambulance arrived about a half-hour later, and the neighbor was brought out on a stretcher, covered by a white sheet and a halo of loneliness. Even as he crossed the threshold of the front door for the final time, he'd never lost hope his wife would cross it again.

A few years later, my mother received a letter from Ontario, Canada. My grandfather settled there after leaving the neighbor's wife in Maine. He said he liked how clean the city of Hamilton was and that he'd met a nice girl from Ottawa and they'd moved in together in a high-rise apartment with a balcony and a view. Quite a change. He thought she should come up and visit when she had the chance. She knew he didn't mean it. He also wrote that he hoped she'd meet a man nothing like him. That, she noted, he meant with all his heart.

My mother kept the black and whites of her parents in the same shoebox as the photos of my own father, barely fastened together by a disintegrating elastic meant to keep them separate. In one photo, my grandfather cut a sophisticated silhouette, dashing in his fitted suit, dark porkpie hat tilted to one side. He was tall and narrow shouldered, straight up and down like a cut of lumber, his eyes, so blue the film found them white, wandering away from the camera toward something more interesting, much like my own father. My mother, like my grandmother, was attracted to men with short attention spans and roving blue eyes.

There were no pictures of my grandmother and grandfather together, near each other, embracing or even standing close together. Even the group pictures, though there were only a few, featured one or the other, not both. It's possible my grandmother had passed down the habit of melting and griding the pictures she believed were offensive or disappointing or upsetting. Men in my family were good at being offensive and disappointing and upsetting.

My mother never made it to college, never followed her dream. One would think she'd encourage the next generation, would respect her future children's educational wishes, their dreams. One would also believe, with hindsight on her side, she would know to keep her limbs out of whirring machinery and to not marry someone just like her father.

Questions (Bobby)

The front seat of the car was warmed by the noontime sun pouring through the windshield. I'd been parked at Kilkenny's office for fifteen minutes, but hadn't turned off the engine. It's up to me, I thought. I can turn off the engine and walk into my appointment or I can put the car into gear and ride away unscathed. For a fleeting moment I felt in charge of my life, in charge of my destiny. I even felt like there was a life and a destiny of which I might be in charge. When I opened the office door and stepped into the foyer, my mood turned sour.

"Hi Bobby," Nurse Heidi said, "How are you feeling?"

"I've been better," I growled.

I immediately felt like a heel; Nurse Heidi was being polite. She was always polite, chatty, caring. She was doing her job and there wasn't a need to be short with her. I tried to lighten my tone, but it came out the same way.

"I'm not sure how I'm feeling to be honest."

"Dr. Kilkenny will figure this thing out," she assured me

then laughed to herself and shook her head. "He always does."

Then she smiled at me the way I'd always hoped my mother would smile at me, warm and without judgement. She escorted me to examination room 3. It was the one with the canyon theme, giant photos of different canyons from, I assume, out west. I'd already seen the photos, studied them, fell into the canyons, hypnotized by them. I needed to pass the time awaiting the courtesy knock, the one where the doctor doesn't wait for an answer before opening the door.

"How are you feeling?" Kilkenny asked. It was sincere, but he lacked the optimistic compassion of Nurse Heidi.

"Terminal." I was beginning to feel a little frisky.

Kilkenny stiffened and his eyebrows pulled close together. For a few seconds he appeared at a loss for words. He rubbed his right eye with the knuckle of his index finger. He pulled up his clipboard, clicked his pen and began the routine:

"Coughing?"

"Yes."

"How often?"

"Daily."

"Headaches?"

"Yes."

"How often?"

"Daily."

"Nausea?"

"Daily."

"Dizzy or fainting?"

"No. Can we just say everything's the same as three months ago?"

"No. Taking all your medications?"

"Yes."

"Have you been following my other instructions?" Kilkenny asked.

"Yes."

"There's just so many unanswered questions," he said while looking through me, like the mysteries of my disease remained somewhere off in the distance.

"We don't need to go through this again," I said and raised my palm up to indicate "stop."

"Ok, fine," he said. "They took blood and urine?"

"They jabbed me with a needle and I pissed in a cup."

He nodded his head and pursed his lips. "We'll have to see if there are any changes in your other numbers."

I nodded. He put down the clipboard.

"Have you figured out how it spreads? How I contracted it?"

"Could be more than one way, still not certain. It's been found in blood, saliva, semen, tears. It could be all; it could be none."

I shake my head in disappointment. I have the feeling he knows how it spreads, but isn't ready to tell me.

"The question," he continues. "Is not simply how it spreads, but when it becomes contagious."

"Do you mean I could be contagious already?"

"Yes, and still."

Silence, then.

"Your weight's steady. You look good," Kilkenny said, his hands in the front pockets of his gray dress pants, his paisley tie impossibly straight, his eyebrows and shoulders raised upward.

I offered a fake smile. “For a dead man.”

“It’s your one-year appointment and you look very alive to me.”

My Wife Claire (Bobby)

"What the fuck are we doing, Bobby?"

That's what she wanted to know. A fine, reasonable question. What the fuck *were* we doing?

I didn't have an answer, so I stared at her. Empty. Hollow. Vacant. My mouth hung open.

"Is it possible you've become a bigger asshole?"

Hmmmm….

"Because you were a pretty big asshole before."

Claire didn't swear often, but like a sailor on leave, she was making up for lost time.

"What did the doctor say at your physical?"

"He said I have an attractive prostate."

"Really, Bobby? Do you ever just answer a question?"

For a moment I didn't answer, then I ticked off the measurables like I carried my own clipboard.

"My blood pressure is good, cholesterol is reasonable, sugars are good. Everything's good. He said I'm a heathy man in his forties with decades in front of him. Oh, and he said my weight's good."

Claire was sitting at the kitchen table, biting at her lower lip and looking out the sliders. It was dusk and the gray of the evening had settled over the backyard grass, the woods in the distance.

"Is there a reason you're avoiding me?" she asked.

"I don't think so."

"You don't think so?"

"No."

She pursed her lips and nodded, "Do you even have any idea what I'm talking about?" Her voice was shaky and higher pitched than usual.

"Whatever it is," I said, "it's probably in your head."

I walked out of the kitchen and from the lightless hallway said, "I have to go to the studio tonight." And from that lightless hallway I heard her exhale full through the nose, then the first sniffle.

She was right, I'd become even a bigger asshole. What else was I capable of?

In the movies and on the news, guilty people claim they didn't know. They didn't know the gun was loaded. They didn't know excess dryer lint could cause a fire. They didn't know a car engine low on oil could seize up. They didn't know they had a crush on their best friend's wife.

But I knew. I knew I was destroying my marriage. I

knew Claire was suffering. I knew none of this ended well. I knew I wasn't telling her I was terminal. But I didn't do anything about it.

I called Maddy from the safety of the studio.

"Can you talk to Claire?"

"About?"

"Christ, I don't know! Talk her down from the ledge. She's asking so many questions and I don't know how to answer her. What do I tell her?"

"I don't know, the truth maybe?"

"That's not helpful."

"Fine, I'll talk to her. I'll figure something out. Maybe I'll say it's a midlife crisis."

"More of an end-of-life-crisis, but yeah."

"Are you calling me from the studio?"

"Yeah."

"Why are you there?"

"Rochelle."

"Ah. Good luck," she giggled.

"Thanks."

"Bobby?"

"Yeah?"

"What did the doctor say?"

"He said I look alive to him."

"Could be worse," she said and hung up.

Rochelle was a professor of anthropology and her husband

was a neurosurgeon—or she was a neurosurgeon and he was a professor of anthropology. I'm not really sure. She walked into the studio like she owned the room, well-heeled heels clicking against the floor in quick succession, and spoke to me like I was parking her Benz and she was concerned about scratches to the paint.

Even at night, she wore brown, tortoise-shell sunglasses and flung them off her face to greet me with a hot-breathed kiss. Her lips were always warm and wet and coated in waxy lipstick, but her cheeks were cold and dry. Her dark brown, mid-length hair was held by a pink Jackie-O headband.

Whenever she arrived there was energy in the air: a hot, confident, rabid energy. It was an energy that wasn't necessarily conducive to my work, and I often found myself unable to concentrate.

Rochelle required of me a grace and patience I no longer controlled, no longer yearned to control. In my early years, I wanted to please and was willing to do almost anything to garner a commission. I knew one commission would lead to another commission, then another. Now, it felt like death was watching my every step, gawking from behind a neighbor's tree-shaded window or taking cover beyond the rusty hinges that stained the front gate's white paint a reddish-brown. I was being hunted. I tried to ignore it. All I wanted was to create—to assemble as I myself was slowly being dissembled.

Rochelle insisted on posing nude.

Her breasts were lolling, heavy, but shapely, and she insisted I see them, admire them, twisting and turning her body in an effort to make them front and center. Our conversations typically consisted of her compelling me to make "the girls" the center of my study. Of course, our conversations were also one-sided: she didn't shut up.

"Do you have what you need?" she asked. Then while curled on the red velvet of the sofa, one arm spread along the ornate wooden frame of the backrest, she answered. "Well, of course you do."

"Can I buy this sofa from you? I need it. You know I love it. No?

"It's the third session and you said three sessions. Is that right?"

"Do we need another session? You said three, but do we need four?"

"That's fine if we do, but I'd like to get it on my calendar."

"Can you turn up the heat a smidge?" She looked down at her breasts. "As you can see the girls are a little cold."

"Did you hurt yourself, Bobby? You're walking a little funny."

"Really? You always walk like that?"

"Can I see the sketches?"

"Later? Why later?"

"How about seeing them now?"

"I'd like to see them now."

"Maybe just a peek?"

"Fine, after."

"No need to be snotty."

"Do you love your work, Bobby?"

"Are you feeling my essence?"

"Is my future clear to you?"
"How about now?"
"Would it help if you fucked me?"

Something Else About Jack (Bobby)

There was something else I haven't told you about Jack. Or rather something that happened to Jack. Or happened to me and Jack.

There's more to the story about Tammy's mop-headed boyfriend. He didn't like me. He didn't like the thought of me, either. One afternoon, Jack and I were hanging in his room, door closed, listening to music and talking about girls we might dare each other to call on the phone. I heard Tammy come home and she wasn't alone. Jack's bedroom was in the rear of the house, overlooking the backyard, so we didn't hear the car pull up to the front curb.

"Is he here?" Mop-head asked out loud to no one in particular. It was clear he wasn't asking Tammy a question, but rather hitting the bush with a stick to see if anything fell out. His question was loud enough for us to hear over the stereo.

"Where's your friend Bobby?" he asked, again to no one.

We could hear them out in the hallway, feet shuffling, hands banging against walls.

"Shut up," Tammy protested. "Leave him alone. They might not even be here."

Undeterred, Mop-head knocked on the door to Jack's room. It was a full knuckle knock lacking kindness or respect, almost a dare.

"Don't open the door," I mouthed to Jack as I shook my head. He looked at me like he understood, then opened the door anyway.

"There he is!" Mop-head squealed. He was four-years older and a head taller than me and much wider than Jack.

"What the fuck do you want?" Jack growled. He breathed in deep, expanding his still hairless chest to make himself appear bigger.

"That's quite a foul mouth your brother has!" Mop-head said to Tammy.

"Leave them alone," Tammy insisted, pulling on Mop-head's arm with full strength yet unable to budge him.

"How about you?" Mop-head said to me. "Anything to say?"

"No."

Jack tried to close the door, but Mop-head stood firm in the doorway.

"You had your fun," Tammy said to him. "Let's go to my room."

He wasn't having any of it.

"Please…" she begged.

"What wrong with this room?" He asked. "We have a

couple of pussies right here."

With that, Jack lunged at him. His fists flew, striking Mop-head on the chin and shoulders, sending him backward more out of shock than fear or injury. He pushed Jack backward and began to pummel him. Tammy was screaming, trying to pull Mop-head back out of the room. Jack continued to swing his fists, great looping swings that sometimes connected but often didn't.

Despite Mop-head connecting on several significant blows, Jack didn't stop and wouldn't back down. Jack was a whirlwind, a twister, a force of nature. There was blood now, Jack's blood, streaming from his nose and mouth, his upper lip split wide open. I could hear his labored breath as the blood sealed his nostrils, preventing air from passing. Tammy had blood on her shirt, Jack's blood, as she continued her attempt to separate them. Eventually, Tammy got in-between them, eating a couple of punches in the process, her long, red hair hiding her own injuries.

Mop-head was winded, his face blotchy red and scratched while his hair was somehow even more mussed than usual. Unsurprisingly, he was ready for more.

"I'm not done with either of you," he laughed as Tammy was finally able to push him out the door and into the hallway.

"Go fuck yourself!" Jack yelled before he wiped blood from his nose and lip onto his shirt sleeve.

And what was I doing? What did I do as Jack fought my battle and Tammy took punches for me?

I wasn't laughing—Mop-head was.

I wasn't bleeding—Jack was.

I wasn't crying—Tammy was.

I was doing nothing.

No, that's not true.

I was hiding.

I was cowering.

I was frozen.

My best friend and my dalliance were fighting for me as I stood silently, withering.

I didn't come out of my room for three days. After school, I walked directly home from the bus stop, grabbed a sandwich and locked myself in my room. I didn't answer the phone and, if someone called for me, Maddy told them I wasn't home. Mother called me down for dinner, but I didn't budge and she didn't persist.

"What's his problem?" She asked Maddy.

"A girl."

"Not that redhead, is it?"

"That's the one."

"Oh, great," she scoffed. "She's just like her mother."

I slept mostly, listened to music, read a bit and filled my drawing pad with various images of no particular significance. Even though I didn't want to admit it, I missed Tammy and flipped back through an old drawing pad to her sketch, admiring her as well as my work. I'd offered Tammy the sketch, but she insisted I keep it. I think she wanted me to keep the sketch so I could look upon her, pine for her when the time had come for pining. Sure enough, the time had arrived.

On the fourth day, Tammy stopped by unannounced and apologized and we spent the afternoon listening to music and, unlike Jack and I a few days earlier, we weren't disturbed.

"He's not going to stop by here is he?" I asked.

"We broke up," she said. "It's done." She curled up in my arms as we lay on my bed. Her translucent lips pecked my cheek, her head buried against my collarbone. And as I pulled in a breath of her hair, apple shampoo and conditioner, she fell asleep.

If he'd stopped by, I'm still not sure what I'd have done. There were some bullies I stopped cold with a clenched fist while others I continued to fear.

Must I choose between being the hero or being a stooge? Did it matter? Did it matter at all? Who was I meant to be? None of it was clear to me and I refused to choose, refused to take a stand once and for all. And that, perhaps, is the biggest reason I remain a coward. I like starting a book, and I like finishing a book, but it was torture to read into the middle, purgatory, neither halfway done nor halfway started.

A few months later, Tammy was gone and Jack was gone. There was only one bully left.

Success and Excess (Bobby)

Overnight success, as the *Times* called it in an over-the-top article entitled "The Gift," didn't happen overnight. But when it did, there was much to celebrate. My bank account as well as my ego swelled to bursting. Art became a blank check and I was able to pick and choose my commissions, negotiate for larger rates. Much larger rates. There were exhibitions and shows and even books with glossy photos and luminous quotes. I had no idea my work "beguiled and bewitched" and left one "gutted and marveling."

Maddy became my de facto manager, negotiating commission rates and amenities, demanding private jets and hotel suites. Maddy also kept the accounts up to date, freeing my time to do whatever it was I did, giving me time to share this so-called gift.

Claire doesn't possess an ego or at least not the kind that needed reassurance or stroking. Her love was teaching English and literature to high schoolers and it made her happier than

I dreamed a person could be. I often wished I could find in myself such solace, her comfort in her own skin, her place in the world. It all would have been so much simpler.

Claire was reluctant to move to Boston proper. She preferred a quiet life on the coast, north of the city. I wanted the Back Bay, a brownstone on Marlboro Street or Commonwealth Ave, maybe Beacon Hill. I was in demand and demanded to live as such. I wanted to catch the rising tide and let it cast me upward. There were restaurants to dine in, museums to visit, galas and fundraisers to attend. A new world opened its mouth wide, bared its teeth, and I was determined to let it consume me, to grab it before it vanished.

She was a girl of the *Mayflower* with simple needs, not a girl of pomp or Buckingham Palace. In the end, she won out and we stayed in our modest home on our modest street in our reasonably modest town. But I was determined to wander far and wide, to snatch beauty while it floated within hand's reach, to test the perimeter, to find where the boundaries could be stretched or breached. I'd been unleashed: someone had foolishly left the fence gate open and I ran out into the world at full speed.

These were days of great excess. I embraced sins, none more than gluttony. Actually, perhaps lust more than gluttony, but at the very least it was a tie, a photo-finish, too close to call. Often Maddy would fish me out of the hotel room tub before I drowned. Sometimes she'd pour me out of an overly expensive bottle of Scotch and onto the bathroom floor. All in good fun.

"Not bad for an ugly kid," I'd say.

"Not bad," she'd respond. "Now go change your clothes."

I took pains to make sure Claire didn't see me in such a state. The *Mayflower* wasn't built for excess, at least not of the sort I found enticing. She saw little need to make up for lost time since, for her, time hadn't been lost at all.

We also learned around this time that I, too, was barren. We wanted children, tried our darndest for many years, but some ingredient was missing. I insisted on finding out why. My yeast was dead or, at the very least, mortally wounded. Claire handled the news with her usual quiet dignity and a grace I couldn't hope to match. She retreated into the types of books only someone like Claire could appreciate or understand.

"We're the end of the family line," I said to Maddy one night. I offered a toast with some overly expensive red wine that I'd overpaid to purchase.

"It's not fair that we are," she replied, but touched my glass with hers anyway.

"No, it's not fair," I agreed.

A few years later she added: "Shouldn't at least one of us go out in a blaze of glory?"

The Woods
(Bobby)

Jack ran away when we were ten years old. He didn't run away from me. As a matter of fact, he told me he was going to do it and then he did do it. He packed a few peanut butter sandwiches wrapped in tinfoil and a green army canteen filled with tap water, put on a wool sweater and his play sneakers and off he went. I found him in the woods a couple of blocks from my house, tending a campfire (he'd also packed a box of safety matches) made from twigs and fallen branches, whatever dry leaves he could gather.

I stayed with him until I heard my mother calling me in for dinner. I didn't like to miss dinner, so I told him I'd come back and bring him something on a paper plate, hopefully something good as I didn't know what was being served. Before I left, he made me promise that I wouldn't tell my mother or tell his mother or Tammy where he was. Tammy and I weren't close yet, so it wasn't an issue. But I did tell Maddy.

After dinner, I asked my mother if I could use the tent in the basement as a fort for the back yard. After all, it was

August, so the weather was pleasant. Soon afterward, I convinced Jack to stay in the tent rather than out in the woods. He reluctantly agreed but was convinced it was the right decision when it rained that night. The tent wasn't as easy to set-up as I expected, but eventually I was able to figure it out.

I hung a flashlight from one of the poles near the top of the tent so Jack would have some light and maybe wouldn't feel so lonely. I also gathered some blankets from the linen closet and a couple of the extra couch pillows, including one of the fancy ones that we weren't supposed to use. All in all, it was pretty comfortable.

When I asked him why he ran away he said his mother wasn't very nice to him and his sister. She was always nice to me, I said. Yeah, he said, "because you don't live there."

Around nine o'clock, while the rain was steady, my mother came out to the back yard to get me and, of course, saw Jack, warm and comfortable, looking like he had no plans to leave.

"Don't you have to be getting home, Jack? It's late and I'm sure your mother will be looking for you."

"Yes," he said. "Thank you, Bobby, for use of the tent and all the rest."

But Jack didn't go home. Instead, he walked around the front of the house to the far side, then back around to the tent and resettled himself among the blankets and pillows and what remained of the peanut butter sandwiches. He'd told me that was what he'd do if he was told to go home or if his mother called.

A couple of hours later, Annette called looking for Jack. I heard my mother tell her that he was in the tent I'd set up in the back yard, but that was hours ago, and she'd sent him home right off. She said she had no idea where he could be if he wasn't home. She didn't ask me if I knew where he was—I'm not sure if I would have lied.

It was a cool August night, and I had my bedroom window open to welcome in the comfortable sleeping air. Around ten o'clock, I heard screams and crying and the elevated, panicked voices of Annette and Jack. I went down to the living room to get a better look, though I'm still not sure why. I didn't really want to know what was going to happen to him. I heard the strikes raining down on him, the bite of the snake, over and over and over, until he crumpled beneath her fury and was dragged out of the tent by an ear.

Maddy, despite her usual stoic and steady disposition, pressed her hands over her ears and wrapped her limbs around her torso. After the noise subsided, I found her in one corner of her room, fearful of his screams, fearful of the snake. I put my arms around her and we cried together before she fell asleep. She was always able to comfort me and now I'd found a purpose in comforting her.

My idea of the tent had backfired for Jack and he was dragged back into the lion's den, the place where, in the future, he would lose sight in one eye. It was my fault and for many years I carried the guilt of what was to come. On some level I knew Jack would never fully trust me again and, on some level, I knew I couldn't be trusted.

"You and me are the same," he'd said to me earlier that day. "We don't have fathers and we don't have mothers, either, not really."

The Arrival
(Bobby)

One never expects to get sick. Getting sick is for other people, weak people, those who eat fast-food and drink in excess and don't wear coats in the November rain.

It was an autumn Tuesday, the gray, in-between season, when I awoke on the floor of the studio. Something or someone was pounding a railroad spike into my head with a sledgehammer, driving me deeper into the floor. I was able to get to my knees, but not any further. I was dizzy and cold and sweating. I lay back down on the floor and closed my eyes.

When I awoke again, if I awoke again, I heard Maddy's voice. It was getting closer than moving further away like she was searching for me in the next room, the next house, the next town. But she was above me, kneeling, trying to rouse me.

"I've called an ambulance," she assured me.

"Why?" I wasn't assured.

"Because you passed out! I've been trying to wake you."

"Don't tell Claire." It was the first thing that came to me.

"What?"

"Don't tell her."

"I have to tell her."

"Please."

"I'm sorry," Maddy said. "I can't honor that."

"I know."

The room began to blend, sounds, sights, colors, smells, all melted into a kaleidoscope of the senses, both blinding and attractive, drawing me in, pulling me toward them before pushing me away. Maddy's voice faded again until it was gone, until there was darkness.

The ambulance arrived, and the ambulance people were serious folks. They looked like bouncers at a county fair or local country-and-western bar, burly and bearded and unsmiling. At least they didn't smile at me. When they bent down, their shoes were uncomfortably close to my face; they may have stepped in something during their last stop, their last lifesaving mission down at the stables. I smelled chewing tobacco.

They wouldn't let me walk to the ambulance, or even walk at all. I had to lay on the stretcher, strapped down like I was untrustworthy, ready to be committed to someplace rural and quiet: you know, with whispering nurses who'd tell me everything was going to be okay if I took all the medicine in the paper cup. Those were the rules and the rules needed to be followed. The two burly men lifted me into the van and asked questions I'd already answered.

Did I have a dog? And, if so, what was the dog's name?

No, I don't have a dog. Were they implying that whatever they may or may not have stepped in was the product of my dog? Which I didn't own?

Do you like dogs? Yes, of course I like dogs. Who doesn't like dogs? Maddy, the goon squad wants to know if I like dogs. Yes, of course, everyone likes dogs.

The ride was smooth, exceptionally smooth, the curves of the road soft and gentle, potholes were nonexistent. We floated. We never came to a full stop, only deceleration followed by rapid acceleration. There were sounds coming from the roof of the van: beeps and squeals and whirrs. Were those sounds for me? Because of me? Was my episode being announced to the world? Get out of the way! Sick man coming through! I may have fallen asleep. Or died.

When I awoke, I was dizzy again, dizzy still. We were in a large building, a hospital, I assumed, and the clean white walls melted and flexed, ran like rivers and froze solid in stillness. I threw up. My blood pressure was low, too low for their liking. This blood pressure just won't do, they said. *Lie down! Lie down!* They insisted, but wasn't I already lying down?

There were tests and machines that beeped and pinged and doctors and needles, a bed and an overnight stay. There were fluids for dehydration and vitamin D for lack of sunshine and potassium pills for a lack of itself. And there were questions about my health history (easy), my parents' health history (not so easy). There was too much noise. Too much bustling about. Too many soles of shoes squeaking along the tile floor. I couldn't sleep.

Was there pain, they asked. No. Other than the pain of more questions and the two lumberjack assholes that brought me here on a bed for one.

Was I going to the bathroom regularly? What does regularly mean? Yes, *reg-u-lar-ly.* That was hard to say, so I kept saying it or trying to say it. Okay, Maddy said, I should stop now.

I was in the hospital for too long, but not long enough to get the lunch items I'd filled out the night before. I ticked the boxes on the menu, a white slip of paper, with a blue ink pen and made sure the nurse picked it up. I felt like I was passing in an assignment to my fifth-grade teacher or a note to a cute girl I liked. It was the only thing I was looking forward to eating: grilled cheese and a fruit cup. Fabulous.

They booted me to the curb and said my blood was fine and my urine was fine and I was generally fine. Perhaps I'd caught a virus and my body would need a couple of weeks to clear it.

Claire picked me up and kissed me and told me how worried she'd been and was glad I was cleared of anything "serious." Poor thing.

Her father had died of heart failure, so her first concern was for me and for my heart. As it turns out, my heart was strong, at least strong enough, but the blood that flowed through it was compromised, polluted, poisoned, dank and fishy, a bouillabaisse. I wouldn't learn this for some time, however.

I went back to my usual life, a little, perhaps more than a little, concerned, but, as time passed, less and less so.

The episode never left the back of my mind, but also never stepped foot into the front. In some senses, we were at an impasse, the episode and I, it waiting for the right moment to reveal itself and me choosing to ignore it, refusing to provide it with the power to control me. Soon enough, though, there would be a new bully in my life, one that wouldn't go quietly, one that wouldn't go to the grave without dragging me with it.

About three months later, there was a second episode. This time there was no convenient settling to the floor to be conveniently found by Maddy within the hour. No, this one was much more dramatic in nature, an announcement screamed at the top of its lungs.

Maddy and Her Bed (Bobby)

In her early twenties, Maddy's breakdowns could be counted on one hand, but they were deep and dark and terrible. She'd recount Annette's treatment of Jack and wonder how someone could hurt their own child, how a mother could mutilate her own flesh and blood. Then she'd talk about her inability to conceive, her inability to be a "true" woman, David's betrayal and her unwillingness to make peace with all of it.

Pragmatic. That's how I'd describe her, pragmatic. She was a person of numbers, facts and figures. Which is not to say she didn't have a passionate and emotional side, she did. But her mind revolved around more logical pursuits, and a stoic demeanor. This made her troubles all the more frightening and always unexpected. When the strongest person in your life is knocked to the ground by an invisible demon, you begin to wonder if anyone remains whole or has the required strength to come out on the other side.

She had our father's eyes, but not his free-spirit.

It arrived with the suddenness of a flash-flood, a drenching fever, overnight, slithering out from her darkened closet or clawed paws grabbing at her feet from under the bed. It lasted for days. Now it exposed itself more often and refused to depart without a fight. If I wasn't already aware, meaning my own phone calls weren't returned, I'd receive a call from her office that she hadn't been at work and hadn't been heard from in a couple of days. It was time to make my way to the house.

My first stop was the bakery. Cakes and sweets would not contribute to her initial rise, but they were essential on the way up, like switching on stair lights one at a time to guide the way upward. My second stop: the bookstore. She would need a distraction, an escape, something where someone else was having a problem, too. The goal was to encourage a soft landing, a tuck-and-roll out of bed onto her steady feet, though I was fully aware a soft landing wasn't always possible.

Our childhood home, the roughshod bungalow, was now Maddy's home. The outside was neater than the corpulent home of my memory, squat and with gables, a fresh coat of brown paint and bushes trimmed with care. The roof was redone recently and the grass mowed and edged. The door, too, since Satan was buried, was no longer red.

Maddy liked to garden, knees in the soil and heavy, fabric gloves pulled almost to her elbows. As a result, tulips pushed up for their May bloom and each summer tomatoes were so abundant she parked a red wagon full at the curb and painted a sign that read: FREE TOMATOES. Thorny roses, carefully pruned, climbed white trellises and perfectly proportioned pine trees grew tall and without a needle littering the grass. Built in 1870 as a summer home for some well-heeled Bostonian, it once again looked the part of a peaceful retreat and had regained its calming purpose.

There were men, too, hopeful suitors who, over the years, arrived at the bungalow's doorstep. They took many forms: studious banker types who spoke her language, thick glasses and fancy suits, brawny tradesmen with ladder-strewn work vans who arrived to fix a gutter and never wanted to leave. There was an occasional poet, unscraped teeth and radical politics: they all came calling for Maddy. The girl with the blue eyes and blond pigtails had blossomed into a fine woman.

There was even one creative fellow who claimed to have attended a showing of my work in Denver and was, on cue, immensely impressed and nearly moved to tears. His performance, I'm told, was convincing. However, Maddy, never the fool, cracked open her leather-covered chart of accounts and matched, or rather unmatched, the dates in question. On that particular date, or thereabouts, I was firmly hitched to my studio, a son of Massachusetts. She let him dangle a bit longer, squirm on the hook, before she drowned his ambition in a briny mix of facts and disappointment.

As I placed my key in the door lock, I remembered my spying days, hiding in the shadows and listening to my big sister's mostly uninteresting phone conversations. She'd stretch the curled cord as far as it could go, to the furthest point away from the kitchen base and into the hallway closet, escaping our mother's prying ears while trying to determine where my ears were operating, absorbing information like a Soviet spook. They spoke of boys and jeans and shampoo, and sometimes a band I'd never heard on the radio.

Mostly, though, they spoke about David, or she spoke about David. Or she spoke *to* David.

David had so thoroughly damaged her that, twenty-five years on, and with plenty of suitors along the way, the only one who pried open the door, made it to her bed was another red devil: the demon of depression.

These bouts didn't fade into the background though she did her best to keep them hidden.

And then there was this: she was living my life of worry. I'd contracted wasting disease, yet I was not tied to the bed. I was living my life and continuing my work while Maddy fought the fight. Was she my portrait in the attic? She took the news harder than I did. I'm not sure why, but it barely registered for me.

I had a plan, a way of dealing with my ever-shortening life and it was unfolding through determination and deception. A grand plan to be sure and one that lifted the weight from my shoulders. I did not come to the decision lightly and I hope it's not presented in a manner that makes it seem trivial. It was strange, though, even to me, that I would live carefree even while dying and Maddy died a little while trying to live. I was going out with a bang.

Ghosts (Maddy)

The morning copy of the *Times* was tossed onto my doorstep as it has been every morning for the past twenty or so years. After a cursory glance at the headlines, I roll it up for later. It's not often I read the entire paper, and it's usually not until dinner.

Today the headline is something about politics, how one side or the other is holding up an agreement that one side or the other believes benefits one side or the other. *The usual Wednesday*, I think to myself. But it's not the usual Wednesday. On this Wednesday my brother is nearing his final run, his sprint to the finish, and there's little left to be done other than wait. I'm not sure if that benefits one side or the other.

Yesterday, I went to the studio to find what Bobby asked me to bring to him, two wood pedestals with something, or rather some "thing" in progress on each. He has his reasons. I wrapped them in cloth and placed them in two separate bags. I've made the mistake of placing two of his works together in one box and I was nearly disinvited to Christmas dinner.

The two pedestals are heavier than expected, weighty like they carry their own thoughts and dreams. I place them on the floor of the car, in front of the passenger's seat that's empty save the now unrolled morning paper. I'm not really sure why, but before I drive to the hospital, I pick up the paper and start leafing through it, flitting by the first couple of pages until something on page 5 catches my eye.

"You just missed Kilkenny," Bobby says when I walk into the room. He's not wearing a mask today.

"Oh, what did he have to say?"

"The usual. Lots of hands in his pockets and confusion," he laughs.

I'm glad Bobby is laughing. If, as they say, it's the best medicine, then he could use lots of laughter, more laughter than a hundred giggling children could produce in a year. But I'm about to put an end to it.

Bobby could always gauge my mood. He also knew I was the keeper of secrets. What he didn't know is there were certain things I'd allow him to see in my face, things, deep down, I wanted him to know.

"What's going on?" he asks. "What aren't you telling me?"

"Have you seen today's paper?" I ask him, knowing full well he hadn't. At the moment, he was so distracted and unsure, he would have looked out the window if I asked him if the sun rose this morning.

"I don't read it anymore," he said and dismisses the notion with a wave of his hand. "Either ads or worthless editorial opinions. I think they even got rid of the funnies. Who would get rid of the funnies?"

"You might want to take a look."

"Why?"

"Page 5, Obituaries," I say and pass it to him.

He glares at me with a snarled lip, like a child being forced to eat the broccoli on his plate before he gets dessert.

On page 5, in words larger than expected it reads: NOTED NEUROSURGEON ROCHELLE MILLER SUCCUMBS TO WASTING DISEASE.

He looks at me out of the corner of his eye, folds the newspaper and places it on the serving cart, then lays back down.

"She lived a wild life," he says. "That one didn't get cheated."

"No, she didn't," I agree.

"Grown kids," he says.

"Yeah."

"They'll do fine."

"I hope so."

He sinks into the bed and his face grows even narrower and paler, something I couldn't fathom until I saw it with my own eyes.

"Her bronze, her essence, was slimmer than expected, she was more her past. That happens sometimes. She was happy with it. Very happy."

"I remember."

"She even made that book over there," he says and gestures off into the distance.

"I didn't remember that."

"Take a look. I don't know what page."

"I will."

I took a moment.

"Bobby? You understand what this means."

"Yes."

A shitshow.

I decided no one would be invited to the funeral and no one, save Claire, would attend. What would be the point? He would already be dead.

It will be more important to avoid the reporters, bloodthirsty fuckers with recording devices and red-tipped noses and brown leather shoes that pit-pat along the ground and the floors. They'll camp out in front of the house, in back of the house, trying to worm their way through the ductwork. They'll want a scoop, an angle, information, something saucy, an admission even with the body still warm. My only brother, my Bobby, gone and the crows nip and peck, squawk, try to pull the roadkill from the asphalt. Yes, yes, there's blood on his hands, but he'll sleep his sleep.

Do they see what's been wrought upon our family? Do they even see it? Barren, lifeless, childless, we're the end of the family line. Yes, yes, everyone will cry poor me! Poor me!

That's our nature. But in the end, we all get what we deserve, what we've earned, regardless of class or income bracket or pedigree or education. Fine, I'll say it if it makes you feel better: including me. I'm not ignorant to that fact.

Why is an abusive mother blessed with the ability to have children while others have eggs rotting on the vine or sperm that swim in sluggish circles rather than toward their goalpost? Why do those with the least right to happiness somehow find it? I'll have nothing. I'll have no one.

It didn't make it to trial. Or, rather, he won't make it to trial. Everyone loves a good scandal, especially when it happens to the rich. Everyone enjoys when they get theirs, poking the body with a thick branch to make sure the noose has done its work.

I've seen the headlines. Stories need headlines whether accurate or otherwise:

Wasting Disease Patient Zero

Famous Sculptor Is Infamous Patient Zero

The Great Equalizer: Wasting Disease

There was something else I forgot to mention. I few weeks ago, I brought Bobby a couple of statues he'd been working on for a long time. There were two pedestals, his versions of the sketches he used for his clients.

One of the statues represented Bobby when he was young, younger at least, it was twisted, perhaps in pain, all of which makes sense when I consider his childhood. The second represented him mid-life, just earlier than now, he was jumping toward the heavens, strong, lean, in the prime of life. There was no third statue, no future, no what he would become.

He placed the statues on the meal table near his bed and stared for several minutes.

"Just as I thought," he said and almost laughed. "It makes sense now."

"What does?" I asked.

"Two statues representing two sketches."

"Did you not finish the third?"

"The third never made sense. I couldn't see it, my future didn't make sense, now I know why."

Now he allowed himself to laugh.

"It's not the future statue that's missing, it's the past."

"What do you mean?"

"You see the present, well, the one that until recently was the present."

"Yes."

"The first one, my childhood, isn't my childhood, it's my future, my now, I guess."

He continued.

"My childhood, it's still unmade. it had no essence and therefore didn't need a statue; I hadn't become who I was until the middle. The beginning was a work in progress, something yet to be molded. No, I've become the third, wretched at the end."

Wasting (Bobby)

I'm not afraid to die; I've been dead most of my life.

And when you're not afraid to die, it makes everything easier, clearer. You become more focused and your energy returns, your cheeks pinken and your eyes twinkle. Passions become passionate again and loves, true loves, rise to the top like cream.

Kilkenny, the good doctor, isn't very optimistic about my future. He says the right things, heavy, measured words of the healer, but his eyes belie the spoken word. Things will get worse and worse and I will waste away, ounce by ounce, pound by pound until the wind carries me away towards the storm clouds like a discarded page of newsprint or a balloon broken free of a child's hand. It will be less a death and more a never-to-return. Over time, I fear, it will be less a never-to-return and more a never-was.

From the window opposite the hospital bed, I can see the trees as they shed their leaves in autumn, their own choreographed version of wasting away. They shake and sway in the breeze, holding steady through rain and falling temperatures, until, at last, their reddened and yellowed selves are ready to say goodbye. I imagine the leaves holding on tight with tiny veined fingers, gripping the branch in defiance of the life-cycle, then, their purpose fulfilled and feeling comfortable in their station, they smile to each other and wink, before releasing their grip. Finally free of the suckled teat, they ride the wind, and take that final journey, wherever it may lead.

The clouds too, have a message for me. Fluffy and droll, gray and curious, they peek in through the window as they float past, always moving, too nervous to stay and chat, too bored to stop and listen. They want to know how long I will last and want to tell me it's okay. We're all just fleeting they'll say, all on borrowed time and at the will of the wind, at the will of nature. Don't think you're any different, Bobby Shaw. Don't think it for a second.

A nurse delivers lunch. She's the one who's hoping, expecting a signature on the book I refuse to sign. Of course, I will sign it when the time's right. Yellow and white corn, a warm medley, is the only thing I recognize on the tray. Something in a red sauce, but it isn't pasta. Chicken? Maybe it is pasta. I tell her I'm not hungry, but she leaves it anyway and smiles like she knows better than I do. So does everyone else, so the jokes on her. The smell is unsettling, like something gone off while bathing in pickle juice and drying itself in a bowl of paprika. I push the tray and cart as far away as my withered arm will reach. When did this arm wither? It was strong only a few weeks ago.

Claire is supposed to drop in soon. Maybe she'll bring

me something to eat, something from the outside world, something bad for me and wrapped in a greasy, wax-paper shroud. I assume the blue-shirted people in security don't pat you down like they might when you arrive for a conjugal visit at county jail. At least as I assume they do for a conjugal visit. And if they do pat you down, that they still allow outside food for a condemned man.

These are the things you think about when movements, even trips to the bathroom, become complicated endeavors. Wires and tubes replace the metaphors, the leash and collar around your neck are real, tangible, and tighter than you expect. It becomes easier to observe and speculate from the bed than to interact with the world around you. Assuming you can stay awake long enough.

Though running never came easy to me, I do miss it. I remember running in the yard, stealing bases during impromptu neighborhood games of whiffle ball. And running from wasps when we found a basketball size nest, paper gray, in the bushes by the street sign and we, Jack and I, decided, for some strange reason or other, to hurl stones into it, through it. They chased us for hours, but thankfully, we escaped. My legs were good legs then, despite it all.

Mrs. Grace called the other day and asked me if I knew, if I knew when I was with her, if I knew when I was inside her. Yes, I did and I told her I knew.

You see, I think about anything at all, everything but the death that awaits me. The only thing I truly fear is being forgotten and I've already addressed that little notion. I've gone out with a bang. Just ask Mrs. Grace.

A Fundraiser (Bobby)

Claire was beautiful in that black dress, her shoulders bare, hair pulled toward the top of her head so it fell in wisps and curls. It's an evening I'll never forget, the way she looked at me, like I was the most important person in the world and, for that night at least, I felt I was. There were others, a series of weighty speeches given by well-dressed people who looked and sounded like they were born orators. And then there was me, the upstart artist who'd found a way to make enough money to be able to give some away.

We were put up at the Copley Plaza Hotel, a fair indication that our fortunes, at least to the outside world, were looking favorable. Earlier that day, Claire explored the hotel room with small, purposeful steps, her hands running along the raised, velvety wallpaper and painted wainscotting. "I feel like royalty," she said while rolling like a child on top of the heavy, blue quilted bedding of the four-post bed.

While on the bed, she turned toward me and smiled.

Not a regular smile, a Claire-smile that warmed the room. "You did it," she said and winked.

I brought her a pair of white, Copley Plaza emblazoned slippers I'd found in the closet and placed them on her feet. "I'd hate for these to go to waste," I said while she admired them, flexing her feet up and down like that same child, angling for a better view. "Yes," she admitted. "That is better." She wasn't one for being fussed over and had little need for fancy comforts, but she was enjoying her afternoon.

There were oils I kept in a small, leather travel bag just for occasions such as this. I went into the bathroom and took them out, displaying them for her review.

"Ahh," she said. "The good stuff."

I took a towel from the bathroom, white and heavy, and unfolded it on the bed. I stripped off her clothes and she lay on her stomach, centering herself on the towel. I poured small quantities of oil down her spine.

"You're supposed to warm it first!" she half-screamed, half-laughed.

"Sorry about that," I pleaded. But I wasn't sorry and she knew I wasn't sorry. It was all part of the choreography, part of the dance itself.

Her skin was butter-soft, and despite the cool oils, warm to the touch. Her tight muscles collapsed under my hand and I rubbed until she was pliable and, with her face turned to one side of the pillow, her lips formed a devious smile.

"I think it's your turn," she suggested.

"I'm too nervous about the speech," I said.

"Nonsense," she said. "What better way to loosen up."

But I was determined to let the moment pass, my inelegant, ghastly behavior toward my wife had become ingrained, almost natural. It had to.

"Room service?" I asked.

"Hmmmmm..." she considered for a disappointed moment. "No. It's beautiful outside. How about a café on Newbury Street? We can go over your speech."

"Newbury Street sounds perfect, but only if we don't talk about my speech."

"Are you sure?"

"I'm sure."

"You know," she added in a tone without judgement while her chin rested on her palm, her weight on her elbow. "There are pills now that can help."

"It's not that," I said softly.

"Then what?"

I didn't answer.

We walked the couple blocks toward Newbury Street on that late April afternoon, hand in hand, like we used to do. There was no mention of my uncomfortable behavior. The air was dry and sweet, and Boston Public Garden was coming to life. We made a quick detour. Green flower stems reached toward the sun and the swan boats filled with tourists made their way around the pond. A scruffy young man in a heavy flannel shirt strummed his sticker-laden guitar and sang folk songs I didn't recognize. I tossed a couple of dollars into his open guitar case. He continued along his with his setlist, his obliviousness well earned.

When two college students left a bench drenched with

spring sun, Claire was quick to claim it for us. The scruffy man's music was still in the air as we sat.

"Don't you love to people watch?" she asked.

"Not really." I answered.

"Well, why not?"

"I don't like how people walk," I said.

"What's wrong with how they walk?" she asked, her eyes squinted like a sleuth from a black and white film.

"There's nothing wrong with how they walk."

"Then what's the problem?"

"There's a problem with how I walk."

"Oh," she said and looked at me with a frown and raised eyebrows. "No one notices how you walk."

"I do."

"Then you're the only one," she said and laughed. I still loved her laugh.

Afterward, we found a sunny table on Newbury Street and sat in heavy iron chairs made barely comfortable by thick, fabric cushions. I don't really remember what we talked about (though it wasn't my upcoming speech), but I remember being happy. And I remember Claire being happy. She'd forgotten her sunglasses, so she squinted at me and her skin began to pinken before the afternoon sun ducked behind the brownstones. Claire checked her watch.

"We have to get back to the hotel," she said with a faux accent, what I assume was supposed to be Boston Brahmin. "I'm due at the spa for a hair styling."

A few months prior, Claire bought me a tuxedo, or rather accompanied me to be fitted and re-fitted, pinned and chalked as I stood on a small stool as a small man took measurements. "You should own one," she said with a smile. "You're going to need it." As it turns out, she was right.

The fundraiser was in support of public school art programs throughout the Commonwealth of Massachusetts. Near and dear to be sure and an effortless decision on my part.

My speech was simple, to the point, perhaps even sparse. In other words, it wasn't the thoughtful, scholarly speech it might have been had I allowed Claire to help polish the language. She had a way with words that was well beyond my skill. However, when I held the podium and the audience quietly awaited my words, I thanked them for thanking me and presented the check and did something I should have done ages ago. I told everyone, including Claire, how I felt about her.

"My wife, Claire, is here with me," I said. Then I pointed amongst the round banquet tables, past the red roses in a vase at the center of each table, to the woman in black, her hair styled with those small wisps flowing down her temple and forehead. She acknowledged me with a small smile and then ducked her head as the room gave soft applause.

"As you can see, she's the beauty in the family. But she's also the brains. And the talent. Come to think of it, I don't know what I bring to the table or what she sees in me."

Between pats on the back and the shaking of hands, there were toasts of champagne and whiskey on the rocks and the bar stayed open much later than expected. Claire, not usually a drinker, had spritzes and martinis and a concoction John the bartender named "The Claire." She was in good form.

And there were commissions consummated that evening.

"I hear you're all the rage, Mr. Shaw."

"Please, call me Bobby," I said. "I think, perhaps, there's been a bit of hyperbole in the papers," I said.

"You're too modest, Bobby" she said. "Lynda Grace." She held out a ringed hand which may have sunk the Titanic.

"Mrs. Grace," I said and took her hand. "I know who you are."

She gave a bow, almost a small curtsey. She was a tall woman with short, tidy gray hair and a heavy necklace supporting a large ruby around her neck. The attendees brought their A-game.

"You're in Marblehead, I believe?"

"We are, yes," she said before moving on from the small talk. "Tell me, Bobby, how does one get on your schedule?"

"That's a daunting task, I'm afraid," I said with due seriousness. "There's a background check, reasonably thorough, medicals including bloodwork, references from your college advisor…Years."

She stood in front of me, stiff as a board, her mouth hung open, unable to comprehend what she was hearing.

"Mrs. Grace," I said. "I'm kidding."

"Oh, my goodness," she blurted. "You had me going there!"

"My sister, Maddy, is sort of my manager. I can have her call you."

"Perfect," Mrs. Grace said. "Would it be possible to arrange for my husband and I to pose together? I'm not sure if that's something you do."

"Of course," I said. "That would be wonderful."

There were other, similar conversations throughout the evening, people treating me like a pseudo-celebrity, waiting in line to have a word, chuckling at my unfunny jokes. Claire just stared in amazement at the ease in which people at the event wanted to talk with us, wanted a small piece of us for themselves. After hours, while Claire was in the restroom, I stood, leaning heavily against the lobby bar, my bow tie undone, alone with a glass of whiskey, shaking the ice in my glass and shaking my head.

"Mr. Shaw?" John asked. "Can I refill you, sir?"

How far I'd come.

"No," I said. "But thank you, John."

"And, Claire?" he asked.

"I'm thinking we've stayed out late enough."

"Yes, sir."

When we entered the elevator, Claire looked at me like I was the great catch of her life, like light emanated from the parts of me that never saw light. Like I was meant to be her person. Her eyes were the bright eyes of a young woman, before the weight of the world and the burden of relationships could take their toll, take their pound of flesh. When the doors closed, she hugged me tight and, even when they opened again, delivering us to our floor, she refused to let go. The poor thing.

She wasn't one to look for the spotlight. I'd embarrassed her, of course, with my tribute but that night we made love. It had been some time—months, possibly years. I'd forgotten the last time, but she hadn't. It was like the old days when our bodies fit together perfectly, locking in place like we'd been crafted and carved to fit together, honed in superb tolerances and balance. There were no more excuses. What was done could not be undone. In the morning, I awoke to a stinging regret, the bandage torn from the flesh.

I also threw up that morning, filling the hotel toilet with nonsense and whiskey and the aforementioned regret. It was guilt and fear and the realization of consequences that drove the nausea—that and the half bottle of whiskey. If things were as I feared, as I knew they were then, I'd damaged the only human I'd ever loved. The only person who ever truly loved me. I'd buried the ticking time bomb, snuck it beneath the floorboards. *Tick-tock*. In order to achieve balance in my relationship, I'd risked everything. In seeking to see her smile again, to hear her laugh, that wonderful and joyous and infectious laugh, I'd knowingly captained the ship into treacherous waters.

I tried, I did try, to not remain inside at the end, to not poison her with what swam inside of me, what coursed through my veins. But she was insistent and pulled me tighter, closer in the moment until I relented. What was I afraid of in the moment? That she would leave if I refused. And that wasn't an option. There now, I've told you what I've done.

Professor Finlay (Bobby)

"You have talent," Professor Finlay said one afternoon in the washed-out, yellow light of her campus art studio. "But you aren't giving your soul."

She was a slight woman, wispy, but sinewy and strong. Her jet-black hair was pulled back into a tight ponytail and secured by a pink elastic, her signature look. Her nose was thin and turned slightly up at the tip like it knew better. Her brown eyes stared at me, *through me,* when I worked. Her hands grabbed my wrists like vices, squeezing and guiding my hands until I began to sweat.

"No, no," she'd say when she stood behind me. "You're going through the motions. You see it, but you aren't becoming part of it. It's not becoming part of you. Learn to look not only with your eyes, but your hands and your imagination." Often, she would stand behind me and hold me by the waist, resting her chin on my shoulder. I could only hope she didn't notice her effect on me. But she did.

She liked to work in soap and wax, to carve and shape

what she saw and what she felt. "You're going to get there," she assured me. "When you can form a shape while your eyes are closed."

"You're going to sculpt me," she said. "Then you'll understand what I mean. We can use my home studio."

When Claire asked me where I was spending all my time, I explained I was working on my semester project with Professor Finlay.

"She's taken quite an interest in you," Claire remarked one afternoon.

"She has," I admitted. "She's brilliant and I'm learning so much from her."

"I'm sure," she noted and turned her nose, her entire body away from me.

"It's not like that," I explained.

"You don't know anything about women," she snickered.

"It's not like that," I insisted, perhaps more to convince myself.

But it was like that. And she was like that. And I was like that. The ugly child was taking what was being offered to him; he always would, and that would be his downfall. At the moment, however, he was evolving and growing as an artist, and he had Professor Finlay to thank. The training did not come without a catch or without guilt. You don't grow as an artist by taking notes in a cavernous lecture hall of an ivy-strewn building; you grow by believing and feeling and grabbing what you can.

To be clear, this wasn't about feelings and love and the rest of it. It was transactional. Yes, that sounds cold, I agree.

But I was learning, she was teaching and, to be honest, her methods were both sincere and effective. She knew what it would take for me to make the leap and, whatever her intentions, she was willing to provide an environment to foster my development. How many times before or since had she employed these methods? Impossible to say, and I was reluctant to ask. What was also clear is no one had taken such a serious interest in my development.

Professor Finlay lived, alone, in a gray ranch on a side street off of Willow Street, and I met her on Wednesday evenings. It was a short walk down Willow, past the Stevens College library, left at Hammet Avenue, down Hammet for three streets on the left, taking the last one, Green Street, 75 Green Street. How could I forget?

Looking back, her methods were unsurprisingly unorthodox. Her home studio was the largest room in the house and where one would expect to see a living room or family room. The windows had dark fabric sheets hanging from makeshift curtain rods which, by design, blocked out any light from outside. Track lighting was clustered in the center of the room and pointed in every direction. The lighting was so effective and expertly aimed that it gave the room a feeling of being outside at noon.

"Here's what we're going to do," she began that first evening. "You're going to sketch me without looking at me while you work. Eventually, we'll move on to a sculpture."

I may have looked either confused or concerned because she smiled and continued.

"You have to be able to see to fully understand your

subject, to capture it in any art. You have to explore your subject. A musician can't create music until they understand how to listen. It doesn't matter the sound unless you can hear it in relation to the sounds around it."

"Ok," I answered, as much confused as concerned. My body was tense and nervous. I hoped my deodorant wouldn't fail.

"Relax," she said. "Don't think of this as a class and a grade. Think of it as transforming the way you use your senses, the way you use your hands, the way you use your imagination to fill in what you can't see or feel."

"I'm sorry," I said. "I'm a little nervous."

"Understandable," she said and placed her hand on my shoulder. "Let me walk you through what's going to happen. I'm going to blindfold you and you're going to learn every curve of my body. You're going to be thorough and unafraid and you're going to trust me and you're going to trust yourself. Your instincts will be right even if you want to fight them."

"Blindfold?"

"Yes," she said and laughed. "Of course! How else will you develop your non-sight senses?"

"I hadn't thought about it," I claimed. But I had thought about it and I was willing to learn, willing to do what was required of me. Willing to grab hold of what was being offered to the ugly child.

I stood in the center of the studio facing a tall desk made for standing, not sitting, and she placed a dense fabric over my eyes and tied it in the back of my head before she moved around to the front.

"Can you see anything?"

"No, nothing."

She placed my hands on her breasts.

"Can you feel this?"

"Yes," I croaked.

"Okay," she said and removed my hands. "I'll be right back. Get used to the darkness, open your ears, open your mind, forget where you are. Most importantly, try to relax, that's when we do our best work."

I heard her somewhere in the house, another room, perhaps in the back. The sound of a door opening and drawers closing and shoes crossing the floor, then bare feet patting along the same floor.

"Are you comfortable?"

"Yes, I think so."

"Good. So, each session will begin the same way. You'll be blindfolded and once you learn a bit about your subject, in this case, *me*, we'll take the blindfold off. You'll begin work, starting with sketches and moving on to a three-dimensional medium. When you're working, you won't be able to look at me. Got it?"

"Yes."

Her voice and the patter of feet grew closer until I could feel her warm breath on my throat.

"Do you trust me?" she asked.

"Completely."

"That's a good answer," she assured me. I could smell mints and some kind of herbal shampoo.

"It's a little warm in here," I noted.

"I'll need it a little warm," she laughed. "Trust me on that."

She took my wrists in her strong hands and placed them near the top of her head while her hands held my waist.

"Now, explore your subject, learn the shapes, the angles, the textures, the smells, the tastes. Everything. Be fearless."

I began following her hair downward. It was out of the perpetual pink elastic and flowed down her shoulders. She was wearing a loose-fitting robe that dropped to the floor when I nudged it on her shoulders. I heard it crumple into a pile near her feet. My hands moved naturally, and quickly, to her breasts and I cupped them like I was worried they would disappear, evaporate before I had the chance to discover them.

She laughed and said, "Maybe you want to start higher and work your way down."

"Sorry," I said.

"Don't be sorry," she assured me, "you didn't do anything wrong."

"Okay," I said. "Sorry."

"There will be plenty of time to explore, but maybe best to start with the shape of my head, my ears, my nose and eyes."

"Of course," I said and pulled my hands back up near her ears. "Sorry."

She laughed again and said, "Take your time, we have all the time in the world."

My hands spent time exploring her ears, small and soft,

more what one might expect of a child than a woman of forty. I felt the small pinholes where her diamond stud earrings had been only a few minutes earlier, the lobes still warm from the touch of the metal.

"Good, good," she said and pulled a breath in through her nose. "I can tell you're thinking. Tell me what you feel."

"Your ears are small, smaller than I expected, more delicate and the skin is very soft and warm."

"Is there something else you can do, a way to get more information?"

Although she was only a few inches away and facing me, I pulled her closer and used my lips to find her ear. I was careful not to bite though it was my first instinct. She must have noticed my reaction to her body, to the moment, as I had her pulled tight up against me, but she didn't say anything.

"I almost bit your ear," I confessed in a whisper.

"I told you, your instincts will be right, but I appreciate you fighting that one."

I moved my lips down her neck as my hands rolled over her shoulders. She was wearing a perfume of some sort, flowers and a hint of something more, a spice maybe.

"Anything?" she asked.

"Perfume, flowers, something more," I answered.

"Good. Excellent."

My hands again found her breasts.

"Sorry," I said without removing my hands, "Just getting to know all of you."

"Please do," she said.

A few minutes later, she moved behind me and untied

the blindfold. She reached down to the floor, twisting her arms around my knees and picked up the robe and put it back on. It was pink like the elastic that usually tied her hair back, silky and smooth.

"No," she said. "Don't turn around. Walk forward to the desk and use the charcoal and paper to draw what you felt. Every detail you remember and use your imagination for what you don't know yet."

I moved forward toward the desk and she followed close behind me, leaning her weight against me when I stopped in front of the desk. The heat of her body against my back was both comforting and terrifying. I took a deep breath and picked up the charcoal. Her hands moved around my waist. As I began to draw, she unbuckled my belt and unbuttoned my pants, sliding them down downward, the metal of the belt ringing in a new era as it hit the wood floor.

I must have hesitated for a moment, stood straight up, my neck and back rigid. "Start drawing," she said. "Stay in the moment."

My underwear soon joined my pants down by my ankles, and I felt her strong hand grab hold of me.

"Now," she whispered, her hot breath on the back of my neck. "We're going to release all that distracting energy you have built up. We're going to get rid of it so you can concentrate on the drawing, concentrate on what you felt, how my body feels and smells. I'm concentrating on what I feel right now. Do you think it's helping?"

"Yes," I said as I leaned forward and placed my hands on the desk. "Definitely helping."

These sessions were conducted every Wednesday evening for two semesters, each session exploring a little further, a little deeper until I could draw her while still blindfolded. There wasn't a scent, a mole, a single hair I couldn't place with staggering accuracy. As the weeks went on, she insisted on releasing my "distracting energy" in ever more creative ways and in each room of the house. I became more confident in my movements and my work. By the time I was ready to sculpt her form, my hands moved without hesitation, I could see her, all of her, inside and out, burned into my mind.

"You're ready," she said late one Wednesday evening in a tone that was both congratulatory and matter-of-fact. And I was. "But do continue to visit, I've grown fond of your company."

Under the care of Professor Finlay, I developed my senses, my art: when I look at someone, I can see their guilt and their fears. I can see who's been unfaithful, who is a thief and who is pious. I can tell how they've lived by the lines on their faces, by the things they laugh at and the way they look back at me.

Although, as I mentioned, her methods were unorthodox, I owe Professor Finlay, Margaret, everything. Without her showing me what was possible and what I could become, there is no me. Of course, without me, as you'll learn, the world would be a better place.

Campion (Bobby)

I begged and pleaded for months. Maddy did too. I was ten, I think, so Maddy was around thirteen, and we both wanted a puppy. All our friends, most of our friends, had dogs, and it appeared we were making slow but steady progress in convincing our mother. I envisioned a dog making us complete, a family of four, that magical number you see in movies, however unorthodox.

"Six months of good behavior," Mother demanded. "Then we'll talk about a puppy." She believed any reward or success required the requisite suffering and this would be a reward, therefore, it fell firmly under the auspices of Anguish, the patron saint of suffering.

A dog, I pleaded, would fill my nights with joy, a fluffy animal asleep on my bed keeping me company, one eye on the closet guarding for monsters. It would be something to love unconditionally and something that would love me back, unconditionally.

"Do you require unconditional love?" she asked, a scowl,

her upper lip curled upward.

I didn't know how to answer the question. What answer was expected? What my answer might be? I did the only safe thing and said nothing. I felt foolish and small.

On Christmas Eve, Mother carried in a cardboard box from the garage. The way she walked made the weight of the box appear unbalanced. It made a strange noise, not a very cardboard box—like squeak. She delicately placed it on the living room floor in front of the tree. Almost immediately, the box began to vibrate and one side pushed outward–someone or something was attempting to escape. There was another noise, much higher pitched than the original, followed by the unmistakable bark of a puppy.

Maddy and I both rushed toward the box at high speed, the knees of our pajamas worn through by our sliding stop on the living room rug. Maddy opened the flaps on top of the box to reveal a black headed lab-mix that stood up on its hind legs, bobbing, intent on leaping out. Maddy screamed with excitement or I screamed with excitement. Perhaps we both screamed.

Although I could sense my mother was holding back a smile, her words are burned in my memory.

"Remember, good behavior, all of you, or that's it."

She didn't clarify what she meant by "that's it." She didn't need to clarify. It was understood.

I named him Campion after Captain Campion in *Watership Down*. Maddy preferred the name Oliver, but when she heard me call the puppy "Campion," she relented. He was mostly black, but had small patches of white on each paw and floppy ears and a pencil thin tail that hit me in the face when he danced in endless circles.

Even in the cold, I didn't mind walking Campion or stealthily cleaning a puddle off the kitchen floor when he had an accident. I did my best to keep him out of trouble and far from the watchful eyes of my mother. We quickly settled into a schedule: feeding time was 6pm, before my dinner, and 7am, when I was about to leave for the school bus.

Although Campion adored Maddy, he slept in my bed, down by my feet, curled into a tight ball of black fur. Early each morning, though too early for his breakfast, he pushed his cold nose into my neck to wake me. When I left for the school bus, he climbed atop the couch so he could watch me out the window, his whine trailing along the sidewalk and his bark still in the air as I stepped onto the yellow bus. When I came home, he greeting me at the door like I was the only other being on this earth, shaking his tail and smiling his white teeth, his nails clicking against the hardwood floor as he spun in circles. Only when he greeted me at the door could I be sure all was well in the house.

Jack liked Campion and insisted I bring him over to his house when I visited. This was before the days of Tammy (she existed, but hadn't noticed me). We even tied a rope around a tree in the backyard so we could let Campion stay outside for extended periods. He was going to a friend's house, too, and didn't seem to mind spending the afternoon under the canopy of the tree.

We brought Campion with us everywhere. In the summer, we brought him fishing in ponds for bass or rivers for carp. He took to the water like he, himself was a fish. He was a natural, bounding through the water in graceful leaps, swimming his unique, stylish doggie-paddle when the water ran deep. Campion spent as much time scaring the fish as we did trying to catch them. While we rode our bikes to and from the fishing spots, I held his leash and he ran along side of us, proudly trotting along, a confident guide and able bodyguard. There's nothing like the bond between a boy and his dog—it was the happiest time of my life.

When it happened—the thing that caused the problems—I begged and pleaded with my mother. Maddy begged and pleaded, too. But it was no use. "How else will you learn?" my mother asked. And I cried for two weeks, a month, a year. I've never really stopped.

Understand, as I do, it was my fault and my fault alone. I hadn't considered the consequences or at least not *all* of the consequences. What ten-year-old or eleven-year-old considers the consequences of their actions? Yes, I had to face them. That was the rule. That was requisite suffering and we were all clear on it. The patron saint had arrived as we all knew she would.

There was swamp on him, dingy mud water that painted the whites of his paws a reddish-rust. And the smell, that was there too, a pungent musk that made my mother furious when Campion was set free into the house. We'd been doing his favorite thing, stalking the local swamp for polliwogs and bullfrogs, garter snakes when the weather was right and there were sheets of plywood lying about that we could turn over. I wanted him to have a fun day. It was the least I could do. He deserved it.

I didn't tell Jack I was going. He would have insisted on coming along and I knew what task was ahead of me. I didn't want Jack to be a part of it. Jack was too good of a person to get mixed up in this business. A few days before, however, he was at my side, causing the problem right along with me, like a true friend.

Between us we had about fifty cents, miscellaneous change, mostly dimes, nickels and pennies, no paper currency to be sure. But we didn't need much money because the plan was to steal what we needed, or rather steal what *we wanted* from the local convenience store. We didn't like the owner much. We called him "Fruit-face" because, regardless of the time of year, his face was always red and puffy like an apple. I'm sure he suffered from some unfortunate disorder of the skin, something that he was overly conscious about, but we had little time for empathy and things of that sort.

Fruit-face stared at us whenever we entered the store, which was often. Our mothers would send us with bags of coins or dollar bills to pick up the basics like bread or milk or, sometimes, a soda or for the latest copy of those awful magazines featuring the celebrity of the moment and their closetful of murky deeds. Also, Fruit-face drove a fancy car, a sporty, black, foreign roadster which he parked out in front of the building for everyone to see. That told us he had plenty and didn't need our spare change. It meant counting out coins was below his station.

That particular day, the plan was to get chocolate, preferably Hershey chocolate bars. Jack went to the back of the store near the drink coolers and I went straight for the target. Fruit-face appeared confused, keeping an eye on Jack and not paying much attention to me. But he was laying a trap. While appearing to eye Jack, he was watching me out of the corner of his eye as I slipped two chocolate bars into the pocket of my windbreaker. I headed for the door and said out loud, "I guess nothing for me today, thanks." I went to the side of the building and waited for Jack.

But he never came out.

I found him sitting on a stool behind the counter and under the watchful eye of Fruit-face. "He's trying to call my mother," Jack said when I went back into the store to rescue him.

"There's the little thief," Fruit-face said when I came back in. "Time to call your mother, too."

"We don't have a phone," I said. I was as slippery as an eel.

"Your mother left the number a long time ago," he cautioned with a raised finger before pointing to an address book of some sort. Then he picked up the phone and dialed. Maddy answered and he told her we had stolen from the store. While he was on the phone, I took the chocolate bars out of my pocket and placed them on the counter. "I'm sorry!" I pleaded. Fruit-face shook his head "no." He was having none of it. He'd had enough of us.

Maddy was attempting to handle the situation, to take a little air out the balloon before it burst, but Fruit-face insisted. "I'll send them home, but I really need to talk to your mother. Yes, have her call me."

When he hung up the phone, he turned to us and said, "You can go. I'll be talking to your mothers about this. You're banned from the store. Now get!"

The funny thing was, this was a minor hit, at least when compared to some of Jack's handiwork. It was a little like getting caught driving fifty in a thirty when yesterday you hit seventy-five along the same stretch of road. The year before, Jack had made the heist of a lifetime and gotten away free as a sparrow. His plan was both ingenious and executed with the precision of a seasoned museum thief. It was winter, January or February, and Jack had a blue snorkel jacket, a big, bulky thing with fur around the edges of the ample hood. The front pockets were deep and wide, enough to slide in a hand to halfway up your forearm. Though the pockets were sufficiently large, Jack ripped holes in the bottom of the pocket fabric allowing his arm up to the elbow and essentially creating one large pocket that ran between the inner jacket lining and the insulation and all the way from one pocket, around the back of the jacket, to the other pocket.

And in this giant snorkel pocket, Jack lifted and stored what I can only assume is a world record thirty-two Hershey bars. All this in one stop and without a hitch or hesitation. He was the master.

This time, I'd choked. A true amateur.

One can only assume Annette handled the situation in her usual way though I never asked Jack about it. I should have cared more about Jack, but I had my own skin to worry about and things were not going well.

Surprisingly, my mother was calm, succinct, to the point. She sat Maddy and I down at the kitchen table. "The dog has to go," she said.

"What?" From me.

"I told you having the dog required you to be on good behavior. Clearly, you've not held up your end of the bargain."

"Mom! You can't!" Maddy cried.

"I'm sorry, Mom! It won't happen again!" I pleaded.

Maddy stormed out of the kitchen and slammed her bedroom door behind her.

"You're a thief!" she said. "Thieves don't get rewarded by having dogs."

I begged. I pleaded. I squirmed. It was all a waste of time. Just like I knew it would be.

The dog wasn't mentioned in any tense conversation over the next few days and I'd prayed it was all a bluff. I hoped beyond hope it had all blown over. I avoided any and all banter for fear of the topic being revisited. Had the wound my transgression tore begun to heal rather than fester? The answer came too soon.

"There's a nice couple coming to meet the dog on Sunday." Since the problem began, she'd stripped Campion of his name, robbed him of his place in the family. He was now simply: "the dog."

"What do you mean?" I asked.

"I told you already. The dog has to go. That was the deal we made."

It was then, at that moment, I made a decision. The decision.

On Saturday morning, Campion and I headed out to the swamp. As I mentioned, he always enjoyed slopping through the swamp, the mud, the bushes. It was his thing. He was thoroughly tired out from the mere enjoyment of the day. I usually let him run free at the swamp, so I attached his leash as we began the walk back toward the house. We made one last stop, though.

At the end of Rabbit Road, we squeezed through a hole in the chain-link fence that ran along the interstate, the one meant to keep deer and dogs and children off the highway. The highway was crowded, a busy Saturday and the cars and trucks rushed by us, blowing my hair (Campion's fur) with a wind that stank of gasoline and rubber and road rage.

I gave Campion one last pat on the head, one last "good boy." One last hug.

There were sounds of death I refused to hear, sounds of skidding and shouting I wouldn't acknowledge, visions of death I chose not to see. There were black birds in the trees, those I heard, warning their kin with a harsh, guttural call. They knew death was in the air. I'd found the hole in the chain-link fence, the one made by bored teenagers some years in the past, and pushed Campion through onto the side he shouldn't have been. I'd unhitched him again, Campion, let loose the twenty-foot leash from the hook on his collar and pushed him, released him onto the highway. Reckless, yes, and foolish, but necessary. I turned for home, alone again, and never looked back.

"Where's the dog?" Mother asked when I came into the house.

"Around somewhere," I said with a shrug. "Can't be far. He's never too far."

The people who struck him were able to trace our address from the tag on his collar and a man delivered Campion's body back to us. It was wrapped in a dark wool blanket and tied with a fraying rope. The man carried the dog clutched close to his chest, like he was trying to keep him warm, like it was his own dog that had fallen. The man said he was sorry, but he couldn't stop in time and the dog ran right in front of him. He was still shaking; I could hear it in his voice and the words he spoke.

The man's wife was in the passenger's seat, staring forward like she'd witnessed the specter of death, was hiding from it, and would not return for a long while. Her eyes were glassy and distant and her seatbelt remained firmly buckled. There were black make-up stains under each eye, but she made no attempt to clean them off or even acknowledge them. She was ruined.

My mother untied the rope and unwrapped the blanket to make sure he carried what we thought he carried. Was his burden our burden?

"Ah," she said. "I'm afraid it's him."

The man re-wrapped the blanket and re-tied the rope. His face was ghost white and I thought he might burst into tears.

I imagine he believed he'd stolen Campion from our family and he was contrite in his words and actions. He didn't look directly at me and only spoke to my mother. With dry eyes I told him I understood, accidents happen, and with dry eyes my mother told him she understood and Maddy wouldn't come out of her room.

Did the man wonder how this young boy, who'd only recently learned about the death of his beloved dog, handled the news with the stoic indifference of a mortician? He must have. Perhaps he assumed I was in shock—not far-fetched in the least as his wife was displaying just such a thing—and in time reality would catch up with me, sending me into an emotional spiral from which I would not soon recover. In many ways that was true.

Several times I pressed my ear on the door to Maddy's room, waiting for an indication she might want to talk to me, that she was ready. The only sounds from the other side of the door were small sobs and the sniffling of a nose unable to contain itself, unable to stem the flow of sadness. Over the course of the weekend, there were several phone calls for her. I knocked on her door, a polite, one knuckle tap. Each time, before I could let her know she had a call and so-and-so was on the line, she let fly a preemptive and high-pitched "No," that penetrated the bedroom door with a weighty confidence.

Finally, I sat down in the hallway outside her door, leaning against the wall with my legs splayed. It hurt my legs to sit this way, but I would wait for her. In time, she would want to talk to me and I needed to be there when she was ready. After perhaps an hour, I gathered myself and retreated to my own room.

Mother carried the body and placed it on the front porch where it rested, a malignant mound cooling like our collective trust. Flies were beginning to notice it, perhaps not yet for the scent of death, but for the blood, almost dried, that, here and there, stained the dark wool a shade darker. Despite my willingness to part with the dog, I would not leave him to the flies. I took hold of one end of the blanket and dragged him around the back of the house, leaving a trail of bent grass and apathy in my wake.

There was a flat edge spade with an aging wood handle leaning against the house near the basement door, a gardening remnant that hadn't made its way back to the garage. It was short and ill-suited for the task, but I made due. What choice did I have?

Late that afternoon, near a lilac bush, I dug a hole in the back yard and buried my dog, marking the site with a wooden cross I made by nailing together two pieces of two-by-four I found in the cellar. He seemed comfortable in the wool blankets, so I left his body wrapped and tied. Using a black marker, I wrote the word CAMPION in large, block letters.

Maddy didn't attend the make-shift funeral and I didn't have any spoken words for him. I was sure he understood. And, if he didn't, it wouldn't make any difference to explain it now.

Mother called the nice couple and told them there'd been an accident and that there was no need for them to come by on Sunday to meet the dog. Yes, she was sorry too.

"How deep did you dig the hole?" Mother asked.

"Deep enough to bury my dog," I answered and continued to my room and closed the door.

There was no further discussion about the dog between myself and Mother.

Later that evening, Maddy came into my room and crawled onto the bed, lifted the comforter and slid underneath. Her body was cold against mine. She didn't speak, just looked at me and leaned her head against the pillow, waiting for me to talk. She knew what happened or at least figured she knew. Maddy, the keeper of secrets.

"If I couldn't have him, no one could."

"I know," Maddy said.

She rolled onto her back, hands folded behind her head, and stared at the ceiling. Her eyes were red and swollen, but no longer able to produce tears.

"Sorry about your dog," Jack said on the Sunday that the people were supposed to meet Campion.

"Sorry about getting you in trouble," I said.

"It's okay," he said and shrugged. "I was bound to get in trouble for something."

I was beginning to notice something different about Jack. His responses were slower, more labored, like it was taking longer to find his words and organize his thoughts. He was like a cartoon voiceover of himself, his voice just a little behind the movements of his mouth.

"I'm always in trouble for something," he laughed.

To this day, nothing grows near the lilac bush where Campion is buried. Nothing grows in sadness.

I have not had another dog. Or wanted another dog. I love them, though I'm sometimes reluctant to pet other people's dogs. There would be no other Campion.

Dreams (Bobby)

I'm on the operating table. Each time they try to remove her, to cut the disease from the flesh, she slithers deeper into my body, cackles as she slips under a new organ or through a different sphincter. I can feel where she is, but I can't see her, no one can. It's a game of Whac-A-Mole and the doctors are overmatched.

"Please," I beg. "I can't live like this any longer!"

There's someone else on the operating table, a woman, lying beside me, touching me, fingering my greasy innards like she's planning to buy them by the pound. A voice in my ear is asking me if I'm ready to wake up.

I'm naked, raw. Why am I naked?

And the woman beside me is naked also? Why is she naked? Is there a two-for-one on surgeries today?

"I've called an ambulance," she says, but not in a panicked way, more matter-of-fact. "Don't worry, they're on their way."

Slowly her face comes into focus. It's Mrs. Grace. Her

naked breasts hovering over me catch me by surprise. "Where am I?"

"We're at my summer residence."

"I don't have a summer residence."

"No, my summer residence, in Kennebunk."

"Where's Mr. Grace?"

"Oh, he's not here!" She holds back a laugh.

She's standing on the side of the bed, now. She puts her hands on her naked hips and leans over to kiss me on the lips.

"You passed out," she explains. "And right in the middle of the proceedings I might add."

"I did?"

"Yes, you did."

"Sorry about that."

"As long as you're feeling better, that's the most important thing."

"Did you say an ambulance was coming?"

"Yes, should be here any moment."

"Can you cancel it?"

"That's not how it works," Mrs. Grace answers. "They need to make sure you're okay."

"Where are my clothes?"

"I'll get them for you."

The EMTs arrive and take my vitals. My blood pressure is a bit low, but nothing terribly unusual. I refuse the hospital and they make me sign the requisite liability forms indicating my refusal. "Pre-existing condition," I assure them. One of them checks the signature, shrugs and walks out the front door.

"Can you call Maddy for me and tell her I need a ride home."

"I can take you home."

"I need Maddy."

I have no memory of what happened after I drove to Kennebunk. I do remember the drive, no traffic or weather delays, the hum of the wheels, no radio stations I liked, a smooth trek up Interstate 95 followed by the Maine charm of Route 1. I had my sketchbook, and there was a new sketch of Mrs. Grace, an odd sketch of her bent over at the waist like she was dusting a table, her nude backside captured in stunning detail. How I ended up naked next to Mrs. Grace is a mystery. No, not a mystery, that would be absurd. I know exactly how that happened even though I have no specific memory of this particular dalliance. After all, it wasn't the first time with Mrs. Grace so I can fill in the blanks.

Will the broken memories of the day return to me? Time will tell. But what else was lost that day? That's more important than a few hours lost to time and the abyss.

Maddy had her suspicions all along and, let's be honest, she knows me better than anyone. Better than Claire knows me. Perhaps better than I know myself. Now, there was little doubt my days of grabbing hold of what was made available to me, the bane of being an ugly child, remained in full force. How many complications this created!

Things were usually justified under the catch-all

umbrella of "the creative process." Quite convenient. All artists, all people who create have their methods and reasons. Despite the fact mine might be considered dubious, it was *my* process, *my* method of seeing what could not be seen and making it visible to all. A convenient excuse? Sure. Fine. Probably. But it worked. The results justified the means. At least to me.

It was an hour drive to Kennebunk; Maddy had sufficient time to percolate questions. She'd spoken to Mrs. Grace on the phone several times, but this was the first official in-person meeting. I was seated on the living room couch, trying not to listen, but, unsurprisingly, listening.

Mrs. Grace answered Maddy's questions with a delicate hand and a large degree of discretion.

"I'm still confused as to why you were here."

"We thought it best if he observed me in a natural environment, my natural environment, so I suggested we visit the summer house."

"So, he drove up here to watch you hang around the house?"

"More or less. We thought it might be beneficial, easier to find my soul in a place I'm most comfortable, where I'm myself."

"And what happened that made you call an ambulance?"

"He sensed he might faint, he went over to the bed to lie down and see if it would pass, but it didn't."

"He went to the bedroom when he thought he might faint?"

"I guiding him, but yes. Once he was on the bed, he appeared to pass out. I tried to wake him, but he was out of it, so I called an ambulance. He was conscious before they arrived, but was still, you know, out of it."

"What happened when the ambulance arrived?"

"They took his vitals, which were reasonable, I don't remember the numbers, but they were satisfied. He didn't want to go to the hospital and I wasn't going to force him."

"Thank you for calling them, better to be safe."

"I hope he's feeling better. He put quite a scare into me."

"He has a pre-existing condition and this has happened before, in his studio."

"I hope it's nothing serious."

"Depends who you ask," Maddy said. "We're hopeful."

In Maddy's car the silence was eerie, a thickening stew of disappointment and concern, like getting into the car with my mother.

"We'll have to come back and get my car," I said. "Before Mr. Grace finds it."

"Sounds to me like there's some unfinished business here, so I'm sure you'll make it back," Maddy said it with a smile, but her tone was dark, angry, like mine would be if the roles were reversed.

I didn't respond as we turned down Route 9 toward

Route 1 on our way to Interstate 95.

"So," she said finally. "What's going on? What brought you here?"

"Research."

"What kind of research?"

"Just getting to know Mrs. Grace."

"Does getting to know Mrs. Grace including spending time in her bed fucking Mrs. Grace?"

"Research is a funny thing," I said.

"Listen," Maddy said. "In your condition…"

"My condition!" I shouted. "My condition is terminal. There is no *my condition*. It's over, that's my condition."

"Then what are you doing?"

I took a moment to calm myself. My hands were shaking and hot, and sweat formed into a thin layer on my forehead. Maddy was worse, her eyes were red and swollen. Her hands were shaking, too, as they strangled the steering wheel.

"Sorry I yelled," I said. "I've made a decision."

"And what is that?" she asked, her voice thin and cracked.

"I'm not ready to share that with you yet." I looked out the window, watching the blur of trees, counting telephone poles as we passed them.

"When will you be ready?" she asked.

"I'm not sure."

"Look," she said. "I've done everything you've asked of me, right?"

"Right."

"I've even kept things from Claire because you asked and I feel terrible about it."

"I know."

"Well?"

"I'm not ready to tell you," I said. "But you're not going to like it."

Maddy shook her head and gripped the steering wheel tighter, hands at ten and two, eyes forward, lips pursed. She refused to look at me. Who can blame her?

"You're scaring me, Bobby."

"You should be scared."

What's in a Name? (Bobby)

Disease is difficult to define. Especially when you look in the mirror and see dark circles, laughing crescents beneath glassy eyes and wonder what's living inside you that wasn't there yesterday or the day before yesterday. Most days my lungs pull in the air around me, sucking the dry, stale air of my bedroom or the fresh air found while seated on the front porch or the death air of the hospital bed as it waits for you be distracted, seeks a weak moment, then strangles you. One day the air is humid and oppressive, the next it's crushed gravel that scrapes the throat on the way down and the next light and sweet like springtime. It's the lungs, mostly, that carry the burden of my burden.

When people hear someone has cancer, the reaction is typical: "Too young!"

Cancer is a known enemy. Cancer = Bad.

When people hear something isn't cancer, it's also predictable: "Thank God!"

And that's because: Cancer = Bad.

But what about when it's not implicitly bad. Or at least not yet. When it's something new and exotic—wait, that sounds too much like a vacation or a fancy car. And disease is anything but fancy, nothing like a vacation, except a vacation from normality.

So, what if it's something which can't be easily classified and filed, written in a tidy headline or on a blue-inked clipboard chart with any confidence? What if it's not understood? Something that makes you feel like you're the only one in the world to contract it because you pretty much are the only one in the world. Is there hope that they, the doctors, the scientists, the chemists, the researchers and lab assistants, the readers of the charts and results, are wrong? Did they find something that's, when the curtain is opened and the magician exposed, actually nothing? Poof! Or, at worst, a tolerable, minor inconvenience. Take ibuprofen every six hours as needed.

"It itches a little when it rains."

"Here's a cream. Apply it once a day. Only needed on rainy days. Should do the trick. See you in a year."

Is it easier to fight something with a name than something nameless? Was it easier to make a villain of Cuba than Vietnam because it was simpler to market Castro as a bad guy? Once we had his photograph plastered across newspapers, magazines and television screens, it took care of the rest on its own. So, to give it a name (and possibly a face) is an effective means of creating, for lack of a better term, an enemy.

Enemy = Bad.

The thing about something new is it's neither good nor bad until it's no longer new. Or no longer good. Until the time and money and research and determination are applied, it's impossible to know what's possible. We were told in the 1950s that smoking can be good for us, soothing what ails the throat and calming the nerves. When that research was new, it was branded as good. With mature research it's branded as bad. And when they wanted to make it bad, they let us know a big, bad, greedy corporation was steering the ship. There had to be a bad guy.

Bad Guy = Enemy and Enemy = Bad.

We haven't reached this point with what ails me. This malady doesn't have the marketing cachet of cancer or Castro. I hope it never does. I pray a ubiquitous flowering vine in the Peruvian jungles is found to contain the cure in quantities so vast and accessible, it will join the likes of scurvy and smallpox, but preemptively, without the requisite scourge and before my clock stops ticking.

Is that better or worse? Is confusion better than lost hope? Is it better to have a filing cabinet full of files or just one sheet of paper with scribbles of notes in red pen ink? In other words, it is better to be given a finite length of time or to exist in an unknown? Will it be tomorrow or after three thousand tomorrows?

It's been given the name, at least temporarily and uncreatively, wasting disease (doesn't give one a warm and fuzzy, does it?). It's a virus, that much they know, but a relatively new discovery, one that causes organs to age at an accelerated pace, albeit a different pace in each person who has the pleasure to contract it. It, being equal opportunity, settles in whatever organ it finds accommodating (or maybe attractive), the liver, the lungs, the heart, the kidneys: perhaps even the brain. And from there, it begins its impenitent work, dissembling that which spent a lifetime functioning at just the perfect rate, the desired speed, the natural way.

In the medical field the virus was originally named, uninspiringly, E5, after the room at the lab in the Netherlands, that isolated it. Its origins are unknown: A monkey? A walrus? A tiger shark? Did it incubate in a shampoo bottle, taking hold as I showered, thinking my hair was being squeaky-cleaned? Or did it float in the air, a weightless assassin finding its mark, something my lungs pulled in and ate up like candy? My lungs seem to think so.

Was it ingested during a seemingly innocuous meal or even a tasty, memorable one, somehow skirted the virus killing stomach acid and bored its way into an unsuspecting internal system? Was there a cook in some backwater café or metropolitan grill whose organs were aging at an accelerated rate, him none the wiser? Perhaps it was the doctors and nurses themselves, the very healers exposed to myriad disease, too many to understand fully the unique qualities and tendencies of each.

Or was it, as I feared, in the bodily fluids, percolating and festering, waiting for their moment to pounce. In the blood flowing out into the world from a nick of the razor while shaving or in saliva waiting to sneak into another's mouth during a deep kiss of affection or jettisoned across the room by a bone-shattering sneeze. Was it in the tears of those who already suffer? It's also possible it flows from the fluids produced during sexual contact, the warm, lubricating process, a trembling of her body or the sudden, coiling release of sperm.

Does it matter in the end? More than you know.

The thing is, the truth thing, is that I was already aware of what ravaged me. At least the doctors were fairly certain of a number of things and all the numbers were unlucky. The dice were rolled: snake-eyes. The number thirteen. Six-hundred-sixty-six. There, I've given it some much needed marketing.

So, to say none of this was known is untrue. Not completely, but mostly. There were theories and concerns and hunches and guesses. Perhaps that's always true of something new in medicine. I listened and nodded and mostly understood. I asked questions, but not many, not challenging enough. I took the medicines they gave me, lots of them, though they unsettled my stomach in ways you don't want me to describe. Nothing was for sure and I wasn't going to live my life, however long it may be, on hunches and ifs and mostly and maybe.

I'd met with a series of doctors after the first episode, a gaggle, a team, however disjointed. They were mostly stumped. Blood, saliva, pee, poop, pressures and temp. All of it was gladly provided and more than once. Then again at the next appointment.

Like most of us, I suspect, I wanted to believe everything was just fine. I wanted to believe it was just an episode of panic or anxiety though, unlike now, I felt neither panicked nor anxious at the time. Or maybe I was sick, a little sick, not a lot sick. Could there be a virus, a cold virus, maybe even a flu, that was embedded in my system rather than being flushed out in the usual way? As it turns out, yes, there was. But it was angrier.

III
Night and Morning (Claire)

At night he reverts to the little boy he once was, the little boy he yearns to have never been. His dreams are vivid, visceral; they must be, for he shakes and sweats, the muscles of his face flex and contort and his sex stiffens, makes itself known to the world. He wraps himself in the sheets and heavy, feather-down comforter, tossing, twisting until he's tightly bound, cocooned, and his limbs can no longer flail. At times, he loses his breath, then gobbles up air to fill his lungs double, a thirsty, sunburned man at the oasis. Sometimes he talks to me, tells me his many secrets and his many fears. His arms, when freed from the cocoon, flail about before he wakes, before offering an apology when he sees the bloodshot whites of my eyes, wide and awake, stunned and expectant.

As I mentioned, it appears the plumbing, his plumbing, is intact and functioning. In the morning his ego rises with the sun, demanding attention like a flag hoisted, released to the world, to the yellow light leaking through the undrawn blinds. Over the past couple of weeks, I've conducted a study, an observation of his physical condition shortly before his morning alarm. I only note this because his behavior would have me believe his libido has abandoned him, become one of his fears and now mine.

At times he treats me as if I'm a fragile vase, not the strong bronze he creates and nurtures, casts and fires, but something that might shatter on the floor, rather than bounce. Don't get me wrong, I do appreciate being treated like a lady, a wife, someone he elevates, maybe even adores. But there are times when I just want to be wanted in the way a woman wants to be wanted. Wants to be needed. I need to know his dreams, his rigid morning energy, can still be for me. At least some mornings. Or some evenings.

There is still a little boy in there, one who internalized his mother's odd observations, her doubts, her suffering, too. You don't outgrow these things. They're not forgotten. Instead, you find a place to store them—in a shoebox under the bed, in a punching bag in the basement, buried in an unmarked grave. In alcohol or drugs or violence or debauchery. It needs to go somewhere. Energy, especially negative energy, doesn't tend to sit still.

And his clients, his models, love him like a deity, a second-coming of someone or other. They hang on every word, devour his plans like seasoned thieves devour a rumor that a fortune awaits an easily accessible safe. He's found a way to release them from their own internal prisons and they willingly jump, off cliffs if necessary. He sees them as they want to be seen, as they wish they were. And it's not some parlor trick or lurid sales technique; Bobby believes they are more, sees them as more. It may be because he wants people to see him as more than, too. He wants us all to be immortal in some way or other.

A Letter Home (Claire)

Recently, I found a letter I'd written to my mother during my junior year of college, soon after I met Bobby. It seems strange now that I would write a letter. We were allowed to have cars on campus and if there was something important to say, I could have driven less than an hour and spoken to her in person. And there was a pay phone on each floor of the dorm. Yet, for some reason, unknown now, I wanted to write it down in ink and on paper. I wanted it to be permanent, a romantic view of letter writing, I know. Or perhaps I feared I wouldn't go through with it if left to my own devices. A letter, after all, was (and is) a commitment: once it's dropped into a mail slot, the message is no longer in your control.

My mother and I always had a strong relationship, generally open and supportive. Why would I have wanted to do such an old-fashioned thing as send her something in the mail. Was I embarrassed about having a new boy in my life? Perhaps, but I don't recall that being the case. I'd only had one boyfriend, but such limited experience, I like to think, was more a choice on my part than some sort of curse thrust upon me. I had my books and they had me and, up until the moment I met Bobby, we were all just fine with the arrangement.

The day I met Bobby he was hiding behind his hair. Actually, he was literally hiding behind a shelf of library books, but also hiding behind a bush of curly brown hair that hid his eyes like a cartoon sheep dog. I half expected him to lift up a clump of that bird's nest with his hand in order to get a better look at me. He was sweet and shy and clumsy, like most freshman boys, but he made me laugh and my mother always told me to find someone that makes you laugh.

I hate to use such a cliché as opposites attract, but there was an element of it. His eyes had a bit of the devil in them, blue and oddly dark, and I'd never spent enough time with the devil. That's not to say I was looking to be a bad girl, far from it, but perhaps a little adventure was an enticing thought. High school me noted that he had an edge to him.

Warren was that one boyfriend I'd mentioned. He was also a student at Stevens College. I met him freshman year and after a couple semesters the relationship had run its course, fizzled and burned out. But Warren wasn't a big believer in things running their course unless he was the one who felt the course had been run. He was typical of the guys I'd grown up with: entitled, well-off and a bit of a bore. Actually, he was just fine. The temptation is to paint him as a villain (he wasn't), but the truth is there just wasn't enough chemistry for us to linger. No one likes to linger.

Things became complicated when he saw me walking to class with Bobby. I hadn't spoken to Warren in a couple of months, but our too slow march into oblivion was sufficiently interrupted. I noticed Warren out the corner of my eye and knew he'd have something to say. That night, Warren stopped by my room to have a talk about this "other guy."

This was funny to me: A boy who I wasn't seeing wanted to talk about another boy that I wasn't really seeing.

"A freshman?"

"Yes."

"You're seeing a freshman?"

"What does that matter?"

"I don't know how it matters, but it matters."

"And I'm not really seeing him."

"Sure as hell looked like it."

"I didn't know walking to class was tantamount to a serious relationship."

"It's your body language."

"Is there a point to this conversation? I have to study."

"And what's with the limp?"

"Are you serious?"

"I'm just asking! Looked like Hop-Along-Cassidy."

"Jealousy is an unattractive trait."

He could see by the scowl on my face that he'd pushed the wrong button. His face filled with what I can only assume was contrition, his brown eyes wide and his ears pulled back, his lips pulled so thin across his face they lost all color. He attempted to settle the issue on his terms with a dismissive: "Whatever." Then he was gone.

I was uncharacteristically bothered and the little devil I'd been awaiting got the best of me. Now, it's true that Bobby has a birth defect that gives a little hitch in his step, but it's just that: a little hitch, a hiccup, a nothing. It's also something that someone with a little hitch might be self-conscious about. And I was well aware of the self-consciousness. In a seething whirl I couldn't let go, I allowed myself something out of character: a rage, a fire, a taste for blood. In my quest to hurt Warren, I unleashed the self-conscious pain of Bobby. Yes, I told him. I told Bobby what Warren said knowing full well the ramifications on both sides. I hurt both of them because I could, one the blunt instrument, the other the bag of flesh, and for a fleeting moment it was empowering. The devil. I thought revenge would taste sweet and I was wrong. And I've spent over twenty years repeating my mistake, I've also spent twenty years regretting it.

And after the fleeting moment, and a moment too late, a weighty regret took hold. This was the reason for the letter to my mother. I needed someone to tell, a confidant for a confession of sorts, and it seemed easier to write a letter, stuff and stamp an envelope and drop it into a metal box than to face another human.

So, you see, I'm not so much the lofty prize Bobby likes to keep on a pedestal and to which he blows dry, distant kisses. Our closets stuffed with skeletons are bursting at the seams.

There was another letter, the content more weighty, more devastating.

Tit-for-Tat (Claire)

I was seated on the living room couch, legs crossed, hands fidgeting, each small movement drawing me deeper into the soft cushions. I looked around the room for a clock, but the walls were bare, I didn't find one. I played with my hair, twirling it around my fingers, searching for split ends. He'd said he'd just be a moment, but that was several moments in the past. I hadn't expected to be so uncomfortable. I'd poured and downed two overfilled glasses of Chianti in only a few minutes. The wine bottle, now three-quarters empty, sat on the glass coffee table, wagging a disparaging finger in my direction. My head swam with wine and foreboding.

What was I even doing there?

Professor Connelly returned from the bedroom wearing nothing more than a thin robe, almost transparent, made of a light, shiny silk, sky blue. The robe was barely closed, tied in front by a loose knot of narrow fabric that wouldn't withstand a light wind. The light behind him poured through the sky blue creating a lustful silhouette. His brown hair was combed perfectly (except for one lock), as it always was, erudite, like the head of a Greek statue. I couldn't recall the color of his eyes and, anyway, I didn't look at his face. I couldn't.

Even though I had a car on campus, I'd walked to his apartment, following handwritten directions he'd penciled onto a lined, yellow sheet from a legal pad. He'd handed it to me with a fun-uncle, "don't tell your parents" wink and smile. 74 Green St., white house, black shutters, a phone number in case I got lost. I'm not sure I would have called if I'd gotten lost.

Green Street was a tidy side affair with iron streetlamps and granite curbstones, the kind of street they used for outside transition shots in 1950s television programs to illustrate the wholesomeness of the entire endeavor. It was the kind of street professors would live on if they'd received a well-kept house along with their doctorate. Yet, each clicking step on the sidewalk brought me further and further from wholesomeness. I pulled the yellow paper from my coat pocket and gave it one last look, one last chance to turn back, one last grasp at sanity. I was close now.

Had I completed the legendary, off-quoted, "walk of shame"? Could I tick that shadowy activity off the shaded column of the bucket list? Since the shame would typically be on the other end, the shoulder-slouched, chin tucked into the coat collar, return home, it would have to wait. But tick-it, I would. This, I told myself in the meantime, was the walk of opportunity, of adventure, perhaps even of scandal. It was deliberate, confident, a purposeful stroll down into the cobra hole. I knew exactly what I was getting myself into. Or at least I had a pretty good idea. Why then, was I so nervous?

According to rumors, there were plenty of other students who knew the way, the path, directions often written in his own dense handwriting and probably on that same yellow legal pad. I could have asked one of them for advice, the others, the notches on the bedpost. After all, they were students with experience, valuable experience. But I found myself too shy, too self-conscious, too guilty to ask for their wisdom, their wizened list of do's and don'ts. As I sat in the living room reconsidering the entire affair, he stood a few feet away, what God gave him reaching up into the light, gesturing toward me with an ivory ambition.

Many of the girls at Stevens thought he was the most handsome man they'd ever seen. They'd giggle and make mention of his square chin and high cheekbones, the subtle, oddly sensuous cologne he wore. He certainly looked the part: brown herringbone sports jackets and wool trousers perfectly fitted and pressed, uncomplicated, as if he'd been dressed by a fashion magazine editor each morning. When the weather turned warm, he left the jacket at home and wore a vest over white shirts, effortlessly complementing the look. His leather-soled shoes click-clacked along the hallway floor, calling for attention all on their own. He had one rogue lock of brown hair, a curl, that fought the rest and hung down over his forehead like a misbehaving child. No one ever mentioned his eyes. I think that was for their own sanity, their own protection.

Now, in the time of need, the ticking clock I couldn't locate, I thought about tomorrow and the next day and the next week. Some of the girls whispered to friends who whispered to their friends who whispered to all the girls in school that they'd caught something sinister, a hitchhiker, a parasite that gnashed its teeth and clung to his naughty bits. Yes, they said, it was he who carried such things and he refused to hide behind the numbness, the inhumanity of the latex condom. Those were the things that were talked about—who he got pregnant and who got creepy crawlies. I tried not to get caught up in the flavor of the day, the rumor mill, the grapevine, however accurate. I'd yet to hear stories of penicillin or amoxicillin or any other "cillin" being needed. It was guilt they felt swimming in their brains, nothing more, and long overdue.

In those not-too-distant days past, if you wanted to get married in Massachusetts you had to submit to a blood test for syphilis. At least at a future point I knew I was clear of that particular scourge. One down.

"I'm not technically an employee of the college," he assured me with a confident wink and tilted head. And why wouldn't he be confident–I'd walked right into his nest.

"Oh?"

"I work for an institute contracted by the college."

"Are you saying my visit is not a sanctioned college activity?"

"That's exactly what I'm saying."

There you have it. A technicality. A permission slip, if you will. A note signed by somebody's mom saying it was just fine to fornicate with students. Feel free! Have at it! It was all the proof he needed.

As you might imagine, it, all of it, everything I did, everything I said that night was an act. On the inside I was terrified, a twisted stomach in knots, nearly vomiting, while outside I was confident, playful, coquettish. So, what was this? This dalliance? It wasn't an affair—I wasn't married and Professor Connolly wasn't married. It certainly wasn't courting. I had no interest in him and I doubt he had any real interest in me. Alas, it was tit-for-tat. An even exchange.

I knew exactly why I was there. My mother always told me a relationship must be equal and I was there to equalize my relationship, bring it into balance, allow it to prosper and evolve and continue. My intentions were pure or so I reasoned. And only when we were even would I offer Bobby what I know he secretly desired, my unconditional love.

There's no mistaking the scent of another woman. It lingers on a man with a lusty sourness. It festers, burrows deep into the skin, in the hair, on the clothing and no amount of soap can completely cleanse it. To a woman that's aware, one who pays attention, it can be sniffed out quicker than a pup finds a cookie stuffed into a coat pocket. That little professor of sculpture, she was dedicating an exceptional amount of time to Bobby's development and her ways were rumored to be unorthodox and personal, cozy. (Yes, I would ace a class on euphemisms if Stevens had offered one.) I could detect her scent from the next room, almost feel its heat. It clung to him for dear life and I snipped it off with gentle shears, clean and tidy as a eunuch.

This, of course, wasn't a craving for revenge. I'd like to think I held no such ambitions (other than Warren's medieval punishment). But what else could it be called? It looked like a duck. It smelled like a duck. I refused to watch the way it walked for fear it might confirm everything unsavory.

Bobby, when all was said and done with his little professor, Finlay, that was her name, came away with a reason to live. I, on the other hand, came away with a reason to die. These are life's paradoxes and I don't claim to have the answers.

As for the walk back to my dorm, my memories are a bit clouded. It was late that evening, not the next morning. I'm sure of it. Reasonably sure. What I don't recall is regret or the requisite "shame." It certainly wasn't pride, either. This wasn't a conquest. To use one of Bobby's words, it was transactional. A lurid quid pro quo.

It was a crisp New England night, the kind where your breath streams out of your nose and mouth like a whistling teapot and your nostrils pull together each time you draw a breath into your nose. There was a full moon and I thought I might turn into a werewolf or some specter haunting the streets, haunting Stevens College in perpetuity. Perhaps I would dry into dust and crumble into a pile to be swept away by an old man with a broom sweeping at sunrise or simply be blown away with the wind. Being transactional felt like being a temporary person or a train jumper passing through town on the way to somewhere else.

It's fair to wonder the significance of this minor blip, the minute corner of my life. Why mention it at all? I wanted to illustrate that I was not always so innocent.

I, too, am capable of shocking the unsuspecting listener. Bobby's childhood was complicated and, often, unsettling, and in me I believe he looked for the idealized family, the perfect upbringing, normalcy. Some of this I may bring to the table but not as much as he thought or hoped. The bookish girl is not all libraries, pigtails and homework and that's neither pride nor shame. There's some baring of the soul yet to be fleshed out.

Sleep (Maddy)

I'm falling apart.

In Bobby's eyes, I'm put together, stoic, rational, solid, the big sister to lean on. I've cultivated that image over the years, the thespian embracing her role despite the typecasting or miscasting. I've felt I needed to be the strong one. But some mornings I can't get out of bed. I just know I can't. It's that simple. I'm much more fragile than Bobby will ever know, than I will allow him to know. After all, he needs to know, to believe, I'm the rock. That's all he's meant to see. He's not meant to sneak a look behind the curtain or place his hand into the magic hat.

My eyes won't open, cemented by the morning pollen or the dry crust produced by the winter air. I slap at the alarm clock, hit snooze until it cycles out and no longer works, leaving me to doze until night returns again. It's a guilty, cannibalistic circle, feeding upon itself, feeding on time and destined to repeat. For reasons yet understood, I desire to kill the day rather than conquer it.

One particular grumpy morning, I pulled the clock out of the socket by the cord and flung it against the wall. Despite the dull thump of the impact and a high-pitched scrape as it slid toward the floor, it still functioned, and we began the dance again the following morning. I was never a sleeper; it never suited me. I'm too high-strung, too controlling to let sleep take over and whisk me away to dreamland. The somber act of falling asleep holds no appeal to me; it's rather like being sucked down into darkness, into a pit with no bottom, hair being pulled out of my head from the vacuum, a dizziness that I fight to the end. I await the fleshy thud of the pit's bottom, but it never arrives. Instead, it makes me wait and wonder when and if. Sometimes I attempt to brace the fall with my hands and feet which only serves to startle me more.

Sleeping pills were prescribed, liquid filled capsules that made my head fill with helium and float around the room like a barrage balloon protecting the night from my attempts to dose. Under the influence of these pills, I've awoken on the front porch at 3am in nothing more than a nightshirt, watering imaginary plants with an imaginary watering can. I've also purchased a gallon of chocolate milk from the twenty-four-hour convenience store. I have no memory of it, but there it was in the refrigerator along with dollar bills and coins given as change and a receipt of the transaction sitting on the kitchen counter. The car was in the garage, none the worse, despite my dream-induced drive. Although there's no indication I failed to dress myself before leaving the house, no front-page photograph of a naked woman purchasing a gallon of chocolate milk, it was the last time I risked sleeping pills.

I'm afraid of dreams and I don't like mornings. Not a combination for success, I know.

But it's not just a reluctance to let sleep control me and there's more to the mornings than simply the result of an unrestful night. Some mornings my head is too heavy with the night's thoughts to rise from the pillow and my neck is too feeble to support its weight. Remaining in bed is the most logical conclusion or at least the most common conclusion. Sometimes, the morning air is too cold, and I refuse to relinquish the warmed pocket of air trapped beneath the blankets. As the baby bird will not abandon the nest for fear her wings are not developed, I am not always ready to fly. "What's the point?" the morning asks me, knowing full well there's no good answer; there is only the self, and sometimes it is beaten into oblivion.

There are also pains in my extremities, tingling in my fingertips, a dull bloat or swelling of my feet, numbness that runs the length of my legs. It all may be as simple as too much time in bed, too many mornings and afternoons and evenings in positions meant for nighttime. The muscles, the nerves, the joints all endure stress meant for a finite number of hours. Or is it something worse? What swims in the blood of the ignorant? I dare not ask too many questions for fear of learning the answers.

As Bobby would say, Ignorance = Bliss.

Often people ask the existential: "Why are we here?" There are days I simply ask: "Why am I still here?"

It's possible I'll lose my job even though I'm really good at it, and they don't want to fire me. But there's a limit, we're all expendable to some degree, and it's possible I've overvalued my skills. If I did lose my job, I suppose I could live off of a percentage of Bobby's commissions. He's wanted to give me 15 percent as his manager for as long as I remember, but I'd rather keep the status quo and bill him an hourly rate. Sometimes I don't bill him at all. I don't want to be a burden.

Who am I? I was the favorite child, I'm not blind to it. I was the hope, the future. That's who I was supposed to be. That was their plan. But nature has a way of correcting course, shifting the wind and challenging us. Life would be boring otherwise.

Actually, I know who I am: I'm the keeper of secrets.

My tiny hand held my mother's hand when they told her Marcus was dead. I found her loose, blue fingers during the blizzard. They were not lost, only not found in time. It was me, not Annette, that hugged Tammy tightly with both arms, her face clammy against my cheek, and drove her to the out-of-the-way clinic that provides abortions if you ask the right questions and quietly pay the full fee. And, yes, I'm well aware of the irony. I was with Bobby at the doctor's office when the news was delivered. I'm also the keeper of Claire's secrets, the unexpected secrets of someone who is not expected to hold any. I'm crumbling under the weight of it. My narrow shoulders were not meant for these burdens; my eyes were not meant to see them. There's something else.

The reason I am the keeper of secrets, the reason I do not freely offer the information I'm entrusted to hold, is the one time I did offer, the one time I did blab and gossip and spread the news was when I told my father that Marcus was dead. Had I not told him that afternoon, had I let my mother tell him or someone else, anyone else, would it have made a difference? Marcus, of course, would still have been dead, but the shock may have been lessened, dulled, cushioned if it were not for his two-year-old who ambled into the waiting room and bluntly set fire to his world. I can't help thinking, perhaps, he wouldn't have left, would have waited longer to vanish, would have embraced Bobby as his new hope. But I did. And my father did.

I've thought about it, as we all do in troubled times. I struggle with my world, the world that lingers behind my eyes, a world that's hidden, the pieces poorly matched and impossible to put back together in a satisfactory manner. That's how mornings feel—dissembled. Would a quick exit be the best course of action? Would it solve my problems (I would have to think so), but cause additional problems for the people I love? Today, this does not seem a viable option and is not under consideration. But tomorrow. No, not tomorrow.

Who or what was I meant to be? If I could sculpt as only Bobby is able, what would this person, this creation, look like? How would her soul shine, if at all? In this daydream, she is a mother of three: two girls and a boy, all three rambling and rambunctious. It's not perfect, mind you, but it doesn't need to be unspoiled to be perfect in my eyes. I can't help but think it could have been that way with David if I could have kept my end.

Let it go. That's what Bobby tells me whenever I bring it up, when I speak of David. Even Claire became fed up with the David talk over the years. Too many years of sniffling grief over someone who put his own needs first is enough to piss off anyone. I know it. I'm trying to let it go, but it refuses to leave quietly. One day it might.

I think David is happy. Once in a while, I hear from him. He writes or calls to ask how I'm doing. He doesn't contact me as a taunt but as an old friend. He doesn't know my life, my emotional life at least, has never really moved forward—how would he know? When he called to tell me his daughter, Kimmy, was born, I invited him to stop by so I could meet her. He asked me if I was sure and I told him I was. I don't think his new wife, or his only wife, knew of the visit since it took several months to materialize. He had to pick his moment.

The first time I held her, Kimmy, she was warmer and heavier than I expected. I took in a deep breath through the nose, pulling in the sweet, slightly damp scent of new life. I was standing on my porch as David looked up at me from two steps down, his feet firmly planted on the walkway. He was the one who'd reached the pinnacle, but I was higher up. He knew I would never fully forgive him, but he also knew I'd keep trying.

One time, after a Saturday morning soccer game, David stopped by with Kimmy. She's was ten years old and a fierce soccer player. That's what she told me, anyway. She said her mom knew they were stopping by to say hello, so that must mean she realizes I'm not a threat. I can only assume she looks like her mother because in her soiled soccer uniform, I saw very little of David, very little of his guarded personality. It had been a couple of years since I'd seen them both.

"You certainly look the part of a fierce soccer player," I agreed.

"Everything is good?" I asked David.

"Can't complain," he said and shrugged his shoulders.

He was wearing a pressed button-down shirt, white with a soft pattern of colored lines, red and blue, tucked into a pair of fashionable blue jeans. On his feet were black dress shoes, not office dress shoes, but not Saturday soccer game shoes, either. Guarded.

"Do all the coaches dress for success?" I asked.

"Oh, I'm not the coach."

Had he dressed this way on my behalf?

"I hear Bobby's famous now," David said to me and shook his head like he still couldn't believe it. "I read an article about him in the *Tribune*. I remember he always had that drawing pad with him."

"He's done very well for himself," I agreed from the porch while he looked up at me from the walkway. The subject of Bobby meant the conversation was nearing an end. Kimmy had already grown bored and started to soccer kick the yellow heads off the dandelions of my front yard. David, though, had something on his mind.

"I wanted to apologize for missing your mother's funeral,"

he said. "I would have come, but I didn't hear about it until a week later."

"What's the point?" I asked. "She was already dead."

The words emptied from my mouth before I realized I had a leak. Kimmy turned towards us, mouth hanging open, unsure if she'd heard what she was sure she'd heard. David looked at her for a moment, then back at up me. His eyes were narrow and his brows formed a peak on his forehead.

"That certainly sounds like something she'd say," he said and smiled.

"Oh, Kimmy, before you go, I have something for you," I said and walked into the house. During a bout of insomnia, I folded a large origami butterfly, green and yellow and red.

"Last time you told me you loved butterflies," I said and handed it to her.

"I love them and I love this!" she said and looked upon it with great pride.

"What do you say?" David prodded.

"Thank you!"

"You're welcome. I know it will have a good home now," I said.

When they turned back toward the car, David waved to me and said to Kimmy, "Wave goodbye to Auntie Maddy."

"Bye Auntie Maddy," she said and waved, a big smile filling her mother's face. "See you soon."

"Bye, Kimmy," I said in return. I couldn't wipe the smile from my face even though I knew she didn't mean it, I wouldn't see her anytime soon.

After they drove away, I stood on the porch listening to the day. The honeybees were fast at work, buzzing about, bouncing from spring flower to spring flower, even to the felled dandelions, enjoying the peaceful months before the wasps arrived in full force to terrorize and assert their dominance.

For now, there's a fear of being alone though I've already been alone, mostly alone for so many years. Being with your thoughts, however visceral, is not the same as speaking to another person. Is it better to be alone with thoughts then to spend a life with someone incompatible? I'd like to find out.

Sometimes I take medications, but they leave me lethargic and unable to remember things from five minutes earlier. It's a frustrating circle: take these to settle the running thoughts, to ease the burden, but the new burden will be memory loss and lack of concentration. Wonderful.

Now, when I try to sleep, I hear my mother's voice: "No man is going to want a woman who can't have a child and no man is going to want a woman that loses a child. You and me are the same, cut from the same cursed cloth. That's just the way it is. You'd better get used to it."

What's the point?

The Next Morning (Claire)

It was 6am, gray, cold and unwelcoming, typical of the bridge season New England weather they don't feature on the tourism commercials. The night before, I'd taken the long way home from Professor Connelly's apartment, the route where it seemed like it was always uphill and pulled at your calves like piano wires. As I mentioned, I don't have a clear memory of the walk, just that it wasn't my normal route. Or rather it wasn't the route I'd normally take considering the neighborhood I'd visited. The normal route, the familiar route, was about a mile, but I'd managed to turn it into a mile and a half, maybe more. It was circuitous, as Bobby would say. Perhaps it was to throw someone, anyone, off the scent, to cover my trail and make it look like I was returning from a place I hadn't visited. The cloche and dagger approach, more for me and my peace of mind than anyone who might care. Bobby might care.

It was Saturday morning and I was flat on the bed, staring at the ceiling of my bedroom. Despite the chill in the room, the ceiling fan squeaked and churned cool air, matching my thoughts. My pillow was on the floor beside the bed, the victim of a poor night's sleep. My apartment roommates were still out when I returned the night before, so there were no questions, no wondering. No one cared. I'm not even sure I did. There was no shame, yet my thoughts would not cease.

Was there a hiding place? A place to keep *her*, my her, the other me now that she'd been unleashed? What was she capable of, this other her? Where would this will lead? Will I wake up one morning with a pang of regret, or the opposite, an appetite for more adventure? Will it be worth it? Who was she? Who was I?

I don't want it written on my gravestone that I was a bad person. I do think I'm generally a good person, but sometimes one needs to dabble a bit, to heat the cauldron to a rolling boil and add an eye of newt and a drop of your enemy's blood just to be sure what one is doing on a normal day is right and good and fair and just. We all have secrets and if we don't have secrets then we haven't lived. And I've lived. At least I believe I have.

Of course, to Bobby, my life has always looked perfect, an innocent snapshot from behind the camera's eye. It's always looked just so. My house, the one I grew up in, looks perfect, stable, along with my parents. And perhaps it was on some level, but there was always something in the background, a small hum, perhaps to keep us grounded. Sometimes when things are too perfect, you need some sport, a little game to be played that makes you feel a little dirty, a little sinful. it allows you to appreciate when you're clean.

What I'm trying to say is my parents had their positivity and success and balance—all of which is true—but there is always a "but." There is always something they hid or thought they were clever enough to hide. They had friends they vacationed with: strange, odd friends who liked to drink whiskey and cognac and were always on the lookout for a hot tub. On the surface this isn't so strange, but there were photos in my mother's nightstand of husbands and wives with other people's husbands and wives. The photos weren't hidden, but they weren't in plain sight, either. Sometimes the camera's eye captures those who aren't so innocent as well.

It turns out, even the buttoned-up, cardigan-wearing folks have their moments. Perhaps that's what keeps them sane. I asked my mother what she was doing in those photos and she didn't panic. She really didn't react at all.

She simply said, "What do you think I was doing?"

"I'm not sure, but it certainly doesn't look good."

She laughed and said, "No, it certainly doesn't."

And as the smile dropped from her face, she said, "That's because it wasn't."

My mother confirmed what I was just discovering: yes, sometimes you need a little sport, to be a little unclean in order to value all the cleanliness around you.

A Thief in the Night

Bobby was fast asleep beside me. His chest rising and falling in uneven intervals, a snore gurgled in his throat before dissipating in soft murmurs and slowly fading. Even though it was 3am, I wanted a cup of tea and set a kettle on the stove. Minutes later, I was on the back deck listening to the night insects clicking and buzzing as they searched for mates. The sky was mostly clear, a heavy navy blue, a few stubborn clouds glowed white when they swallowed the moon before moving on to their darkness.

The tea steamed upward from a dainty porcelain cup, a family heirloom, one of the "Mayflower cups" as Bobby called them, old as my family crest. "Getting your weekly requirement of lead," he'd say whenever I used one of the *Mayflower* cups for a cup of hot tea. He never seemed to tire of that one. The tea itself tasted stale and sour. Something had gone off.

When I opened my eyes, the clouds still glowed from the moon's reflection only it was different, I was different. All was brighter than I remembered. The sounds of the backyard were replaced by blips and beeps and there were people, people I didn't know leaning over me.

"Claire?"

"Can you hear me, Claire?"

Yes, I can hear you.

"Can you hear my voice, Claire?"

Yes, I can hear your voice. Who are you?

"Still not responding."

There's a light in my eye. I don't like that.

"She's following the light. Dilating."

"Ok, good."

Who are you?

"Her blood pressure is 130/82."

"That's an improvement, good."

"Pulse is still high."

Why is my pulse high?

"Increase the fluids and give her a few minutes. Make sure to monitor her blood pressure."

When the phone rings at 5am it's seldom good news. Come to think of it, unless it's winter and the call is confirming a snow day from school, it's never good news. Add that to the fact it was Bobby calling, someone who would never call before 9am. Ever. Except now. Maybe he was on a bender and needed a ride home from the police station.

"Jesus, Bobby, it's awfully early."

"I had to call an ambulance. Claire's at the hospital."

It wasn't a snow day.

"What? What happened?"

"I don't know. She fainted, passed out. I don't know. I was in bed and she wasn't, so I went looking for her. She wasn't in the house and the outside light was on in the back. I found her out on the deck. I don't know how long she was there."

"Did she pass out like you pass out?"

"I don't know! I didn't see her pass out and I don't know how I pass out because I'm too busy fucking passing out!"

"Ok, ok, are you at the hospital now? Saint Rosalie?"

"Yes."

"I'll be there as soon as I can."

Claire's eyes were open. Otherwise, there wasn't a lot of information. I was waiting for Maddy to get here. She'd know what to do, what questions to ask. I also know if I knew the answer to thirty questions, Maddy would want to know the answer to thirty-five and because I didn't have the answer to those five questions, I'd never hear the end of it. Yes, it was better to know less at this point. I tried to sit on the orange plastic chairs lining the wall of the waiting room, but as soon as my bottom hit the chair, I got back up, pacing the room with nervous energy, a zoo lion prowling the enclosure.

My stomach was churning, growling, making noises not found in nature, eating itself spoonful by greedy spoonful. By chance, I caught my reflection in the glass of the empty reception desk. Looking back at me was something or someone I didn't expect. The man in the reflection was a dark specter, his face contorted and vile, blackened by his own actions, a figure so wretched and despicable, I had to look away. But he drew me back into this morbid game of chicken, this face morphing into something familiar, his stare growing magnetic and irresistible, even attractive. Now I understood his reflection to be exactly as he was, as I was: guilt.

This was it. After all this time, all this avoidance, avoiding her, ruining my marriage to save her life. None of it mattered in the end. I'd killed her anyway. I imagined myself the subject of one of those investigative reporting shows that masquerade as news programs. A handsome man in voice-over: "Who is Bobby Shaw and what else was he capable of? What you will learn will shake your very soul. Stay tuned!"

There's little traffic at 5am and for good reason—no one wants to be out of bed. I barely had time to brush my teeth, and my attempt to comb down the mop on my head ended before it began. I gave up after thirty seconds. I put on the first things I found: a pair of blue sweats and a gray zipper sweatshirt. After tossing several pairs of dress shoes over my shoulder and into the hallway, I located a pair of sneakers in the back of the closet and dashed out the door. My stomach was in knots.

The hospital is about ten minutes away and I drove like I was playing a video game. Red lights be damned! I heard the screech of the tires each time I hugged a curve. At this rate, I thought to myself, I'm going to end up in the hospital myself. I passed a patrol car while well above the posted speed limit and likely not within the lines. The cop looked at me sleepily and shook his head like I should know better, but didn't drive after me. I slowed down a bit and took a deep breath before my nerves overloaded again, then I sped up. Although it felt like half-an-hour, I arrived at the hospital seven minutes after I left, squealing into the parking lot like a doctor late for surgery.

The tears were tugging at my eyes and the pressure in my sinuses was growing. I had the beginnings of a headache, one that was likely to linger. I found a parking spot, a good one, a 5am parking spot, but sat in the car unable to move, my fingers curled tightly around the steering wheel. No! I won't allow a panic attack! This isn't the time.

The ceiling lights, rectangular, glowing blobs, whoosh by one-by-one, making me dizzy. The hum of the wheels on the bottom of the bed makes me sleepy. Dizzy. Sleepy. Where are we going? How long is this hallway? Why isn't anyone answering me?

"Room 337," someone says.

That sounds like a good room, the third floor is safe from floods, but only two flights of stairs down in an emergency. A fine room. Tell me, is that a good room?

There's a strange face, a woman's face, brown eyes blinking quickly and eyebrows thick as a forest. There's a blue mask covering her nose and mouth.

"Can you hear me?"

Yes, of course I can hear you! You're a foot away from my face. If you weren't wearing a mask, I'd be soaked in spit.

"Her eyes are following my finger," she says to someone I assume is not me, someone I can't see. Her voice sounds optimistic and friendly. Someone else says something but it's garbled and I can't understand what they're saying. We turn a corner at a speed that doesn't seem safe to me.

The lights going by, bright then dark, bright then dark, are making me sick. I might throw up. Dizzy. Sleepy. Sick. Make it stop! Make it stop!

It was strange that she hadn't come back to bed. I assumed she was getting a drink of water or using the bathroom, something that would take a few minutes. I must have dozed off after she got up, but when I awoke, her side was still empty. I ran my hand along her side of the sheets: cold. I'm not sure why, but something told me I needed to find her.

She wasn't in either bathroom and the kitchen remained dark. Had she run away? Was she finally leaving me? Good for her!

It would have been due time, the leaving. I'd provided her a myriad of reasons to escape from the loveless marriage. No, it wasn't a loveless marriage, there was love, deep love, but it was no longer expressed physically. At least not for my part, not often. I'd placed a moat between us, deep and murky, something she couldn't possibly understand and something I refused to explain despite her questioning, her desperate queries.

In an effort to preserve her image of me, however tenuous, it was necessary to hide my condition. Taking pity on me was not an option, at least not an option for me. For me to remain whole, I must have Claire's love, the old, unconditional love, not a new love of pity. And, also her respect. My fading condition, however slowly I was fading, would change it, all of it, and that I feared more than any disease.

My only fear is not that I'm dead, though I might be, but that Bobby will see me. He doesn't have the strength to see his wife on a hospital bed, skin gray as cement, eyelids pulled down by the attending doctor as he calls out the time of death. Bobby thinks I'm the strong one, the put-together one, the fastidious one. None of it is true, at least not completely true.

I'm already preparing to haunt him. He wakes up when he snores, which is often—now he'll wake up when my ghostly hands pinch his nose shut, cutting off the heavy pull of oxygen and causing him to sit up straight half in shock, half in distress. He'll think he sees me, a blurry, gray skinned apparition floating near the closet door. He'll reach out to me, thinking it not a dream, but he can't quite reach as I'll float just far enough away, just out of reach. Even if he lunges out of bed, which he might, I'll move ever so slightly so he can never touch what remains of me. It'll be fun to taunt the living. They're so gullible, so wanting to believe in ghosts so they can justify letting us go.

Is this what it feels like, to be a ghost? At once here, and not here? I'm in many places at once: in the bed with my body, in the waiting room as Bobby paces back and forth, in the car as Maddy races along at dawn. Or am I here, in this bed, in this hospital room and I can't see them, I just know what they will do. In movies they say when you're dead you don't know you're dead, so how am I supposed to know?

The strange thing is—sure, most of it's strange—that I'm wearing clothes. Pajamas. Not that I expected to be naked, but why would I be wearing pajamas? They look like the pajamas I had when I was ten, full-footed bottoms with rubber pads and a tight, long-sleeved top. Is this the outfit I selected for the afterlife or did my subconscious choose that which was most comfortable? Was this period in time when I was happiest? This is all so confusing and there's no one to ask. Where is the promised light, literal and metaphorical?

Across the room there's a bird, a blackbird, at the window. No, not at the window, on this side of the glass, inside the room with me. The window is closed, so I'm not sure how it got in. It turns its head from one side to the other, twitching, studying me.

"I bring news!" it squawks.

You can talk?

"I bring news."

What news?

"News from someone," it replies and buries its yellow

beak in its wing to scratch an itch.

Who?

"A professor, yes, a professor!"

What professor?

"Connelly! Connelly!" it squawks louder.

Professor Connelly?

"Yes, yes, that's him!"

Wait! That makes no sense!

"It makes perfect sense."

What news after all these years?

"He says he's sorry."

Sorry for what?

"For everything."

Why would he be sorry after all these years?

"Because it's time."

Time for what?

The bird hopped twice on spindly legs while stretching its wings full, looked out the window then back at me. "Time for him to go," it said and flew out the still closed window and disappeared into the dim blue of morning.

Wait! What is he sorry for? I asked, but the blackbird had already fluttered off, my imagining of it ceased. Tricks, I thought, tricks of the dying mind…

But I did go to see him, Professor Connelly, well after college. He'd sent me a letter and I needed to speak with him.

There was no one at the front desk to answer questions

and no cell service. I'd assumed these places were twenty-four-hour out of necessity, but my assumption was being challenged. I tapped my fingers on the counter, kept looking at the same places, the desk, over the desk, past the desk, around the empty lobby, at the ceiling, each time expecting someone to be there, someone to have materialized. Finally, a bored woman with a fresh cup of coffee wandered behind the desk, carefully placed the cardboard coffee cup down like it was a crystal goblet, then took her time getting comfortable in her chair, testing the wheels to make sure they still rolled smoothly across the floor, before looking up at me.

"Can I help you?" she asked though she really didn't mean it. She stared at her computer screen as if awaiting a query result, though she hadn't typed anything.

"I'm looking for my sister-in-law," I said quickly. "She was brought in by ambulance maybe an hour ago, less than an hour ago."

She looked at me in confused silence and bit her lower lip as if the village idiot had wandered into a local diner and asked about a woman in an ambulance rather than ordering the two-egg special. Was I not supposed to ask questions before she'd had her coffee?

She pointed a reluctant finger over my shoulder. "Through the doors and follow that hallway," she said and yawned. "The emergency department is at the end of the hall."

I'm not sure if I said "thank you," but I hope I didn't. As I hurried down the hall, my sneakers slapped against the tile floor, echoing off the walls and ceiling, announcing my presence to no one in particular.

Thankfully, it didn't take long for Maddy to arrive in the waiting room. I heard her hurried steps in quick succession, *pat-pat-pat*, as she came down the hallway and turned through the doorway. She was ghost white, white as winter, her hair was uncombed and un-Maddy-like. I already knew the mess I looked like.

"Any news?" she blurted before I could open my mouth to tell her I didn't have any news.

She wasn't one to wait.

"I'll get some news," she said and turned back into the hall, intent on shaking down the nearest nurse. When in doubt, call Maddy.

She returned a few moments later. "I can't find anyone in this fucking place," she said and put her hand across her forehead. "I'm not sure anyone works here."

She turned and looked at me. I didn't think it was possible, but her face bleached even whiter than before. Her eyes grew larger and tears formed in the corners.

"I don't know," I said and shook my head, answering the question that burned in her belly, answering the question before she could ask. We sat on two of the plastic orange chairs, she leaned over and buried her head against my collarbone. I put my arm around her and pulled her closer.

"God, I hope not," I said and let my emotions take me.

There's and odd sense of relief when you're finally caught, when the jig is up, when it's time to face the music. Imagine the stress of being an escapee, you name the circumstance, a prisoner who scaled the fence, a serial killer hiding in plain sight, an imposter living the life of another. Starving, naked, alone with only one's thoughts to keep you sane. I'm none of these things, and I'm all of them. And now, at least temporarily, there was a sense of relief. I could breathe even though it appeared I was labored.

There were machines beeping and pumps pumping and nurses nursing—all working as part of this sensation of relief. I've been waiting for time to catch me. Not age—I've been aging right on schedule—but time itself. Don't get me wrong, I don't want to face it, time, but there's an exhale, a peace with looking in the mirror. There's an old saying: "Your time will come." That's usually associated or at least I would usually associate it with something positive. Until now.

I wanted to be what Bobby expected, a good person, a good wife and in many ways, I like to believe I lived up to the expectation. But to think my soul is unsoiled, pious or otherwise, is simply a fantasy. Now, now it must float to the surface, that which was sunk in the murky waters of the past. My love has been unwavering, unconditional, of that, I am sure. But there was a price. There's always a price.

The bed has finally stopped moving, the lights have settled above me, angelic in their glow. There are more needles in my arms now, more tubes delivering more liquid, dripping. The nurse's faces are masked, but I can tell by their eyes, wide open and hollow, that they're nervous about something or someone.

There's a warmth down below that's spreading underneath my legs—I've peed myself. Another indignity piled on top of the current one. Controlling one's bladder is an expectation for the ambulant, not some woman they hoisted from a faceplant, so I'm sure they'll understand. It's all I have at the moment. Dignity has died.

Another Letter (Claire)

A few years ago, quite a few years ago now, I received a letter written from someone I hadn't heard from in years. I found it odd at first to both receive a letter (even I consider it old fashioned) but also to receive a letter from a very old friend, Professor Connelly. He told me he'd requested my address from the alumni association (he hoped I didn't mind) and it was important that I meet him. The envelope and letter itself, were heavy in my hand, a weight to consider.

When Bobby asked about the letter with the Stevens College logo on the envelope, I told him they wanted money, as usual. He shook his head and rolled his eyes—he'd seen a hundred such letters over the years. There was an internal struggle, a brief moral debate of whether to tell Bobby, but I made the decision to meet Professor Connelly in a very public place: The Boston Public Library. And I made the decision to not tell Bobby, at least until after the meeting.

Neither decision seemed right nor not right. Meeting

Professor Connelly was out of character for me, but I also knew meeting a man twenty years my elder in a public place held little real danger. On the other hand, not informing Bobby of my decision to meet Professor Connelly carried a certain amount of risk. I keep going back to trust and expectations and this was something, a blunt instrument, to rough-up and scuff that perpetual shine of trust. I justified it by acknowledging Bobby himself was a keeper of many secrets, a great many secrets. I was sure of it. Perhaps it was time I began, or rather continued, my own diary of mysteries, kept under lock and key. I couldn't have known that morning just how many secrets my diary would keep.

The commuter rail into Boston took about an hour and offered magnificent views of saltmarshes and mud flats before it wound into a more expected city view of graffiti and industry, back alleys and abandoned buildings. Once at Boston's North Station, the library was a short, though bumpy subway ride on the Green Line, a gritty assemblance of trollies that slowly creaked and crawled their way under downtown like herded cattle. My father lovingly called the Green Line a "chiropractor in a can," but I'm not certain whether he meant the bumps and jumps and starts and stops loosen the stubborn stiffness of your spine or cause you discomfort which requires you to see an actual chiropractor. Perhaps both.

While on the Green Line, I was tempted to abandon the entire affair, change subways and detour to Harvard Square, to a bookstore or two. This would likely have proved both cathartic and expected as well as spared me what lie ahead.

Ignorance would've been blissful. Bobby would be none the wiser, which he would be either way, and my own sense of regret placed in a folder and filed away. But I convinced myself, adventure awaits.

Before I had the thought of abandoning the journey in favor of a new one toward a bookstore in Cambridge, I considered just what it was I was doing. And what I wasn't doing. I wasn't meeting someone to begin an affair, far from it. There was little interest in him during my scurrilous senior year, never mind now that I was a married woman. Back then, he was more an experiment in a laboratory—let's see what happens if we add a little of this to the beaker. What then was my reason for the covert meeting? Curiosity? Closure? Or was it all simply transactional.

All of these things needed to be considered if I was taking an honest look. There was an officialness to it, a letter, like being summoned to collect a prize overlooked during my academic career. There was a phone number too, and I left a message saying, yes, I could meet on the day, at the hour and the location as requested. If the hour was an evening hour and the location the bar at a swanky hotel downtown, I may have viewed this in a different manner, a scandalous manner. But a public library in the middle of the day? All seemed safe. Strange, perhaps, but safe.

I was twenty-eight which would make Professor Connelly around forty-eight. He could be my father, though that fact held little weight in the past, so I couldn't see it being an issue.

Once off the Green Line at Copley Station, I wandered

up and down Boylston Street passing the library once, twice, thrice, craning my head to look at the building before turning up my nose and walking away. Would my nerve hold? Would I go in? There was a strange shadow outside the library entrance though I couldn't tell which building was blocking the sun or if it was a well-placed cloud raining dark on that particular spot. For some reason, the shadow gave the entrance a funerial look, a haunted, foreboding coolness. Was this a funeral of sorts, perhaps even my own?

The security guard at the library entrance, a burly, wide-shouldered man, his brown head shaved smooth, evidently meant business. He asked if I had a library card with the voice inflection usually reserved for demands. I fumbled through my purse and handed him my teacher ID. His demeanor softened almost to the point of allowing a smile before he let me through. In many ways I wish he hadn't. I wish he'd given me a big-voiced, pointed-finger lecture about the library being for Boston residents and how he was sorry, but he couldn't possibly let me through. Have a good day—somewhere else. Anywhere else. I truly wish he had.

"Miss Haddish," the security guard said as I was navigating the turnstile.

"I'm sorry," I said.

"She was my favorite teacher," he said with a smile, his bald head shaking and his mind wandering years into the past. "Fifth grade."

"If you still remember her, she must have done a fine job," I said.

He nodded his friendliest nod and turned back to his duties.

Was I here to see my favorite teacher? Hardly. But, certainly the only one who'd seen me naked, I thought to myself and laughed.

It was what? Six years since graduation, since we'd last seen each other? If I'd not heard his voice, still strong and silky, I wouldn't have recognized him and walked straight by the table where he sat hunched over. His tweed jacket, only a few years ago filled so solidly with his muscular shoulders and chest and arms, now may have fallen off him if a stiff breeze made its way through the hall. Such was the fullness of his demise.

Here, now, he was not a forty-eight-year-old man. He wasn't even a fifty-eight-year-old man. He was seventy-eight, thirty years older than I expected. Something, a disease, an accident, an addiction, something had robbed him of his youth, played on him the cruelest of tricks, and left him a shell, flesh barely holding to the bones. His eyes were sunken into his face and a scraggly, gray and white beard grew hither and tither, covering what remained of his once pristine jawline. His hair, though, was still a dark brown and perfectly combed, unmarred by the aging gray, and one brown lock still spun down onto his forehead.

Despite the warm weather, he wore a heavy wool sweater underneath the tweed, yet he shivered while I attempted to ignore my damp brow. Though unsure what to expect, this was not what I expected.

"How is Stevens treating you," I asked. The easy breaker

of ice as this day was threatening to be an iceberg.

"I can't complain, some things, like Stevens College, never change," he said and fiddled his emaciated fingers on the table in front of him. "I've taken a sabbatical to focus on a few things."

I nodded along expecting him to say, "For health reasons," but he didn't.

"Claire, I have to tell you, though you won't believe me and I can't blame you if you don't believe me, but you were always my favorite."

"Favorite what?" I asked.

"Favorite student, favorite…everything."

"There were a lot of 'everythings' in your day." I may have rolled my eyes.

He managed a laugh, dusty and raw, like a lawnmower engine that won't quite start after you pull the cord with all you've got.

"Well, yes, I can understand you thinking that way and I suppose in many ways that's true," he said and smiled. "I've lived a full life, but not everyone would agree a good life."

He caught my air of discomfort as I sat across from him wondering both what had happened and why he wanted to speak with me. And, as importantly, why me? Where was this going? Was he making amends with those populating his mistake filled past? I began to wonder what mistake I'd made, or rather the series of mistakes I'd made in traveling to Boston.

He cleared his throat as though he were taking the podium at Stevens he commanded for so many years. The throat clearing brought back Stevens College: the sounds, of course, but also the scent of old books and paneled walls. Was that because I was surrounded by old books and paneled walls? Despite my discomfort or perhaps because of it, I laughed.

"It smells like Stevens, but look where we are. Of course, it smells like Stevens!" I said.

He managed a smile, still perfect teeth, before clearing his throat once again in preparation for a speech he was determined to make. He tapped four fingers on the table in front of him, index to pinky, index to pinky, the grayish nails hitting the wood added a sharp beat to each finger tap. The uber-confident Professor Connelly was nervous.

A large book lay splayed open in front of him. He'd been reading something heavy with history, a glossy hardcover with black and white pictures that screamed "military."

"What are you studying?" I asked.

"I'm a military history nerd," he said and laughed. "I've been researching the role of bayonets in war. Riveting, I know."

He quickly morphed into professor mode, cleared his throat again and delivered an impromptu lecture, those same emaciated fingers springing to life in professorial gestures. "The British did a lot of research on how to make the bayonet more lethal. Rather than a flat blade, they designed a triangular one. This made the wound more difficult to close which caused more bleeding and, because the wound wouldn't close properly, it was more susceptible to infection."

He made sure he had my attention as I nodded along, looking up at me before continuing.

"So now not only do you have the indignity of having to be so close you can smell your enemy's bad breath, you now also know you'll likely die of infection. And you will die, you already know."

His brief lecture had run its course. Or perhaps he caught himself relying on his professor persona when this meeting was meant to be more personal in nature.

"I see you're married," he said and pointed to his own hand to indicate he was referring to my ring. He wasn't wearing one.

"Yes," I said. "A boy, a man now, from Stevens. Did you know Bobby Shaw?"

"No," he said and squinted in thought. "Doesn't ring a bell."

"Three years now," I said.

He smiled. "Congratulations. Kids?"

"No," I said. "Not yet, anyway."

He nodded along and said "good." Who says that? What an odd thing to say.

"And you're teaching English literature?"

I nodded. "High school. So far, so good."

"I got that from the Alumni Office," he said thinking perhaps I hadn't figured it out.

"Why did you ask me here? Is there something you want to tell me?" I said, sensing the small talk had run its course.

"I don't know."

Sometimes, a busy street can feel lonely. Boylston Street was full of people hustling about, cars were honking and buses stopping and starting, but I felt alone. The traffic continued unabated, buses, cars, cabs, weaving, accelerating, almost in unison. There were giggling groups of women in the midst of a girl's day out, their voices shouting with confidence, slouching college students who refused eye contact and may or may not have showered this week, and a reasonably well-dressed, twenty-something woman with clear blue eyes claiming she'd lost her wallet and was asking strangers for a dollar, *a mere dollar* she pleaded, so she could catch the train home. The last of the afternoon sun was about to duck behind the skyline, about to cast a long shadow on Boylston.

Now I had to double back toward the library, to find the trash barrel on the sidewalk that I'd used to toss the unopened envelope Professor Connelly had handed to me after he clammed up.

"Open this later," he said and slouched down like one of his introverted students, like one of the miscreants shoving their way past either side of me when I slowed my pace on the sidewalk.

I shoved my hand into the barrel to retrieve the envelope. Part of it was wet from something, the paper darkened, but I didn't want to know what kind of wet it was. It was better if I didn't know. I looked up to find clear blue eyes a few inches from my own.

"You have a kind face," she said confidently. "You've come back to help me."

"I'm afraid I wouldn't be of much help right now," I said.

"Only a dollar," she reminded me. "All I need is a dollar and I'll have enough to buy a ticket home. I really want to go home."

"I really want to go home, too," I said as I reached into my pocketbook to stuff the envelope in while pulling out a dollar.

"You have a kind face," she reminded me, her smile filled with chippy, gray teeth while her eyes remained clear.

My mother once told me that no matter where'd I'd gone or how long I'd stayed, I didn't leave any footprints. Sometimes, you never even knew I was there. Now, that had changed. My feet had stomped, up, down, up, down.

Up.

Down.

Stomped hard and unknowingly left a trail of destruction. Do not be fooled by my kind face. We're all judged the same in the end.

Being Remembered (Bobby)

They say there's no such thing as bad press; there's only press. Therefore, I conclude, there are no bad memories, only memories. And I'm determined to be remembered. I welcome the bad press if it's the only press I'm destined to conjure up.

The studio has wonderful light in the evening. It's reddish and yellowish and pours through the large windows like a stream engorged after a spring snow melt. The stool, the foam padding leaking out from under worn black leather, was always the most comfortable seat. It makes no sense, of course, it's spindly and old and lists to one side requiring me to keep one foot on the floor to keep the sensation of toppling over at bay. It brings back memories of my shortened left leg and a time when my more innocent world spun upon its axis. Things are going south when your worst memories are better than future ones.

I sat at my work table gazing across its emptiness. The huge, square table, six feet by six feet, usually allowed me to work on several projects at once. Now it was bare, devoid of anything interesting or promising. It held no life. Perhaps life had come full-circle. It was a difficult time this not working–a dancer not dancing, a teacher not teaching, a philanderer not philandering.

I'd been discharged that morning. It was my third stay in the hospital, two weeks, enough to put some weight back on, reduce muscle mass in my legs and disrupt my bladder routine. I'd been working on Mrs. Grace, both her and her likeness. She's a wonderful woman, I admit, and I do enjoy working with her. She has a solid quality, grounded, confident, traits I admire. And we'd been getting along quite well.

She asked me a question or questions a couple of weeks back, something I had to think about more than I expected. At the time I didn't give her an answer—I didn't have one, at least not a good one. It was one of the few things I remember about speaking with her that day. Before everything went dark, the black aperture of the lens closing from all around in slow, but steady motion.

Before the lens closed, while leaning against the warmth of her rosy skin, a hint of perfume teasing my nose before I fainted (strange the things you remember), she asked something like: "Do you want to be great?"

I surely said, "Yes."

And she asked, "What are you willing to do to be great?"

The seemingly innocuous discussion was serendipitously interrupted, but, during my two-week vacation at the Hotel Bedpan, I gave it some thought. When you're laid out with needles jabbed into and tubes spurting forth from your arms, you tend to have a lot of time to think. Naturally, most of the time spent there is time spent on worry. Worry is priority one, the star of the show. Sleep is the second priority and the most elusive. Once worry is achieved and sleep remains elusive you try to think, to ponder your life, your dreams, your future. All of it tied into Mrs. Grace's questions.

What does one need to sacrifice to be great? Everything? Nothing? Is it everything because only one thing matters? Is it nothing because everything else is "nothing?" In speaking with clients over the years, it's clear all of them seek immortality. They don't know it, mind you, but it's what they want. They also have no idea of the true cost, the sacrifice. They don't know I'm the toll taker. I'm the gatekeeper. I am death.

I made a decision and it was a decision I did not make lightly. Let me explain. I've made giving people a sense of immortality my life's work, and along the way it's cost me everything. It's cost me my life, or a portion of my life and now, I fear, a portion of Claire's life as well. Was it too much to ask, a portion of these brief lives to achieve immortality, to be remembered, perhaps revered for all of time? It certainly doesn't sound like it. When I'm dead, they will remember me.

What am I guilty of? It's simple. In creating art, in creating statues that reflect the soul of the subject, I requested—no, *required*—my subjects to succumb to a process that laid bare not only their inner selves, their souls if you will, but their bodies also. It was necessary and expected and there were dangers inherent in the process. They were warned. None heeded the warning.

Okay, what does this mean in layman's terms? Again, it's simple. They allowed me to experience their minds and their physical selves, to explore both in any way I wished. This often, very often, led to sexual encounters as well as deep discussions. Both were necessary and fruitful. And fraught with danger.

Let me take this deviance one step further: once I learned this recently termed "wasting disease" was coursing through my veins, my tears, my saliva, my semen, it was paramount to cease any and all activity of the flesh. I learned this earlier and longer ago than I care to admit and in the course of my work, I ignored it. If I'd taken the poison into consideration, I would have failed as an artist, failed as the keeper of immortality. I asked them, all of them a simple question: Are you willing? To the person, the answer was yes.

Again, I take a moment to remind you that my whole life I was determined to grab hold of what I could for fear of never having another opportunity. Yes, it sounds and feels like the excuse of a hormone-driven teenager; it very well may be. But I've remained consistent and true, have I not? Was I not a true scorpion upon the frog's fleshy back? And were all the willing participants not destined to drown part way across the river of life?

A fantastical fable? Here, however, is where the fable ends. Here is where I'm unable to forgive myself. Despite years of murky avoidance, earnest attempts at marital abstinence, I've wrought my curse upon my love, bequeathed her a death sentence. The one person on earth I was committed to protecting has, sometime during the blur of life, contracted my poison despite my attempt to shelter her, to sheath my stinger. After all, how many stings does it take to kill another? In truth, only one. I spend my last years (maybe), months (likely), days, hours, minutes knowing that I am the cause of her pain. Each tick of the clock deepens the regret.

But what do I feel, really? There are equal parts of me that carry both the nagging guilt and the lightness of knowing it will all end soon enough. I move between sobs for my beloved Claire and shrugs of an apathetic pair of shoulders. Rest assured, I do not like myself more than you could ever not like me. It's been that way always.

And, looking back, what have become of my casual friends? How have they fared? How will they be judged when the judgement is upon them? Where and what is their station? Has it been tethered to the ground or soared to heights? What has become of the lot of them? Were there two alcoholics? One devastating car accident? Three divorces? Four failed attempts at a bachelor's degree? Were there also multiple STDs from multiple prostitutes? I haven't asked. I don't pity them or look them up or hold a particular contempt. My hope is they've forgotten me, too.

And even though I walk a little better, a little straighter, with a bit less hop, I know what they thought of me, what they didn't say in my presence. The poor man, a cripple and he doesn't even know it. Good for him! The poor fool better to not know than be anchored by it, to be ground down by something so long in the making.

The Process (Claire)

Look, I'm not stupid. At least not that stupid. I, too, have a sculpture, a gift, a representation of my soul, my spirit.

Bobby calls it "The Reader" —how appropriate, how accurate and endearing. How much it represents true love. But it's wrong. At least some of it is wrong.

Three sketches: the past, the present, the future. He guided me through it—the exploration, the talks, the getting to know my body with his hands, with his mouth, the sex. And when I say I'm not stupid, I mean I know this is his process. Which means I'm not the first to allow the exploration; I'm not the first "client" whose body was splayed full in his presence. It's what makes him who he is, what makes him successful. It's his gift. But I don't have to like it.

That said, the sculpture is beautiful. Yes, of course I hold a bias, how could I not? The Reader sits on a craggy half of a park bench, hunched over an opened book, protecting it. Her very essence was focused on the text, her eyes wide, her lips beginning to form a smirk, perhaps having just learned something only she and the book will ever share. She wears my favorite pajamas, Winnie the Pooh, red and white, comfy and worn thin, only a slice of Pooh's ear and one eye decorate the fabric. Only she and I can be sure they're the pajamas of my childhood. A light wool blanket, reddish, flows over her warmed lap.

She takes center stage in our living room, watching over her book and, though her eyes never raise, watching over our home. Watching over me. In the morning, a ray of sunlight slips through the front window, envelopes her, casting a grayish-brown shadow on the white wall, ten times her true size.

Bobby says she is his best work, his truest essence, but I respectfully disagree with the image. The amalgam is, in my eyes, lacking my future, my future end. The old woman he envisioned, the grandmother snuggled under a thick blanket, content with her life, her family, her sunset years. No! That's not me. That will not be me! Bobby Shaw lies!

My future is not happy, it's not a glowing sunset gradually sinking toward an ocean horizon, a beach lined with giddy spectators. Despite his gift, this is all wrong. I don't have the heart to tell him and I don't have the heart to tell myself. Even he can't see it.

The Reader was a gift on my thirtieth birthday. He wanted to show my perfection—his words—and my place in the world as a purveyor of truth and knowledge, a teacher of humanity's place in the world. Perhaps he knew I had a secret, one between me and my books, that should be, must be, hidden from the world. But no longer. It must be known.

(Bobby)

Funerals are a rite of passage. As we get older, we know more people and the people we know are getting older each day, each hour, each minute. And the more people we know, the more people that we know will pass. Only hermits, and hermits devoid of emotion, will elude the numbing sting of the death of others.

A year ago, Rochelle passed. She battled something in secret, cancer maybe—her husband didn't say. She was buried along with her sculpture, her gray arm wrapped around it; this was how she wanted to be laid to rest, according to her husband.

"That must make you a little proud," he said to me. I nodded to be polite.

Rochelle lay peacefully in the casket, not unexpected, as I reached out to touch her arm, waxy and cool, almost artificial. I'm not sure why I touched her or what drove me to do such a thing. Did I want to know she was really dead? Claire was beside me, her eyes burned into my cheek, but no words followed. We all have our own way of grieving, and who was Claire to question mine?

She was not the Rochelle I remembered, the gregarious vixen, leaving trails of bubbles in her wake. Then again, I imagine few of us are at our own funeral. But she did remind me of something intimate, her third sketch and I stared at her, studied her in this final pose, for longer than expected.

"She was very fond of you," her husband said as we shook hands. He always had a vice grip for a handshake, and my hand emitted a worrying crack when he wrapped his hand around mine. He was a tall man with wisps of thin gray hair and eyes like Caribbean water. I tried to not look into them for fear they would hypnotize me.

According to Claire, I smiled as I shook his hand, but didn't say anything. I don't remember not saying anything. As a matter of fact, I would have bet I'd said something like "I was fond of her as well" or "she became a good friend." But, as I'm told, I said nothing of the sort.

Claire said she found it strange that I had nothing to say to the man during his time of grieving, no sage words, no words at all.

"Couldn't you have told a story, something that would make him laugh, make him smile at least? That's what he was looking for…something. An anecdote to lighten the day."

"I didn't realize he would want to laugh at his wife's funeral," I said, my tone harsher than I meant.

"For God's sake, Bobby," she growled. "You know what I mean. He was hoping to gather some memories, positive memories. That's what gets us through the tough times."

I stiffened and looked at her out of the corner of my eye which only made her angrier. It always does. A round mirror with gold leaf trim held me in its refection as I walked out of the room and into the hallway. My gray wool suit and baby-blue tie looked wholly inadequate for the day.

And I did know what she meant. The problem was, is, and will forever be that I did not keep these kinds of memories, did not jot them down in a diary or keep them in a shoebox for later retrieval. My clients were not my friends, nor my lovers; they were, are and forever will be transactions. Art is a business, and I am a business man as well as an artist. And let's not be naïve, my clients are well aware that I, too, am a transaction. They hire me to perform a service and I do my part to fulfill the contract. I flit through their privileged lives like a hummingbird, magnificently vibrating near their ear, heart pumping impossibly fast before my course is run and I'm dead to them. I'm a luxury item that goes out of style too soon, replaced by my art which, I pray, endures. They understand the risks involved, the risks of business, the risks of this sort of business.

What am I left with? Not stories. No, I am left with fleeting success. And cash. More cash than my mother would have made in three lifetimes of being bent necked in front of a dinging adding machine.

What else was left for me? Acquaintances? Maybe, and not much more. Certainly, there was no emotion to be garnered, even in this time when I should be emotional. There was little more than an acknowledgement that I'd known Rochelle. But I had known her well. I had studied her and, I believe, found her soul, something she gave willingly and often. Why would I not be affected more by her passing?

What did this say about me? Was I the monster I'd always expected to become or always been? I had the likely answer and I was oddly comfortable with it.

When most of us think of a monster, we think of something lurking under the bed, a growling beast with teeth and claws and a nose that can't be fooled by burying ourselves under wool blankets. Or perhaps we see a cold-blooded killer's beady eyes, a well-honed butcher knife in hand ready to separate an unsuspecting neighbor into bite-sized pieces. I was a different kind of monster—still a monster, mind you—one that operated in an emotionless vacuum. And what were my claws and teeth, my butcher knife? Transactions. The ability to conduct transactions without needing to involve emotions. I've died a little each day.

The thing is, she didn't look dead. At least she didn't look *dead* dead. Not to me. What a strange thing to think that someone who has passed on doesn't look dead even though she very much is dead. What does that even mean? Shouldn't the dead look dead? Yes, she looks more than dead to me. Her skin has lost its luster, her smile devolved into a nondescript, perhaps purposeful scowl, frozen, permanent. Dead. What else could she be?

Did she not have more time? Obviously, not. But why not? There should have been much more time. She wasn't an old woman. Not a young woman, mind you, but not old enough to die. Are we ever old enough? You see, I'm questioning my actions, but there is nothing to question. What is done is done and cannot be undone. To question it now is a fruitless exercise for the question implies there's a cure, an antidote, a magic elixir. There is not.

Have I not made you immortal? Did I not do as I said I would? Yes, the trust was thin, perhaps nonexistent, but you see what's been created in your image. I see her there in your arms, her flowing gown, once yours, her beautiful face, once yours, all now belong to her. You hug her tightly, hugging yourself, your past, your present is your future. Is it not all I said it was, immortality? It is and more. More than you could have hoped. You will be remembered because you cannot be forgotten; you will always exist even though you will be six-feet under. Once this state of preservation is achieved, all say the same thing—what was I waiting for?

Do you see my face admiring yours? An egomaniac? Perhaps, but it takes such a person to create immortals. And through you, through my work, I too may achieve immortality. But that's not my objective. What is my objective, you ask? It's embarrassingly simple: to be loved unconditionally. It is only recently that I've come to this conclusion. It's more difficult than I imagined, though I imagined it to be quite difficult. I've only had it once in my life and it was taken from me. Stolen. Ripped from my scrawny arms as I wrapped them around it.

Now, it's true, I've taken as much as I have given. But I've kept my end of the bargain, have I not? Perhaps I've taken more, but there's always more to be taken, and I am going to consume that which is in front of me without consideration or consequences. As I've told you, the ugly child always does. When a kitten is abandoned, left to fend for itself, it will always eat its food quickly and fight for every bite even long after it's been adopted to a good home and its appetites satiated. My appetite is for attention and confidence and unconditional love and it will fail to be satiated before my body is ravaged by wasting disease.

And what's been traded? Aging flesh that peels from your skull, weary eyes and uncooperative hair that fights gravity and resists chemicals. You're free of aching bones and failing muscles, digestive systems that no longer function with youthful efficiency, memory that no longer serves. I have liberated you, freed you from this fading shell, pulled you from the husk of skin and bone. Rejoice!

The question, my question, perhaps a question for Rochelle, is in our immortality, are our mistakes also remembered. Even if the events and decision are known and remembered, are they considered mistakes on judgement day? Are they held up to the light to make sure there are no embryos hiding within the hard shell of the egg? At heaven's gate are they sniffed like a warm gallon of milk to see if they've turned? Are our mistakes baked in, our bad decisions, our imperfections? If so, do they fade over time or do they morph into the stuff of legends and rumor?

Everything is transformed as it ages, becomes brittle and subject to sickness and decay. My work freezes the sickness, reinforces the brittle, encapsulates the soul. It does not make you young, but rather impervious to age and reinterpretation. You will forever be known as you should have always been known. Even when it's not obvious. In a thousand years you will still be. Your beauty will remain, your soul will linger, the memory of you intact. Do not abhor me for my methods, as harsh and unyielding as they are. I have given you what you wanted and you willingly paid for the service, given something of value for something of greater value even if you were ignorant of the actual cost. You cannot be two things at once for very long. At least, one part of you cannot fly while the other remains tethered to the ground. Leave one behind for the eternal other. That's the choice you willingly make.

I am the darkness. I hide under the bed while you sleep, making little clicking noises with my tongue, using my hands to press on the floorboards until they creak. I live in the hallway closet behind the long coats, waiting for a cold night when you reach for comfort. I am the starry-eyed visitor with the charming accent, the one conveniently lacking a hotel room on a stormy night.

What will be etched into my weathered gravestone for all to see?

Husband.

Brother.

Son.

Artist.

Lover.

Monster.

This, of course, assumes, out of an abundance of caution, the grave is marked.

There! It's done. I've made my peace on this subject.

Now I turn forward and only forward. My eyes turn to Claire, for Claire and only her, as always. She is my best hope to be seen as I wish to be seen, to be loved as I want to be loved. It's all I ever wanted. She is perfect and good and just right and I want her to be happy. Only her happiness can satiate what haunts me.

"I'm sorry," I said to Claire when we reached the car. "The thing is…and it sounds strange even to me… I've seen her before."

"I should hope so," Claire responded as she buckled her seatbelt. "We don't usually attend funerals for people we don't know."

"I've seen her looking the way she did today," I explained. "That was her third sketch."

"That's a little creepy," Claire said.

"It is," I agreed.

After a moment, Claire said, "Do you mean somehow you knew she didn't have that much time left?"

"Yeah," I continued. "I must have."

"That's interesting."

"But she wasn't old. The way I sketched her was old. She looked old even though she wasn't."

"That's what happens when people get sick," she said. "Even when they're young, they age quickly. It's a brutal process."

I'd assumed Rochelle had more time. A slow-acting poison should act slowly, but each of us is different, our systems process different inputs at different rates. I'd assumed it wouldn't want to kill her. So, what about the others?

(Claire)

There's a blueprint, a roadmap—whatever you choose to call it—something I was able to follow, at least initially. As a young man, according to my mother, my father was full of wonder, immature wonder mind you, but wonder and curiosity and potential. He was good with numbers, very good with numbers, and logic was as natural to him as breathing. He wanted to make a difference and was willing to work at it. The problem, it seemed, was the *what* he'd work toward. Medicine? Engineering? Chemistry? Biology? Physics? My mother believed, still believes, great men and great women, great anyone, are made, not born.

In my father she saw the right ingredients that, if mixed in correct proportions and baked just so, would rise into something more. That became her goal, not through manipulation (or at least not overt manipulation) but rather with patience and persistence—a gentle, guiding hand, sometimes more. She put him through law school, called in favors to secure summer internships, gave him opportunities in which he himself would blossom. She wasn't completely sure he needed a shove in that direction, but why leave it to chance?

My mother had a vision for the world, her world at least, and it required a certain station, both social and professional. If my father was to be a part of that world (since I am a part of that world, we have to assume he was also), then he would need to be molded, his edges honed sharp with a whetstone. He, of course, was most of the way there when she met him making her task somewhat easier. Then again, he was a boy just out of college, unfocused, untethered, uncommitted. There was work to be done.

Now, I don't want to paint my mother in an unflattering light (as it would paint me in said light as well). At first, it looks like she was a master schemer, a puller of strings and levers. She is one of the most positive and nurturing people I've met, genuinely. But the offering of kind words and encouragement that so easily flows from her lips doesn't mean she isn't moving toward an objective. My grandmother didn't raise a fool.

My maternal grandfather was a pediatrician and his son, my uncle, followed in his footsteps. My grandmother was an educator and my mother followed in her footsteps and I follow in hers: the blueprint in full view.

"We owe it to them," she said almost casually, like I should already know and this was a quick reminder. *Them*, of course, were the hardy souls of the *Mayflower*. "They sacrificed for us. We strive to make them proud."

With this philosophy in mind, I began to steady and guide Bobby. The talent was there in spades, but like most young men, he was unfocused, undisciplined, unsure where he fit into the world. I undertook a role as a beacon, a guiding light, a guardrail. After all, great artists are not born, they're made. And I was making one. Not a traditional profession, I agree, but Bobby was the perfect clay.

There were demons in his past, but useful demons, ones that allowed him to look at everyday life through a different lens. He'd been bullied, but found ways to strike back. He'd been ugly, but blossomed into a handsome man. He'd been denied, but grabbed all he could when the opportunity presented itself. He was damaged just enough to make a mark on the world. And I would not allow myself to be the first female in a half-dozen generations to fail to make a king.

(Maddy)

And just like that he was off again, jetting away in the middle of the night, the recline of his first-class seat set all the way back, a gin martini with stuffed olives balanced casually on his fingertips. I envisioned him flying into her arms, the singer with the hips and curly hair. She's the one responsible for that wretched "Shake, Shake" song that people can't get out of their heads. You know the song, we all do, the one that causes the involuntary shaking of the hips like you're making that same gin martini. It doesn't matter if you're in the car on in line at the bank, it gets you. That's right, the blond hair and the tight ass and the trips and the private meetings; all is supposed to be hush-hush. That's how he usually works, behind the scenes, in their private lives, doors closed, a spare key in an envelope to be found by following the coordinates. These lives are meant to remain private. Far from the spotlight yet close enough to get burned from the heat. At least her checks arrive early and clear immediately. Unlike Bobby, that's the closest this accountant will get to achieving a work orgasm.

He was running with the in crowd and they ate whipped

desserts off his smooth stomach and laughed at his jokes and were, perhaps genuinely, impressed with his work, enamored by his gift. His statues were the new Orgone Accumulator and the Hollywood heavyweights were eating them up. All good for business.

Was I jealous of his success? Of course I was! Wait, jealous is an ugly word with ugly connotations. I was envious, but I was also proud of him. Bobby had made quite a name for himself.

It was around this time, at the peak of his powers that he told me his decision. Presented the decision he'd made. Something that would change lives, other people's lives and not necessarily for the better.

"If they want immortality, there's a price," he said to me while sipping a vodka tonic, seated on my front porch. It was a quiet evening, dull gray and cool. He was cooler. The gentleman was oddly calm. Was he waiting for me to ask the question? He wasn't one to play games, but this aloof air begged me to ask the right one.

"What price is that?" I asked and looked over the front yard in need of a mow, toward the quiet street, away from him. Moths gathered around the dull, yellowish porch light, slapping against the glass enclosure, attempting to sacrifice themselves to the electric sun.

"A roll of the dice," he answered as much to himself as to me. Then, he raised his eyebrows and widened his eyes. "The price of immortality is life, is it not?"

"How the hell do I know?" I said with arms raised, palms open to him like I was surrendering.

But I did know. Not because he told me, but because I now understood the price he'd set. The price he'd been setting for several years now.

"Do you remember Campion?" He asked and folded his hands behind his head as he leaned back.

"A character from my favorite book and a dog I loved?" I asked. "No, I don't."

I thought for a moment, "Did I ever ask you why you named him Campion?"

"I don't think so," Bobby replied and pulled a long inhale through his nose. His brown hair had a red tint in the fading light of the evening. I'd never noticed it before.

"Captain Campion found his place in the world despite his circumstances. When the crazy was removed and he became chief rabbit, he was a steady hand, like he was always meant to be. That's what I wanted, for the crazy to be removed so I could just be."

He turned to me and asked: "Why is *Watership Down* your favorite book?"

"Because dad sent it to me long after he'd left, even though he hated me."

"He couldn't have hated you."

"No," I said. "But he did."

"You still have it?"

"The book?"

"Yes."

"I do, yes."

Bobby didn't say anything else, just stared off into the fading daylight as it failed him, blended him into the dark wood of the shingles until I could barely see him.

I sat back into the wicker chair, it creaked and complained and another story from our childhood took me far away.

"Be careful. I am Death!" Said Karait the snakeling before Rikki-Tikki the mongoose paralyzed him with a bite to his back. Karait was death, more dangerous than a cobra because no one noticed him, no one expected him to be lethal. Bobby's world, it appeared, was fresh out of mongoose.

(Claire)

"Be careful. I am Death."

That was all I could think. All I could feel. All I could confess to myself.

I'd opened the envelope Professor Connelly handed me at the Boston Public Library, read it once, twice, thrice. The words remained the same, giving up their secret while hiding something more sinister.

It said simply:

"Contact Doctor Kilkenny at the Boston Infectious Disease Center and mention I asked you to call.

I'm sorry. "

Below was contact information.

Nothing more.

I did make the call. And I visited Dr. Kilkenny. And nothing would be the same. Be careful.

I was twenty-eight-years-old.

That was twelve years ago.

I am death.

And I've killed Bobby Shaw.

He's the end of the family line and he doesn't know it.

Fuck! Fuck! Fuck!

Dr. Kilkenny didn't smile much and he wasn't smiling that day.

"Is it AIDS? Please don't tell me I have AIDS!"

"No, we've run it twice. Both negative."

"Thank God!"

But the Doctor's eyes didn't soften, his face didn't brighten. Not even a little.

"What is it then?"

He exhaled slowly through his nose and rubbed his right eye with the knuckle of his index finger.

"Something new."

"New as in new and fatal?" I asked.

"The cases I've seen vary substantially," he said while summoning his most reassuring voice. "I've seen more than ten years and, unfortunately, I've seen much less."

"Is there a name?"

"The Dutch researcher who discovered the virus called it 'Kwijnende Ziekte' or wasting disease."

"I assume it's sexually transmitted."

"It hasn't been conclusively proven, but considering it's found in bodily fluids, it's safe to say it's likely."

He took a deep breath.

"The biggest concern is the potential transmission from mother to child."

The room began to spin and the temperature rose, the

black aperture closed from the edges of my eyes inward choking out the light. When I awoke, I was lying on the examination bed with an IV in my arm.

When I saw Kilkenny's face, I remembered his last words.

"Are you saying I can't have children?"

"Take a few minutes to catch your breath," he said.

"I don't want a few minutes! Are you saying my child will be born with this disease?"

"That's likely as it's been the result in other cases."

"So, I shouldn't get pregnant?"

"Please, take a moment," he said. "This is a lot of information."

"I want to know."

"There are considerable risks."

"That's a no."

"I wouldn't recommend it."

My running thoughts found another question.

"What about my husband?"

"He should probably come in for a test."

No, I thought, he can't know. I won't be able to face him. He's only twenty-six. I don't want to ruin the time he has left. He'll know soon enough that I am his executioner.

"I don't want him to know," I said.

As for next steps, medically, there were few.

"If you don't have any symptoms to treat, there's nothing I can give you."

Dr. Kilkenny shrugged his shoulders and, what seemed a habit, pulled at his long, gray beard.

"We're in a holding pattern."

"A time bomb," I offered as words he couldn't seem to find.

He shrugged his shoulders again, but this time he nodded in agreement.

(Bobby)

And now there comes a time to think about death, my own. I've ignored it for as long as I could. This bed will hold my last sleep and my last awake. These legs, useless during the best of times, have lost their will.

I think of her often, Degas's subject, the fourteen-year-old girl, and what was taken from her. What was taken from both of us. That poor innocent, probably the pawn of a fierce, determined mother, found her way to model for the artist. She would become known as ugly, regardless of her actual appearance, once the statue was unveiled. Such a pity. I can only hope she was unaware of what was being said about her likeness, in essence about her. But it likely found a way to her ears, one way or another, her innocence stolen by the jackals, the critics, her mother.

Did she cry into her bed at night? Was she able to face the day each morning? It would be understandable if she pulled the covers tight and slept and slept.

Me? My crying was done long ago.

I cried when my legs hurt.

I cried when other kids pointed at me and snickered.

I cried when Jack couldn't remember what we did the day before.

I cried when David spurned Maddy.

I cried when Tammy found a boyfriend.

I cried when my mother lost her hand.

I cried for Campion.

There's no more time for it.

I should cry for the others, my models, as I have poisoned many of them, sentenced them to death with full knowledge I was doing it. Judge. Jury. Executioner.

I should cry for the others.

But I won't.

There's a price for immortality. That price is mortality.

(Maddy)

This morning's headline read: FROM MASTER TO MONSTER. Even though Bobby insisted on reading the newspaper each morning, I've been pretending to forget when I visit. Of course, when I see his emaciated body occupying only half the space it should, I see a different monster altogether.

It's hard to argue with the headline, the damage is done and people are dying. And, yes, it's Bobby's fault. At least most of it. The article listed a number of dead and dying, a who's who of the famous and wealthy. All were associated with Bobby, all were clients, his models. But when I look at Bobby, I still see the child, crippled enough to garner attention, persecuted to tears. Now, again, his ability to walk is compromised. It was taken from him long ago: the ability to walk unnoticed and to blend in with the other when he ran, his waist turned slightly, perhaps to compensate for his listless, uncooperative limbs. Then he took from others, their bodies, their affection, and, in exchange for immortality, their lives. At the end of his life, he began to walk in those counter-clockwise circles of his six-year-old self. He was breaking down, the pieces, the parts, the gears of life worn down. Only at the close does he understand the impact of his existence on the rest of the world.

And he will leave me soon. Him, too, as Mother, as David, even Campion. I always considered myself strong, aggressive even, rowing against whatever storm set upon me. But no. I am weak, narrow shoulders and ruddy disposition. Despair brings clarity.

When we were kids, we often played in the woods near our house, muddying our pant knees and contracting poison ivy. One day we found a burlap sack, light brown and stained by some sort of liquid. Inside we found a rotting, maggot-infested carcass of something we couldn't identify. We poked it with sticks and threw rocks. It was a game, this expiration. It smelled worse than death as death often does. Now I associate this smell with Bobby, his actions, the consequences of his actions. Perhaps it was a game to him all along.

Some call it myopia; sometimes we just don't see what's right in front of us until we no longer have a choice. When a few rich, self-important people became ill, no one, other than those directly affected, seemed to notice. But when the Shake-Shake girl collapsed on stage, no longer shook her hips, the world began to shake. She was a few songs into her set, doing her thing, a screaming crowd, flashing lights, bass moving the building off its foundation. She turned her head to one side, then the other, her blond curls swinging wildly, her lips, red lipstick and gloss, were sultry, pouty, drawing the crowd in. For a moment, she floated across the stage, feet barely touching the floor, then dropped like she was throwing herself before an altar, the altar of music.

But she wasn't. Consciousness deceived her, left her limp and at the mercy of the evening. The music still pumped for a few more seconds as the band weighed whether this was impromptu choreography, or something more. Paramedics rushed the stage, surrounded her, loaded her onto a gurney as the cameras rolled and security attempted to empty the arena. The nightly news pounced, pumping the footage into a hundred-million living rooms.

Those of us close to Bobby knew; it was too coincidental. Rochelle and a few others were dead, their bodies wasting away until their essence could no longer be contained. Bobby, too, was fading. Now Shake-Shake. Connecting the dots did not require a great mind.

And what did Bobby do? He shook his head and told me, "There's a price." His words were unemotional, a shrug of his shoulders, almost a "what can you do?"

When Shake-Shake canceled her world tour—something changed. People took notice. Their eyes opened. They wanted to know what felled their favorite star, their dancing, singing Goddess. Several months later it was announced she was ill with what was known as wasting disease. Within days the eyes of the world were upon Bobby Shaw. They were no longer the kind eyes of admiration but the cynical eyes of accusation. What did Bobby Shaw know? What was the connection? Did he too suffer from the disease of wasting?

Some people talk about suffering, their own suffering, other people's suffering, and there are others who simply suffered. He was not one to complain, at least not about this. His suffering, it appears, was good for the soul and good for the business of art.

(Bobby)

How long has this percolated in my blood, hiding in the shadows, biding time?

Forgiveness? No. Do not speak of it. I forgive none and none forgive me. Besides, what's the point? I'm already dead.

If you ask me what I've done I can answer it simply: I have given them what they desired and I have taken from them what's been taken from me. My essence has leaked from me for many years, pooling into a corner of my studio, pulled down a metal drain as I watched, helpless. Many times I've tried to cup it in my calloused palms, each time it squeezed through the small spaces between my fingers, finding its way to the drain.

I have no regrets. I learned at an early age to grab, instinctually, whatever was made available to me, for in an instant, all could be taken away. This wasn't a secret and I never shied away from expressing it even though many thought I was joking.

My young life so often seemingly out of my control became a life where I wielded a power that I couldn't have imagined in my wildest childhood dreams. There was no one to hold my ego in check despite Maddy and Claire doing their damnedest. Even they became an ego which needed to let me be. Even my legs, so often the source of misery in my youth became a trait which made me almost interesting. The boy who dragged himself from the bed each morning only to hear his mother scoff at his unmatched clothes. Yes, the lonely child learned to see.

Now, I wasn't mad about death any more than I was afraid of dying. Looking back, I could say no matter what, in my time here I'd accomplished more than could have been expected of me. Despite those cursed legs, I walked further than Mother would've expected. No! I still sleep at night, the soothing sleep of a clear mind. When you begin with little, when you're born an ugly child that can barely see over the fence, your crash is more subtle. The born monster does not need to soar to great heights, nor be exceedingly monstrous, to leave his mark.

(Maddy)

To be honest, I thought it was a joke. Claire handed me a heavy white envelope (the fancy kind with foil on the inside) and asked me to hold it for her.

"For what?" I asked.

"These are my last wishes," she said. "I want you to keep them safe."

"Isn't this more something for Bobby?"

"You're the keeper of things, so I thought it best if you held on to it."

"Are you going somewhere?"

She laughed. "Not specifically, but someday."

"What if I'm gone before you?" I asked.

"Not possible," she said and shook her head to indicate I was not to ask further questions.

"You have that book of yours, *Watership Down*," she said. "Is that not the keeper of things?"

"It is," I said. I hadn't thought about it in some time. But why would a twenty-eight-year-old woman be concerned about something as morbid as last wishes?

I opened the dusty book just a few days ago. There are pictures of our father taken in the 1960s I imagine, dull and grainy, but real. There are also pictures of our mother, unfortunately clearer, too real. There's the envelope from Claire, at first a secret I could never imagine, but that is now also clearer and more sinister.

I never open the envelope, never let curiosity get the best of me. I fought the urge to remove the letter, leave it unread, fold the thin paper into a crane or dragon, watch it fly away. But I don't need to open it to know what it says. I know what Claire has wrought.

(Bobby)

My body fights to stay warm under four blankets and the nurse assuring me the room is set to my temperature. It's funny the things you remember when, despite having no more time, you have nothing but time.

"Bring me the book," I say to the nurse though I'm not sure she's the one who requested it. "I'm ready to sign it."

I lay deep into the pillow and remember…

The song *In the Navy* was on every radio station, blaring from every car radio. I hated it.

"You shouldn't brag," my mother said. "No one likes a braggart."

I sank deep into the chair at the kitchen table and, using my fork, moved the cooling mashed potatoes back and forth on my plate, mixing it with the cold kernels of corn.

No one likes a braggart. Therefore, no one likes me.

Three months earlier I'd sent a letter to one of the cereal companies, my favorite cereal (In my tired and fading state, I can't remember which one) and by default, my favorite cereal company. I'd won their contest, finally, and was writing to claim my promised prize: a treasure chest full of board games.

Starting a few months before the letter, I'd eaten their cereal to the bottom of the box in order to claim the colored tiles with pictures on them: anchors and boats and fish: all of them surrounding and guarding the treasure chest sitting on the bottom of some faraway ocean and also pictured, conveniently, on the back of the cereal box. But there was only one, and I was the one, the contest winner—and soon the pirate's booty would be all mine. I double, triple checked to make sure I had all the pieces, laying the cereal box down on its face and placing the pieces in each designated spot on back of the box. Yes! I had them all! Nothing could stop me.

I dropped the game pieces—small, cardboard tiles—into an envelope with a handwritten note with my name, age and address. The stamp was affixed, and I walked a couple of blocks and dropped the letter into the blue metal box myself. No one else could be trusted with such a weighty task. I imagined there were spies everywhere, behind every tree, watching my every move, waiting for me to accidentally drop the envelope so they could pick it up when I turned my back to frantically look for it. They knew what I carried tightly in my dampening hands. I walked a little faster toward the blue box, but not so fast as to attract attention. A delicate balance.

My hands shook as I pulled open the lever and let the letter slide from my fingertips. I opened and closed the lever several times, more times than necessary, to make sure the letter was safely in the box. There's a covenant between senders of letters and the post office, and I was sure they would hold up their end as I had held up mine. My part was done. All I could do was wait.

And waiting is what I'd done. But I'd also bragged. Bragged to my friends, my classmates, my teachers, my sister. Certainly, there was much to brag about! This would lift my station, elevate me amongst my peers. It had, too. No longer the kid with the squirrely legs, but now the one with the treasure. A contest winner! I'd take my fifteen minutes of fame. Perhaps even stretch it to sixteen minutes.

I watched our mailbox every day, doubling and triple checking it. I knew this humongous treasure chest wouldn't fit into such a tiny mailbox, but before it arrived via two burly men struggling to carry it to our front porch, perhaps there would be some correspondence, a congratulatory letter, a certificate of accomplishment proceeding the arrival—perhaps scheduling a date so we could call the newspaper and arrange photos. "Local boy wins big! Treasure chest arrives being carried by two grown men!"

I dreamed of it every night and every day. And evidently, I spoke about it every day too.

"I know, Bobby," Maddy said when I was listing off what I imagined was in this colossal treasure chest. "You've already told me a hundred times."

Had I? I didn't remember mentioning it to her. My classmates, too, were beginning to show fatigue.

"Yeah, but when's it coming?"

"Don't worry," I answered to all questions. "Any day now." I was quite confident. "I'll bring it to school the next day so everyone can see it."

Jack loved to hear about it. Of course, he knew I would share the contents with him, so he had reason to let me drone on and on about it.

"Tell me again what's inside," Jack said.

"Well," I entertained. "We can't be sure, but I imagine there will be this and that..."

Days turning into weeks and weeks into months and nothing arrived. There were no burly men, no towering truck billowing exhaust and screeching brakes, engine shaking the house as it idled in front. There was no one from the newspaper asking me questions or taking my picture. My mother rolled her eyes.

"Are you sure you had all the game pieces to begin with?" she asked.

I remained confident—the cereal company wouldn't disappoint its most loyal customer. Yet, I couldn't shake the feeling something had gone wrong. Had someone followed me and, later that day plucked the letter, winning tiles and all, from the mailbox? Had our mailman, driven by greed, taken the letter and repackaged the winning tiles under the names of his own children? No, I convinced myself, there's not that kind of evil in the world. Maybe mother was right, the braggart didn't have the right pieces in the first place. I still dreamed of the treasure chest, but less frequently.

The walls began to close in on me first at school, then at home. The questions became louder and more frequent. The disappointment in their eyes more obvious. The very people I'd hope to impress with my luck and savvy were slowly, not so slowly, souring. Soon I'd become the lying kid with the squirrely legs. I thought about the song and running away to join the Navy, to find someplace safe where no one would know who I was. My confidence, if I ever had any, pulled me deeper, like an anchor. I drew a self-portrait, a boy caught underneath a treasure chest, crushed and bleeding, my crayons almost melting from the friction of wax on paper.

The great gift, the treasure chest, never arrived. Even Jack forgot about it, or at least he stopped mentioning it. I still thought about it nightly, but less about the chest of games and more about the disappointment. I'd put myself out for all to see, I'd bragged and inflated my chest, threw my head back as I walked.

Looking back with the luxury of wisdom, it's likely a summer intern at the cereal company placed the letter in a pile of incoming letters and promptly forgot it existed. On his last day before returning to college, he came across the letter pile and, embarrassed he'd overlooked them for the duration of his stay, dropped them into the trash bin. Poof! Like they never existed.

I hear mother in my head, her voice faded by the years, but still clear: "What can you expect. They have eyes, don't they?"

(Maddy)

It didn't necessarily appear they were there to hate him as much as they were celebrating his death. Are funerals supposed to be fun? No, of course not. But Bobby's funeral was even further from it. There was yelling and cursing and spitting, large gobs of green and yellow spittle drummed up from the lungs of the young and predominantly healthy. Most of the trouble came from rabid fans of the Shake-Shake singer, the golden-hipped girl who'd succumbed to the wasting disease delivered with a tidy bow and a kiss by my brother's sex. And the fans were not pleased. Not at all.

Bobby himself, when he was alive, never elicited an "eh" or a "well" or a "hmmmm." You either grew to love him or hate him. And all of it over a very short period and with minimal interaction. Many were fooled into loving him, and many, as you've learned, paid with their lives.

The headline in the morning paper read, tongue-in-cheek: "ROCKSTAR ARTIST DIES: DID HE ALSO KILL A ROCKSTAR?" He did, yes. Massachusetts sent several state troopers to help with crowd control. Someone high-up in the department understood that Bobby was not a popular figure these days. They couldn't have known just how unpopular. Even I didn't know the extent of it.

They were dressed in white shirts splashed with red paint. They weren't subtle. They pounded on the hearse as it inched through the growing crowd, foaming at the mouth, shouting words that could peel paint—words I'd only heard in British gangster movies on the pay channels. Bobby had become, not unearned, a hated man. Perhaps the most hated. His death, it seemed, did not satisfy the hatred, it may have even intensified it. They smashed statue reproductions (at least I assume they were reproductions) on the pavement and the cement sidewalks. I'll give them credit: they'd brought along appropriate props and effigies. Some shouted that death was too good for him. Perhaps they were right.

Claire hadn't blinked. She sat next to me in the black limousine, leaning back into the dark leather seat, staring forward into nothingness. She hadn't spoken that day, not even to me. The shouting and ruckus outside the car didn't appear to affect her—what was the point? He was already dead.

A statue (or a reproduction) bounced off the hood of the limousine, shuttering the car like we'd been hit by mortar fire. One of the troopers grabbed someone in the crowd and began to wrestle with him. This stirred up the others, and they began to cheer and jump in place like they were at their beloved Shake-Shake concert. A second trooper joined the first in subduing the statue thrower as we rolled away. More protesters filled in the space we'd rolled out of and I was unable to see what had happened to the troopers.

It didn't take long for the crowd to catch up with us. This time, imagining our limousine contained people relevant to their anger (I suppose it did), they began to push our car from the sides, one side and then the other until it seemed we might capsize there in the cemetery. I held onto the small handle above the door wondering if this day would bring our end too.

Claire remained unsettlingly calm, her hands flat on her thighs, wobbling this way then that, effortlessly riding the waves like a weather buoy.

Finally, she called to the driver.

"Call it off," she said like she'd decided on soup instead of salad and was correcting her lunch order. "I should have thought this through," she said and shook her head. "If they know where he's buried, they might dig him up and do who knows what."

Then, at the end and even though we were no longer being chased, I heard it, a deafening sound. The sickening sound of tires melting on pavement. Old cries of Maddy, poor Maddy even though I was safe.

(Claire)

The moment's as clear as yesterday. I can't be certain it was *the* moment, but I'm more certain than I've ever been. My body warmed, dampened, and the heat between my legs burned like fire. This fire, tangy, almost acidic, was foreign to me and determined to make itself known. The heat spread downward into my legs and upward toward my chest. Soon I was fully consumed, my breathing labored, a piano on my chest. Couldn't he feel the fire? Didn't it burn him to be inside me?

My body began to percolate; the hot liquid pumped through my veins. No, if veins are for returning to the heart, then this poison must have travelled by artery, away from me and toward him and at great speed. It was its nature to spread, to propagate and carry forth future generations, I was only a vessel in which to multiply and pass along via my body's system of lubrication.

Yes, that was it. It must have been. It was the moment. I knew it was begging to escape, to spread, to ferment, to infect. It flowed through my fingertips, my toes, the tip of my tongue, all of me. It didn't come without a gift, however, the power to be great, a sinister, heartbreaking ability to change the lives of others.

How can I be certain? There were scents, too, salty and sweet, fully cooked as we were both. I passed a lifeline as well as a death sentence. Is it better to achieve your dream, to achieve a greatness even if for a short time? Or better for one to toil in anonymity for a full lifetime, waiting much too long? I'm sure the great books, the ancient books would offer opinions on the subject, opinions that differ from my own.

Did those brave souls who endured the *Mayflower* crossing believe it was not worth it? The motivations were different, of course, but no less rational. Do not fear success. Do not fear the cost. Embrace both and live a happy life otherwise it was all for naught.

And why did he see me as the bookish waif, the academic, the good girl? I haven't fully moved on from this. Could he not have conceived a vision of the monster before him, the one who bore swirls of whorish make-up and bed-worn thighs? My statue, in my eyes, could have gone either way. Or even a third, a carrier of pox to be driven from town by pitchfork and torchlight, her, swimming the moat, running in a high-knee, full sprint, making for the night forest, the trees, despite being leafless, swaying slowly in the wind.

Acknowledgements

My very special thanks to my perpetual early readers, Linette Tong, Amy Corrigan and Jamie Seevers for your time, feedback and unwavering support. To Jodi for the tough (sometimes very tough) love every writer needs. And to our cat, Maise, for not sleeping on my keyboard.

www.ingramcontent.com/pod-product-compliance
Lightning Source LLC
Chambersburg PA
CBHW032348310726
48973CB00007B/1912

9798985465945